BRECHT AT NIGHT

OTHER WORKS BY MATI UNT IN ENGLISH TRANSLATION

The Autumn Ball
Things in the Night
Diary of a Blood Donor

BRECHT AT NIGHT
mati unt

translated and with an introduction and afterword by
ERIC DICKENS

Dalkey Archive Press ▣ Champaign & London

Originally published in Estonian as *Brecht ilmub öösel* by Kupar, 1997
Copyright © Mati Unt, 1997
Translation copyright © Eric Dickens, 2009
Introduction copyright © Eric Dickens, 2009
Afterword copyright © Eric Dickens, 2009
First English translation, 2009

Library of Congress Cataloging-in-Publication Data

Unt, Mati.
[Brecht ilmub öösel. English]
Brecht at night / Mati Unt ; translated by Eric Dickens.
   p. cm.
ISBN 978-1-56478-532-9 (pbk. : acid-free paper)
1. Brecht, Bertolt, 1898-1956--Fiction. I. Dickens, Eric. II. Title.
PH666.31.N75B7413 2009
894'.54532--dc22

                          2009000870

Partially funded by grants from the National Endowment for the Arts, a federal agency; the Illinois Arts Council, a state agency; and by the University of Illinois at Urbana-Champaign.

Special thanks to the Estonian Literature Information Center and Traducta for supporting the translation of this novel.

www.dalkeyarchive.com

Grateful acknowledgment is made to Suhrkamp Verlag for permission to include the poetry of Bertolt Brecht.

Cover: design by Danielle Dutton, art by Nicholas Motte
Printed on permanent/durable acid-free paper and bound in the United States of America

Introduction

Brecht at Night is Mati Unt's last and most openly political novel; it is one of synchronicity and irony. During the late 1960s and early 1970s, when the young Mati Unt was publishing his first texts in what was then the Estonian Soviet Socialist Republic, he was already using irony and other subtle means of narration to highlight the contrast between everyday life in the Soviet Union and that of the West, where most social and cultural innovation was in fact coming from. But Unt's ironic treatment also extended to contrasting the everyday life of the Soviet citizen with the utopian dreams of communism. Unt could do little more than hint, as any open criticism of the system would have landed him in one of the labor camps of the Gulag.

Irony has always been part and parcel of Mati Unt's box of literary tricks. But now he introduces something new: synchronicity. The synchronicity depicted here involves one year (1940) in the life of German playwright Bertolt Brecht, compared with and contrasted to the events taking place at the same time in Europe as a whole and the Baltic area specifically. The author focuses on the Second World War, the short-lived peace treaty between Nazi Germany and Soviet Russia (best known as the Molotov-Ribbentrop Pact), and one of its consequences: the military occupation of the three Baltic countries—Estonia, Latvia, and Lithuania—by the latter superpower.

While Brecht is tackling the somewhat cerebral literary and theatrical problems of dialectics and the alienation effect, writing his plays in the relative comfort of exile in the Finnish capital Helsinki, surrounded by women of his choosing, the Estonian nation is struggling for survival as it is slowly but surely being occupied by Soviet forces and is in effect being annexed by Russia.

During the Soviet era, from the 1960s when Mati Unt published his first texts until the late 1980s, Unt never overstepped the mark regarding what was allowed, politically, by the Soviet powers who kept a weather eye on all cultural matters in Estonia. But once change was in sight, he produced two remarkable novels in one year: *Things in the Night* and *Diary of a Blood Donor*. In both there were hints of Estonian patriotism, disdain for Soviet reality, and the use of what could be termed postmodernist techniques, but still no direct criticism of Soviet rule, whatever may have been implied.

By the mid-1990s, however, after independence in Estonia had been restored for several years, Unt set about deconstructing some of the myths around the "workers'" writer Bertolt Brecht, whose plays, curiously, the otherwise very modern Mati Unt does not seem to have staged during his many years writing, producing, and adapting plays for the Estonian theater.

While Unt appears to greatly admire some aspects of Brecht, and certainly his stage techniques, the reader cannot escape the feeling that he is bothered by something. Unt deliberately introduces a "dialectic" by comparing Stanislavski's techniques, the precursor of method acting, to the aloof brand of alienation of which Brecht was a proponent. This type of nonrealistic drama can be seen in its early form in plays by, for instance, Maeterlinck, and in more recent times, it can be seen in the films of Ingmar Bergman, Luís Buñuel, Hans-Jürgen Syberberg, Andrei Tarkovksy, and others, including, in the theater, the plays of Witold Gombrowicz and the productions of Tadeusz Kantor.

Brecht's life as a whole was riddled with paradox. The first paradox that Unt tackles is the fact that Brecht is often presented as one of the great champions of the working class, a writer who tried to give the rest of us insights into the proletariat's paradoxical lives. And yet, in his own life, Brecht had relatively little to do with the working class. He was the son of the managing director of a paper factory and was university-educated in the sciences and medicine. He was haute bourgeois, through and through.

Brecht made a brilliant career for himself in the theater in the 1920s, which culminated in *The Threepenny Opera* in 1928, one of Brecht's greatest successes during his lifetime. His career in Germany had reached its zenith.

Only when Hitler came to power did Brecht's troubles start. And because Brecht was of Jewish provenance and had also flirted with Marxism, life soon became dangerous for him in Germany on both counts. Hitler staged his own piece of theater, the Reichstag fire, soon after coming to power in 1933. Things became too hot for Bertolt Brecht, and he began his years in exile: Prague, Paris, Amsterdam, Denmark, Stockholm.

■

It is at this point that Mati Unt picks up the thread: as Brecht is crossing the night ferry from Stockholm to the port city of Åbo/Turku in western Finland. By now it is 1940, the Second World War has started; the Winter War, fought by the Finns against the Russians, is already over. Finland is regarded as a cousin nation to Estonia; their languages closely resemble one another, as do elements of their cultures.

The semi-fictional events of this novel take place over the space of this one year. Brecht is portrayed as being in a world of his own. His grasp of dialectics is seen to be based more on a Buddhist detachment than a Marxist philosophy of action. Yet he is shrewd enough to keep one step ahead of Hitler, whom he imagines to be pursuing him in secret.

The novel is fueled by irony. One such irony is that the country to which Brecht wants to flee Nazism is not the Soviet Union, but that hotbed of capitalism, the USA. And the country from which Brecht would like to sail directly to America is Finland, which Brecht regards as uncomfortably fascist in outlook, an ally of Nazi Germany. Throughout the novel, we overhear Brecht justifying his every move to himself, in a nakedly self-centered way. Unt admits on the first page of the book that he has exaggerated some aspects of Brecht, and yet . . .

Brecht, fleeing Nazi Germany with his wife, his mistress, and his children, is supported financially in Finland by the Estonian-born Hella Wuolijoki, now a rotund woman of around sixty, and by her socialist friends. But this woman is as little a member of the proletariat as is Brecht. She owns a manor house outside Helsinki and is a leading member of the Finnish cooperative movement, Elanto. Brecht regards her as civilized—because she speaks fluent German, another sign that she does not belong to the lower strata of society.

Further, Brecht cannot come to grips with Finnish political reality. While he is happy to be sheltered and nurtured by the rich socialist sympathizer Wuolijoki, he tactlessly terms one of her friends, the full-blooded Finnish socialist Väinö Tanner, a "fascist"—a man who had been foreign minister of Finland during the Winter War against the Soviet Union. Despite all the theoretical dialectics, Brecht is found wanting when he has to interpret real examples of dialectical thought.

Another piece of tragic irony that crops up several times in the novel is that many of the foreign communists who fled to the Soviet Union to escape Nazism ended up being sent to labor camps or executed by Stalin's death machine, which resembled Hitler's. These included a former lover of Brecht's.

Interspersed here with the fortunes of Bertolt Brecht—scenes containing often mundane concerns and humorous descriptions—are the events occurring simultaneously in the rest of Europe, particularly the war between Hitler's Germany and Stalin's Soviet Union. The Machiavellian resolve of the two sides, locking horns and easing off by turns, stands in sharp contrast to Brecht's everyday concerns. Nor are other international personalities and events in the arts forgotten. The writers Lion Feuchtwanger and Klaus Mann are mentioned on several occasions.

And through the strand of the novel dealing with the occupation of the Baltic countries, the fates of numerous politicians are also dealt with. Apart from famous international figures such as Churchill and Molotov, we read about some of the Estonian politicians at the time, and their optimism or pessimism as to whether Estonia would survive as a sovereign nation after being embraced by the bear hug of Soviet rule. One Finnish leader of equivocal status is the would-be leader of the Finnish puppet government under the Soviets, Otto Ville Kuusinen (1881–1964). Even the Finnish socialists ultimately rejected this government, and Kuusinen fled to Russia. Still, Stalin was much more successful in the other Baltic countries, a point Unt returns to throughout the novel.

Another aspect of the novel is Brecht's ambiguous attitude to chinoiserie. Brecht disliked the bourgeois fad of collecting Chinese bric-a-brac, yet in his unfinished book, *Me-Ti, Buch der Wendungen*, Brecht writes commentary on and criticism of European politicians, both left and right, in the form of short prose pieces, resembling those written by Chinese philosophers centuries ago. All the names of the politicians are changed into mono- or bi-syllabic Chinese ones, e.g., Sa (Rosa Luxemburg) and Ni-en (Stalin). Mati Unt carries on this tradition by giving Hitler a Chinese name. The alienation technique involved in Brecht's having Chinese people act out common events also comes into play. If a German slips on a banana skin, this is something ordinary for a German, but if a Chinese person does so, the event is suddenly seen at an aloof distance. Unt makes great use of Brecht's stylistic devices.

Within the space of a few pages, the reader will encounter Brecht's "dialectical" approach to his entourage of women, a description of the Soviet military bases being forced onto the Baltic countries, and Hitler conquering France. Unt employs Brecht's own alienation technique and his dialectical view of the world in order to highlight a multitude of real-life paradoxes and contradictions, both historical—such as the Molotov-Ribbentrop pact, when the Soviet Union and Germany both signed a treaty in bad faith, hoping to re-arm sufficiently before having to tackle the other—and personal.

In an aside at the end of Part IV, Unt steps out of his role of narrator and describes briefly how he and his wife were in a parallel situation to Brecht's in 1991, when the coup in Russia was stifled and Yeltsin came out on top, while Unt and his wife were visiting Finland. A case of history almost repeating itself.

Towards the end of the book (shall we continue to call it a "novel," or shall we, like W. G. Sebald, insist on avoiding the term?), Unt introduces the blunt dialectic of Brecht's poems (real ones) versus documents (also real) showing the steps taken by the Soviet Union to conquer and control the hitherto sovereign Baltic countries. Brecht himself is rather alienated from the struggle for Finland going on around him, while, only eighty kilometers away, across the Gulf of Finland, the country where Wuolijoki was born, is being taken over by way of a series of sly maneuvers, principally by Andrei Aleksandrovich Zhdanov—a key Soviet politician who had two roles, both pertinent to *Brecht at Night*: that of a theorist of the arts (Socialist Realism; "engineers of the human soul") and commissar for the Baltic countries and Finland (the new territories of the Soviet empire). The Secret Protocol of the Molotov-Ribbentrop Pact, wherein Hitler and Stalin divided Europe into two spheres of influence, is juxtaposed with a poem by Brecht entitled "Emigrants"; a phrase-book list for the conquering Soviet forces ends up next to the poem "The Mask of Evil." And so on. Zhdanov is termed the "stage director" of the events in the Baltic countries. In this section, there is also a passage, nine pages long, which is surely the antithesis of the Brecht poems included, leading to exactly the sort of dialectical synthesis Brecht always wished for: a detailed description of what happened to the members of what had, up to the year 1940, been the government and parliament of the independent and sovereign Estonia.

This short section, entitled "Where Did They Vanish To?" and written in clinical fashion by the former deputy head of the Estonian branch of the KGB, Vladimir Pool, could have graced Anne Applebaum's history of the Soviet labor camps, had she known about it. Not only did many Estonian government ministers, officials, and lawmakers end up in the Siberian Gulag in 1940, but quite a few were shot. This article was first published in the free Estonian press, just after independence in 1991. The former KGB agent was, no doubt, trying to make amends, in his own fashion. The section on the treatment of the former Chief-of-Staff of an independent Estonia, Johan Laidoner, is an ugly example of the sheer wanton sadism with which Stalin and his henchmen treated former dignitaries from what had now become vassal states. This section certainly sobers the reader after all of Brecht's wacky exploits and the latest alienation effect produced by poetry.

Another interspersed section describes how in Estonia, those joining the puppet government—entirely under Zhdanov's control—include several cultural figures who, during the 1930s, had been Western-oriented poets and literary critics, e.g., Johannes Semper, who introduced the works of André Gide to Estonia and was the head of the Estonian PEN club, and Johannes Vares-Barbarus, a Modernist poet and translator of Apollinaire and Cendrars, who became a puppet prime minister the second time the Soviets occupied Estonia in 1944, and finally committed suicide under mysterious circumstances in 1946. Historical synchronicity is therefore at play throughout this work.

Towards the end of the novel, Brecht is writing his play *Mr. Puntila and his Man Matti*, inspired by various Finnish texts, and is picking mushrooms with his family. Then, in an intertextual passage, Mati Unt recreates an episode from the Finnish epic *Seven Brothers*, written by the mad poet Aleksis Kivi, as described earlier in the novel when the Finn, the Estonian, and the German all compete to describe the best mad poet. One of the brothers, Aapo, tells Brecht the story, and the episode merges, absurdly, with a passage where Brecht and the Seven Brothers fight off a pride of lions. The whole passage is an ironic exercise in comparing and contrasting the real drama of Europe that was taking place with the way Brecht was conjuring up fantasies based, in fact, on other people's work (Aleksis Kivi) and other nations' mythologies (Finnish). It also shows Brecht in rather a bad light: In the original Kivi version, the Seven Brothers are surrounded by a herd of hostile bulls, which they kill. Brecht turns these bulls into lions and puts himself center stage.

But then the tone grows serious again. Has Brecht obtained any insights into life in Finland, the country that surrounds him, or into Estonia, the country of Hella Wuolijoki? Or is he too busy with his theatrical dialectics to notice? Unt leaves this question unanswered. The epilogue is a brief summary of the further fates of Brecht and his women.

Eric Dickens, 2009

PART I

HE ARRIVES

1940

BERTOLT BRECHT ONBOARD SHIP AT NIGHT

When Brecht notices—

This name could well denote the famous German author and stager of plays. But I am principally using it to shorten his name. As this practice is documented (in for instance Fuegi or Haikara), I am bolder about the use of the name. I have obtained all the information here from various sources, but I am intentionally absolving myself of the responsibility of writing what could be termed a "documentary novel." I exaggerate here and there, but this is done deliberately. We all know that famous people do not have the right to an authentic biography. Take Hamlet! Who cares now who he really was!

—when he notices that it is growing dark outside over the sea—he can see this through the misty porthole—he goes up on deck for some reason or other.

The trip has already lasted one whole day and night.

And on the ship there is nowhere else to go when you want to leave your cabin.

The dialectical relation between deck and cabin is something that Brecht is of course not thinking about right now.

On all sides is a slurry of ice, that is beginning to merge with the sky. Brecht looks at the horizon, if you can call it that, for what else is there to look at on deck? When his eyes have grown accustomed to the dusk and his night blindness receded somewhat, he can make out a couple of faint lights. They are not flashing, so they are not lighthouses. If there is not, maybe, something flashing within

Brecht's eyes. The lighthouses are, of course, two in number, but Brecht immediately brushes aside the menacing thought of dialectics. Here at sea today I am going to think as little as possible about dialectics, is what Brecht has already decided. Because when glancing at the sea, you often enough see the proximity of two waves. And when it comes down to it, they are not lighthouses anyway, whether there are two of them or even three.

Maybe they are German warships?

Brecht is now quite prepared to believe that he is being tailed.

By not just anybody. But by *What's-His-Name*.

—As usual, Brecht is here using some supercilious or mocking name for the great dictator.

—What's-His-Name's practices are often unfathomable. Why shouldn't he send a ship in pursuit? These are perhaps neutral waters and here you can do what you like. Sweden claims that she is neutral—so why shouldn't this stretch of water also be so?

If I am arrested in the Gulf of Bothnia it would be a clear sign to the rest of the world that What's-His-Name will no longer tolerate more redundant chatter, whoever's mouth it emerges from.

Oh yes, Scandinavia is not to be considered safe from attack from any point of the compass.

The Nazis are busy infiltrating everywhere, Finland too, no doubt.

On the other hand, it would seem for some reason that some kind of veneer of civilization has been preserved in this part of the world. The reason being that everything happens at a slower pace here in the North. Are North and South opposites? But the Middle, how does it relate to both parts, the upper and the lower?

You see, here we have yet another dialectical thought, another dream of duality or bipolarity, and this cannot have gone unnoticed by Brecht.

He can feel himself smiling slyly.

Brecht watches the lights, until his eyes begin to water. Then even the lights vanish. Maybe they're not from ships, or maybe they were switched off. This watching won't help. If they come, they come—from beyond the breakers, brandishing machine guns.

Look, the deck's wet, slippery, swilling with water, the foam is spraying over the railing. But lo, a miracle is at hand—there's someone else here too! At Brecht's side stand two Scandinavians: genuine ones, chthonic individuals. They remain silent and spit from time to time into the water. The tundra has shaped their mentality, blizzards have instilled in them scorn for conventions. They are intro-verted. They are not only spitting into the sea. Will they suddenly start spitting on everything? On What's-His-Name too. This is an indifference that bodes ill, ignorance that the Aryan race is sowing the seeds of everywhere. Why Aryan? Brecht doesn't understand why, but that is what What's-His-Name's cronies have already decided. Brecht also suspects that the Finns will be categorized as a Nor-dic race. They are, after all, called Finns, a Germanic term, by some. Finn and *suomalainen*—there we have another duality. But everything has two names, and you just have to get used to it.

The Finns spitting into the water give Brecht the irresistible urge to make a poem. And this line of poetry springs to mind:

Fleeing from my compatriots, I ended up in Finland.

But I've not yet arrived, have to seize the text by the tail and be prepared to spit over my shoulder for good luck. Because where is this Finland? Meanwhile, it has grown even darker and now it is quite impossible to make out anything resembling a horizon. Was so before, for that matter. But now it's vanished com-pletely. *Nichts.* Nothing. Everything has evened out into one great realm of dark-ness and spray. Maybe Germany is a part of Scandinavia. But now I am surely approaching the polar circle, and that really is too much. Without What's-His-Name, this would never have happened. Journeying to the navel of the North Pole. To Finland? Only violence and a world war and, of course, the play of world trade, have brought Brecht "up here."

Lo and behold!

A man staggers by.

It's the boatswain, Brecht decides. No problem if it's a sailor. Even in the far North sailors are human. You can talk to them.

"What's the thermometer showing?" asks Brecht. He asks this in German, of course, in which language What's-His-Name also asks things as once did Wotan and Goethe. Does the Finn understand? At any rate, he stops. The Viking, the Vandal, the Aryan—He is thinking about something, doesn't reply, but his lips are moving, as if he is counting. Brecht waits. He is a refugee, a pariah, he should not get too bold. In relation to this Finnish fascist he is in a situation he cannot escape. He should suborn himself to him. The grim-looking person stops his inner monologue and replies:

"Zero degrees precisely."

He replies in German, which is something that worries Brecht, but a reply in Finnish would have been worse still. What more can he ask? Because once you have formulated one question, the next is pregnant for a reply. Ask the time? Ask how late it is, not for time itself. The sea all around is dark, and Brecht just isn't that banal. Night is approaching and this helps a refugee.

"How's it going otherwise?" he asks him instead. Brecht knows that the common people like this question.

"OK," replies the Nordic barbarian, off the cuff, and because of the swell, he walks away swaying slightly.

Brecht is still thinking about this zero temperature. Zero isn't a high number, and the weather really is very cold and raw. Brecht has waited the whole winter to arrive at this zero. Zero is exactly on the border between cold and heat. At least this has become the convention in Celsius's world.

Anders Celsius (1701–1744) invented the temperature scale that is widely in use throughout Europe. The 80-degree Réaumur scale is largely forgotten. In the USA the Fahrenheit scale is still used. Its calibration is quite different to that of the Celsius system. Europeans find it difficult to get used to the fact that water freezes at 32 degrees Fahrenheit. Why can't it freeze at zero, as our beloved Celsius suggested? But we can't dictate to the Americans which scale they should use. Moreover, Fahrenheit himself wasn't an American. He was a German, like Brecht himself.

This zero wasn't just some off-the-cuff number. Brecht had a friend, Professor K., a Marxist, who claimed that zero marks the point at which water freezes and ice becomes fluid. One thing goes over into another. A qualitative change occurs. It is true that this leap only occurs abruptly on the scale of a thermometer. Brecht had noticed that a bucket of water doesn't suddenly become ice at zero degrees. It only does so when the air temperature has fallen below minus three. And at first only the surface freezes over. Then, goodness knows how many hours later, tomorrow or the day after, the whole bucket will be frozen. Sometimes the bucket doesn't freeze right down to the bottom, the weather gets warmer, the temperature rises to, say, one degree above zero. Then too, things don't change instantly. Whatever the state of freezing, the water doesn't just thaw instantly, although the borderline, the chance of a dialectical leap occurring, has been reached. Time is still needed, and the layer on top maybe thaws the next day.

A qualitative leap has its own specific delay factor, as Brecht finds out, but he is not satisfied with this formulation as this has a whiff of Teutonic values about it, something which Brecht here among the mists, near to the North

Pole, feels rather out of place. I have come here, I am trying to escape the dialectic in the shape of "delay," is what Brecht is thinking and walks determinedly over to the other side of the ship: you have two sides of the ship to choose between, and when you've seen one, you go over to the other. There are two further options, philosophically speaking—to go to the bows or the stern. This is on a left-right axis. So Brecht goes to the other side, beyond the superstructure, walking along the slippery deck, and what does he see after this profound little journey?

He sees that there are lights burning quite near, and they are very close to land. This land or island was on the other side, and before Brecht was staring out into the void, into nothing, which forced him to start thinking. Now, however, the shore is here! "Looking out over the surface of the water you forget the islands," Brecht conjures up, in the style of Mo Di.

The port city is called Åbo, but it is also known by another name. Brecht was told that Finland is a bilingual country. Perhaps it is in its own way, and the other name of the city is indeed Turku, but we shouldn't expect that name to stick in Brecht's mind as well.

Brecht can't get the cigar to light because of the wind. And the darkness. Nevertheless, he would like to arrive in Åbo with a cigar between his teeth. An aromatic cigar is his firm's trade mark. When he was young, he would shake the ash onto the ground . . . and now he's old . . .

Brecht's self-centered thoughts cease, because the Finns have begun to talk to each other.

It is dreadful to hear this alien language—on the deck of a ship, in the darkness, among the slurry of ice, at zero degrees, off Åbo, as a refugee.

One of the Finns utters the word *ilmasto (weather)* again and again. The other replies: *ilmasota (air warfare)*! The first one looks up at the sky and says with approval *ilmalaiva (airship)*! The other doesn't believe him, the sky is clear—at least that's what it looks like—can't really see any detail. They talk on a little, and now Brecht has grown seriously interested. I'm coming to your country, I'd like to understand you, whether you're on What's-His-Name's side or not. You are. After all, human beings, is what Brecht is thinking and homes in on them. One Finn or resident of Åbo is saying:

"Ilmalainen, kylmäläinen."

Brecht repeats this to himself: *ilmalainen*. What's that? *Ilmalainen?* Wasn't it Mr Ilmalainen who, years ago, staged, somewhere in the North, his *Threepenny Opera*? Or was that Kylmäläinen? Or Silmäläinen?

Jumalainen? Nainen?

Whoever it was, Brecht can't imagine that the two Finns, on this filthy night, are talking about a play. They're no doubt talking about something else. Maybe slash-and-burn cultivation or going on strike, now that they're nearly home.

Brecht notes very clearly that he is not the center of the world.

Besides, he's entering the country incognito.

Look, here in the North they drink a lot! That was to be expected. One of the Finns raises a bottle to his lips. Offers it to the other man. He too takes a good swig, then notices Brecht, the emigrant. Hands over the bottle.

Brecht doesn't have any. The eternal refugee must be as sober as he possibly can. Brecht, who isn't to know that that very week a ban on alcohol will be introduced in Finland, following the Winter War.

Yes, the Winter War—

In the year 1939, the Soviet Union demanded the construction of military bases in Estonia (and in the other Baltic countries) and got her way. She now also wanted the islands in the Gulf of Finland, plus Hangö. With Paldiski in the south and Hangö in the north the Soviet Union could have effectively sealed off the Gulf of Finland. The Soviet Union wanted the Karelian Isthmus—using the excuse that the border had been too close to Leningrad. Stalin said: if you can't move Leningrad, then you have to move the Finnish border. The talks were making no progress. Finland resisted, saying she did not want to give up any territory. On 3rd November 1939 Molotov said in Moscow: since our civil negotiators are making no headway, it is now up to our soldiers. Finland took the hint and issued an order for general mobilization. On 26th November a curious incident occurred in Mainila in Karelia—the Soviet Union lost two Russian soldiers, and it looked as if Finnish cannon fire had killed them. Finland didn't admit opening fire. At any rate, the Russians now claimed that Finland has entered into hostilities. (It may be suitable to here remind readers of the border incident at Gleiwitz, where "Poles"—whose dead bodies were found wearing Polish uniforms on German territory—had similarly violated the German frontier. This was the beginning of the Second World War.) The next day, Russian troops crossed into Finland. The Winter War had begun. On the morning of the same day, Stalin said: "If we raise our voices just a bit, the Finns will surrender. If they get awkward, we'll fire one shot and they'll soon have their hands above their heads!" Of course, a puppet People's Government for Finland was declared on 1st December headed by Otto Ville Kuusinen. This was supposed to represent the wishes of the Finnish people. The seat of government was the border town of Terijoki, the first town captured. Historians have drawn parallels with the Kuusinen affair: Anvelt (Estonia 1918), Stučka (Latvia 1918), Kapsukas (Lithuania 1919), Pyatakov (Ukraine 1917), Narimanov (Azerbaidzhan 1920), Kasyan (Armenia 1920), Maharadze (Georgia 1921), Khodzhayev (Bukhara 1920), Marchlewski (Poland 1920), Babrak Karmal (Afghanistan 1979). The balance of forces was roughly as follows. The Soviet Union had 3,000 planes, Finland had 100; the Soviet Union had 1.2 million soldiers, Finland 400,000. The Soviet leaders thought that conquering Finland would be a walkover, they perhaps really believed that the Finnish people would support the Kuusinen government. But things turned out differently. The Russian soldiers didn't know how to use skis and were unacquainted with forest combat. The war was fought with changing fortunes. In the end the Finns were nevertheless driven into a corner. Although the Soviet Union was expelled from the League of Nations on 14th December as the aggressor, and other European nations were said to be supporting the Finns, by the beginning of 1940 the Russians were winning. Finland was forced to negotiate for peace. She lost the Karelian Isthmus and a number of other stretches of territory. In all, one tenth of the land area of Finland was lost. On 13th March, less than a month after the arrival of Brecht, a peace treaty was signed in Moscow. Finland had lost 25,000 troops in the war, with 45,000 wounded. As for Russia, Russian estimates say she lost 48,000 troops with 158,000 wounded. (The Finnish Commander-in-Chief, Marshal Mannerheim, said that Russian losses were around 200,000.)

The Winter War attracted a good deal of attention across the world. I mentioned above that the Soviet Union was expelled from the League of Nations. But other voices were heard too. The Terijoki government was supported by—without these individuals taking a closer look at it—people such as George Bernard Shaw, John Steinbeck, Rajani Palme Dutt, Pandit Nehru, Martin Andersen Nexø, Alexei Tolstoy, Mikhail Sholokhov, Konstantin Fedin, Alexander Fadeyev, Leonid Leonov, Mikhail Zoshchenko. Also Hollywood, musicians, Norwegian women and American tennis stars. With the peace treaty signed, the government vanished into the mists and clouds—as if it hadn't been there already. But during that war, Finland introduced prohibition.

—yes, Brecht is not to know that the alcohol border has just been shut in Finland. His own alcohol consumption is very modest.

No! Now that it's Åbo or Bobo, it's all the same to him—and he is within half a kilometer of it—this emigrant refuses a drop from a stranger. His head has to be completely clear. For Brecht is changing countries again.

Brecht's odyssey has been set in stone, and looks like this: he left Germany the day after the Reichstag fire. On 28th February he was already in Prague. From there he traveled to Vienna, then to Zurich. By April he was in Carona on Lake Lugano on the Swiss border. Two-year-old Barbara was brought there later. The child had initially been left behind with its grandparents in Germany, and it is only by some miracle that this wasn't used to blackmail Brecht. In April 1933, Brecht left for Paris, while Weigel and the children went off to Denmark. Brecht followed after, and they moved to the island of Thurø, where they bought a house in August. Grete was with them by then. In the summer of 1935, Brecht was deprived of his German citizenship. When Hitler had invaded Czechoslovakia in 1938, Brecht sought the opportunity to emigrate to the United States. But he was not alone: two women and two children, plus Ruth. The visa was taking its time. He tried to move to Iceland, but ended up being accepted by Sweden, living there on the island of Lidingö, just outside Stockholm. On 9th April, 1940 the Germans invaded Denmark and Norway. The Norwegians put up resistance, the Danes did not. The Norwegian King fled into the mountains in the north. The Danes, however, had no mountains for their King to flee to (as William Shirer notes). Now they were no longer safe in Sweden. Sweden was not helping Norway with weapons or fuel, although they had done so in the case of Finland when the war with the Soviet Union had broken out at the turn of the year.

So Brecht now had no choice but to move on to the equivocal Finland. He knew full well that that country was sympathetic towards the Nazis. But now that Finland had had to pay the price for its pride, things were maybe beginning to change. Finland could not conquer the Soviet Union, and the peace treaty was after all signed on Communist terms, was the way Brecht reasoned. Besides, Finnish ports were still open, so that there was still a chance to flee to America. His friend Ruth Berlau happened to know the famous Finnish playwright Hella Wuolijoki. They had already discussed Brecht's plight, and she offered to look after the Brechts in Finland should they ever be in straitened circumstances.

Now the time had arrived. The Germans were already in Denmark and Norway! Brecht set the wheels in motion. He asked Wuolijoki for an invitation, which he received. Since Brecht claimed—correctly—that his aim was to reach the USA via Finland, they had no problem obtaining their visas.

So they gave away their property. The furniture went to a neighbor who was a locksmith and all they took with them were the bare essentials. They went on board the "Bore I" and sailed across the Gulf of Bothnia to Turku.

Brecht now goes down to the cabin to wake his family.

Helene is already dressed and just pulling on her stockings. She has already got the children ready for landing in a strange country. Grete is the only one still asleep, her pale lips slightly open so you can see her teeth. You have to wake Grete in a good mood. Once awake, she is an engine of positive attitudes. She looks after others and the whole world. But she finds waking up difficult. She wakes up yelling with fear. Only after the yelling comes the usual joy of life—as much as she can still muster with that ravaged body of hers.

"Muck," says Brecht, his usual nickname for her, "we're going to go onto the Isle of Secrets."

Grete's thin eyelids flutter.

Her mouth starts to move.

A voice is heard.

"Avalon," says Brecht. "Terra feminarum."

"That's why I dreamt about lions," says Grete, her voice forming a sentence.

"Not elephants, as you usually do?" Brecht is not quite at ease.

Grete loves elephants and Brecht gives her such animals at every opportunity. Made of wood or ivory.

In the play A Man Is a Man *one stage direction is as follows: you can hear elephants passing in the background. Afterwards, there is an interlude with a baby elephant. In* Sechuan *there is a song about five elephants.*

When Grete and Brecht first met, Grete mocked Brecht's opportunism, flirting as he was in his Threepenny Opera *with bourgeois values, and earning a lot of money. Grete herself grew up in the slums. Her father was an alcoholic. Grete soon became a Communist. She read Lenin in the original Russian. She got consumption early on. While she was being cured in Moscow in 1937, they found, in her right lung, a "goose's egg-sized" tubercle, and in her left lung one the size of a "hen's egg."*

John Fuegi thinks that Grete had her first abortion back in 1928. The second in 1930. She had her first abortion with Brecht in 1932. Fuegi posits that there were also abortions in 1934, 1936 and 1937. Some people are angry with Fuegi because of these claims.

They have both had their appendixes removed. When Brecht had just undergone the operation, What's-His-Name had the Reichstag set on fire. Brecht virtually fled from the operating theater straight to Prague.

While Brecht has always been short of stature, Grete is desiccating, the further north she travels. Once they reach the North Pole, she will die, as Brecht is aware.

But they are not there yet. Not anywhere near. Perhaps they are still below the Arctic Circle.

Brecht and his family collect together their things and go out into the wind and the rain. Brecht helps Grete to get dressed. Lord, she simply can't do anything by herself! A good job that she's got that Brecht. But Brecht can't be bothered to be all-merciful. Once Grete has got her dress on and her shoes on her feet, Brecht mutters:

"Come on. We've arrived in Åbo."

"Åbo?"

Brecht knows that Grete will perk up at almost anything, and inwardly shrugs his shoulders. He goes first up on deck, and now they really are in Åbo.

The earth is covered with patches of slushy snow.

BRECHT ARRIVES IN A FOREIGN COUNTRY

Brecht decides: I'm taciturn by nature. I won't reveal anything about myself or my plans. He remembers that Ibsen came from somewhere up here, and said . . . Yes, what was it he said? Something about silence, and something about being on your own—you were stronger when alone—and silent. No, if Ibsen did say something like that, he refuted it later on.

As a young man in Augsburg, Brecht wrote his first theater review about Ibsen's Ghosts (1919). Brecht was reasonably pleased that the subject of the play was relationships in a family where venereal disease was prevalent. (Later on, he considered Ibsen to be a proponent of naturalism—along with all those other Goncourts, Zolas, Chekhovs, Tolstoys, Strindbergs, Hauptmanns and Shaws.)

Brecht listens, and hears a rushing sound. But this is not the buzz of the city. It comes from the forest beyond the town. It is the darkness itself that is soughing.

The trees are soughing.

Have to be silent in this country, at least to start off with, whether it has anything to do with Ibsen or not.

The customs post is lit up by a small lamp. There are groups of people in the dark. Has anyone come to meet them? Are they secret agents? Friends?

Where is Wuolijoki, the woman who sent Brecht the invitation?

Hella Wuolijoki (1886–1954), born Ella Maria Murrik, a Finnish playwright of Estonian birth. Went to school at the Pushkin Girls' Grammar School in Tartu. Went to university in Helsinki between 1904 and 1908. Was married from 1908 to 1922 to a Finn, Sulo Wuolijoki. During the First World War she went into business (mostly involving the timber trade), and wrote plays on the side.

Brecht has never seen Wuolijoki in the flesh. But he remembers a photograph that Ruth Berlau once sent him. Hella Wuolijoki is pretty rotund. She is a socialist and a capitalist at one and the same time. She is everything at one and the same time, both traitor and patriot—

In Brecht's beloved dialectical style we can list here a few binary opposites which have nothing to do with Hella.
   Lion and Lamb.
   Master and Slave.
   Light and Darkness.

"Mr Brecht!" someone is shouting.
   It's Hella's friends (the composer Parmet and his wife) and they soon say that they are friends of Brecht and his entourage, and they also say immediately that they are socialists. Brecht has no option but to believe them. There are clearly no other friends out here tonight.

Through the dreamlike, dramatic, even novel-like spaces, and—as has been said again and again—nocturnal and dark, with the odd cupboard, the odd mat, the windows covered in the blackout—they finally arrive at the Finnish customs! And that—blacked out too, as if in a mist, though that was no wonder, as it was after midnight after all and in wartime as well, which had not yet reached its zenith.
   Brecht has twenty suitcases.
   I've got my manuscripts in my suitcases, Brecht is thinking. They'll go and take them off me. But they can't remove my head. The contents of my manuscripts are in my head, and what's not in my head, Grete knows, and what Grete doesn't know, Helene knows, and what she doesn't know, Ruth may do. I'm not so vulnerable as all that, says Brecht in praise of himself. But Brecht has no need for all this bravery. No one is interested in his manuscripts. Quite the reverse: the blond beast of a border guard or customs official does not show the slightest

interest in the manuscripts. As if Brecht's papers weren't dangerous, as if they weren't like fuel to the flames, a mine, a bomb. Manuscripts are not regarded as weapons here in the far North, thinks Brecht. With astonishment he even notices that he is a little hurt. Vanity, he thinks. But on the other hand, he has the right to be hurt. The Finnish secret police should have been keeping an eye on him right from the moment he left Sweden. Brecht is even prepared to be sent back. In fact he doesn't really know which of the two alternatives he would prefer. Of course he wants to save his own life. And that of his family. But then again he is disturbed by the fact that What's-His-Name isn't taking sufficient measures against him. They are still so little scared of me, Brecht is thinking, as some Scandinavian rummages through the pile of papers quite desultorily, then shuts the suitcase again. More attention is paid to the bust carved by Santeson in Sweden, which is supposed to be of Helene. The customs official can't connect this bust with Helene who is standing right here; he is looking to see whether it contains anything, pushes his whole head into the hollow underside.

Then suddenly the abrupt question, which sounds, roughly, like this:

"Ilma? Ilmanainen?"

Brecht starts to cough. He is facing a dilemma. He understands quite well that this has to be an antinomian question. He will have to choose, or find a way of making a synthesis out of the thesis and the antithesis. But—at night, near the Polar Circle, in a strange country which is full of What's-His-Name's spies? No! But one of those who have come to meet him interrupts and reassures the official, explaining and explaining until the official finally shrugs his shoulders.

"Ilman, ilman . . . juu-juu, ilman," says the official, says something more and hands them back their passports. The have arrived at their next port of exile: Brecht (42) and his wife Helene (40), his son Stefan (15), his daughter Barbara (10) and his secretary Grete (32).

They get into a car. Brecht has loved cars ever since he was little. He grew up in a time when the motor car, the airplane and electricity were making their breakthrough. They all had a whiff of America about them. Brecht used to love America and American cars. And now he is in an American car.

Brecht's friend Lion Feuchtwanger depicts Brecht as a young man in his novel Success, *as an engineer by the name of Kaspar Pröckl. The good-humored caricature begins with a car drive: "Kaspar Pröckl, in his leather jacket and leather cap, a grim, thin and badly shaven figure, was sitting in an awkward, forced pose next to a stately, fair-complexioned young lady and is presenting her with his boundless thoughts, in his usual uncouth manner. (. . .) Everything that Pröckl said bubbled with witticisms, fantasy, demonstrativeness and erudition. (. . .) He laughed away marriage ironically as a stupid capitalist institution, smiled a wry smile at the phenomenon, as if it belonged to someone else. He noted how ridiculous it was to preserve the concept of a lady in the postwar world they were now living in. (. . .) At the same time, he got involved in an unrestrained quarrel with a carter, who had not heard his tooting nor pulled in to the verge. Pröckl's face grew red and he began to yell. The people sitting in the cart are in the majority and are bellicosely inclined. They could have come to blows. For the rest of the journey, Kaspar Pröckl fell silent and looked gloomy. (. . .) He was clearly surrounded on all sides by a mood of revolution. Granted he had booked success with his utterly vulgar ballads. When he read them out aloud in his usual piercing voice, women would go weak at the knees."*

Now Brecht is sitting in a car, and Helene and Grete and the children are in a second car.

Like pursuers, like attacking lions, they shoot through the nocturnal streets of the port city, and occasionally the beam of the headlights pick out signs of war—sandbags, shell holes in walls; Brecht thinks they are going round in circles when all of a sudden, they turn a corner and are right in front of the railway station.

BRECHT ON THE TRAIN

The filthy light bulb hardly gives off any glow at all, and beyond the window it is pitch black.

Night, night, night—why have we spent such lengths describing it?

Brecht is traveling with his family through the snow-mottled forest of a Northern country. Brecht is convinced that they will end up in the very North of the country, entering ever deeper into darkness and night.

In actual fact, Helsinki is slightly further south than Turku (Åbo), where Brecht landed.

The difference is a small one. But Brecht is still at roughly the 60th parallel. Only he himself thinks he is traveling to Ultima Thule. In fact, this illusion is a real possibility. The east is changing somehow into—he can't even say why himself—the north. In the north there were camps, in the east as well. Easy to lose your orientation. The sun rises at different times in its own peculiar way—in the summer in the east up to the zenith, in the winter however in the west. Brecht never wanted to be clear about all this. And I know why. Brecht already knew where he wanted to end up. He wanted to end up in America. That was, after all, the West, wasn't it? It wasn't. Brecht was in fact traveling eastwards, hoping in so doing to arrive in the West. Brecht was not the first globe-trotter to do this: Columbus too thought he was sailing to the East Indies, but in so doing ended up discovering America. We know that Brecht's real aim was America, i.e. the USA. Brecht was traveling anticlockwise, in the opposite direction to the sun. Why and how he did this is what we are going to write about here.

Forest and yet more forest!

Brecht is sitting in the railway carriage. It is night and the forest is trotting past.

In fact, maybe here in the night, here in the moss, there may be living dog-snouts or even lions. He knows nothing of lions, but Adam of Bremen said he had seen these dog-snouted humans in his day.

Meanwhile, the two women and two children are asleep. All four of them have their eyes shut. They are looking in on themselves. Brecht, on the other hand, is looking outwards. And, as does every train traveler, especially at night, he has his double with him. It is looking at him as they pass the forest, from the windowpane.

Yes, there was nowhere left for me but this country, Finland, is what he is thinking to himself, with an unexpected surge of irony. Who really wants me that much? And here I've found my rightful place, thinks Brecht, looking again out into the night. Dog-snouts, dog-snouts . . . he keeps repeating to himself poison-ously . . . what's all this about dog-snouts? Something far more real is the fact that the Finnish fascists have been attacking long-suffering Russia this past year.

There are conflicting opinions about the way the Finno-Ugrian peoples behaved during the Second World War. The Russians regard them as fascists. Only a few years ago, one angry and drunken Russian on an Estonian bus or in the street was heard to say: fucking fascists, shoot the lot of them, that's what I say! Even in the West, people don't always understand in which predicament the Estonians (also the Finns) found themselves after the Molotov-Ribbentrop Pact was signed in 1939. They now had to be watchful in both directions! So some faces turned to the East, others to the West. Their secret longing was to preserve independence, something the superpowers of the day had already decided to annihilate.

Luckily, Finland did not manage to bring Russia to its knees. Finland was pun-ished. Not one Finn voluntarily handed in his weapon, but they hid in the woods, waiting for their time to come. After What's-His-Name gave the signal they took off the safety catch from their automatic weapons.

Some of these are now pointing at me, without any extra encouragement from Germany, Brecht is thinking. He knows that the Finns are like phantoms. In the winter a Finn is white. You can't see him. Brecht has seen pictures showing a snowy landscape. Two photos have been taken with a second in between. In the first picture, a Finn is standing on a patch of snow-covered ground. A second later he is gone. The Finn has merged with the landscape. Such an adversary really is cunning. You could even say that he just isn't human.

Such occurrences are not just Brecht's fantasies. I remember that this theme of a Finn merging with the landscape appeared in some paranormal research. This surprised me somewhat, as for me the phenomenon is simply a question of a camouflage suit on the one hand, and the genuine love of one's country that small nations have, on the other.

Brecht himself had a peculiar attitude to this war, being an anti-German German. His equivocal attitude to Russia, being himself a representative of another superpower, is natural with hindsight, if anything is normal.

Here I will reproduce most of a certain Sherwood Paw's little essay "The Finnish Miracle" that appeared in February 1940 in a small Swedish magazine called Ungdomens röst (The Voice of Youth):

"The Russians are straying into this country, which is grimly off-putting as regards temperature, fortresses, forests and civilization, cursing the day they were born. All they see of the Finns is fleeting shadows. Their tanks are pounced upon by Olympic pole-vaulters, who then shoot the crew dead with pistols. The Russians are dying, while the Finns multiply in these battles. They are led by a marshal, who many years ago conquered the world's most valiant people—his own. They fight for civilization along with Mussolini, Hitler, Franco and the Pope. (. . .) The Russian army lacks boots, foot-clouts are wrapped round their otherwise bare feet, and those are of poor quality. They have a couple of automatic rifles, with which they mow down women and children. A few tanks, whose doors have been welded shut so that the crew can't escape. (. . .) They have never heard of American civilization. They do not know what they are fighting for. They do not know that Mannerheim is a democrat. They are physically in bad shape. They freeze to death. They have the shakes—the consequence of the Bolshevik rule of terror. The commissars force them

to sing the Internationale by pointing a gun at them. This should not be happening in Finland. Finland is a democratic country where the "Internationale" is banned. The Russian army is remarkable. Constantly harried by the Finns, always on the point of collapse, lacking the sympathy of the civilized countries, lacking a marshal to lead them . . ."

Brecht clearly wanted to mock the great self-esteem of this small country, since it was fighting such a demoralized enemy. In Finnish police archives there is no note of this text, as Kalevi Haikara points out. Otherwise anti-Finnish texts were traced throughout the world with great diligence. Brecht would hardly have received a residence permit for Finland two months later, had the name of the author of the text become public knowledge.

Sinister peoples surround Stalin and his country. For that reason, what Stalin did can, to a certain extent, be understood. Through the dirty carriage window, Brecht can catch a glimpse of the stare of a Finn from the forest. Now the Finn will no longer be white. There is, after all, no snow for him to merge with. He is now melting into the dead grass of spring. Well, well, one night in this barbarian country and it's already getting on my nerves, so how much more it must get on the nerves of poor old Stalin, who has had to tolerate it for years on end . . . decades! It's no wonder that Stalin has gone a bit funny! Even I'm a bit funny, Brecht smiles to himself.

BRECHT'S MORNING IN FINLAND

In the morning, the dozy, half-asleep family of Brecht is taken to a hotel which luckily is near the railway station. Past the national theater and up the hill. The elevator only goes up to the fifth floor.

Grete manages to fall asleep during this short trip up. She slumps against the wall of the elevator, seemingly unconscious. The elevator goes up and the children have a lot to do. The only one who notices how weak Grete is, is Brecht himself. He tries to prop her up, but by now the elevator has arrived at the fifth floor, from where it will rise no further. It cannot do so as there is no more building, no more elevator shaft, as the hotel was built before the grand days of elevators.

BRECHT WAKES UP IN A STRANGE CITY

Brecht is relatively confused on arrival in the Finnish capital, and since it is still dark, he knows that he will be waking up that morning in a hotel. But he does not wake that morning, not until after lunch. His biological rhythm has been upset, but it is natural that when fleeing from What's-His-Name, you can't get to sleep at the right time and have to forego other luxuries too.

Brecht doesn't go outside. The first day he's in a strange city he never goes outside. The Winter War has admittedly come to an end; a month ago in fact, but Brecht decides to acclimatize while still surrounded by the safety of the walls of the hotel. For the time being, a glimpse down onto the street will suffice. The edge of the roof blocks his view. There's a pavement. No people. A city, but devoid of people, is Brecht's logical conclusion. Not surprising that there are so few people, the next dialectical judgement follows swiftly. Who ordered them to pick a quarrel with Stalin? Stalin is unpleasant, but I too would protest, if someone bit me unexpectedly in the leg!

Just as well that there are so few of them!

Brecht finds a note from his wife and children, where they say that they have gone on a "reconnaissance mission." Brecht reconstructs the previous night. The forest, the Finnish butchers in the dead grass, the darkness. Grete has been sleeping on a mattress, the children in a bed. Helene on the floor, Brecht himself somewhere or other.

Now he is thinking about unpacking. Brecht starts doing so, but breaks off halfway. The table is small, there's not enough room for everything. Not to mention for laying things out systematically. But isn't there suddenly someone in the adjoining room? A child, his wife, a sympathizer? Brecht puts his ear to the wall. He's not sure whether to be hopeful or afraid. Both could be the case: next door it is as silent as the grave.

There is, or there isn't, anyone there, but one thing is sure: they can't carry on living here in this hotel. Must be an expensive one. Refugees especially tend to get fleeced. It's not impossible that via some official or other What's-His-Name has given orders for Brecht to be fleeced of every penny he's got. But even without such concerns, the hotel must surely be expensive. Hotels are always expensive. It's imperative to find an apartment. That almost sounds dialectical. But today, Brecht doesn't want to have anything to do with dialectics. Why the fuck should I always be so dialectical?

Brecht sits down.

Through the wall seeps the indescribable atmosphere of Finland.

BUT WHAT ABOUT CHINA?

Through the wall seeps the indescribable atmosphere of Finland, but Brecht is trying to think about China. He does not, of course, know that only a hundred or so kilometers away, a song will soon be written whose lyrics include: *The Estonian border goes up to the Great Wall of China! Russia should vanish in between!* Some Russians take this song very seriously. It can be imagined that these dreadful Estonians will put their plans into practice. They are supposed to be a crazily oppressed people, likely themselves to start doing the oppressing.

Relations between Brecht and China are of a different order.

Brecht has written a play which partly deals with China. Tretyakov—

Brecht worked on his play entitled The Good Woman of Sechuan *for a dozen or so years. During the 1930s, the project had the provisional title* Die Ware Liebe *which is a pun on* A Love of Goods *and* True Love. *He more or less finished the play in Finland and the drafting was done first by Grete, and was then added to by Ruth.*

—Tretyakov—

Sergei Tretyakov (1892–1939) was a Russian author. In 1924 he was in China, in the 1930s he went to Germany and there met, among others, Brecht. Brecht saw Meyerhold's theater group playing Tretyakov's anti-British play entitled Roar, China! *In 1931 Tretyakov came to visit Brecht. Brecht told Tretyakov about all kinds of horrors. He said he'd been a doctor in a field hospital during the First World War and had had to cold-bloodedly amputate legs and do trepanning, "scraping out brains." In actual fact, he had been a medical orderly for three months in a reserves hospital, treating cases of venereal disease. Tretyakov's second play* I Want a Child *deals with eugenics, the improvement of the species and racial hygiene, falling in line with the prevalent Nazi views on such subjects. Tretyakov translated several of Brecht's plays and promoted them in the Soviet Union.*

—Tretyakov, in his time, had drawn Brecht's attention to China. Why was China so important to Tretyakov?

Did Stalin get into a rage about China, or because of something else? In the case of the Great Man there is no point in wondering why he got into a rage. It is enough for us to know that he did so.

Tretyakov was arrested in 1937, accused of spying for Japan and Germany. His wife was arrested too and his daughter was thrown out of the Institute of Aviation; Brecht found out about all this in 1939. Following Tretyakov's death Brecht wrote a poem where, without mentioning T. by name, he cautiously posited the idea that the "sons of the people," good proletarian judges, could perhaps have made a mistake in this particular case. "One person can blow up the work of 5,000. / When 50 are sentenced to death, one could be innocent."

Brecht is reading a book by Mo Di (479–400 B.C. or maybe 470–391). Brecht used the name Me-Ti. He invented this philosopher back in the 1920s thanks to his then girlfriend and co-author Elisabeth Hauptmann. Later, Brecht wrote his own work "Me-Ti," but this was broken off halfway, and only fragments have appeared after Brecht's death.

Some people have thought that Mo Di is a kind of collective name. Wouldn't that be better! Brecht had a certain interest in proletarian works produced by cooperation. (Oh how he wished to merge with the masses, become a simple fellow, become a cogwheel in the works.)

In the end, Brecht is now leading a small collective, a small crew of refugees.

Brecht listens.

A long-drawn-out creaking sound, then nothing.

The silence is suspiciously arctic.

Brecht no longer wishes to listen to the silence, since silence does not express anything.

He opens Mo Di (or, in his own version, Me-Ti) again. There he can read that in times of famine it is not the done thing to blow trumpets or bang on a drum.

Nor should church bells be rung.

Why play the flute to those who are shivering?!

Yes, why do so? Brecht gives a start and goes to have a look at the stove. It is warmish. Thank God. Someone stoked it a bit during the night. On the other hand, it is clear that this fuel is going to cost something!

Cost or no cost, and whoever it is that gets paid, Brecht tries to merge with the stove. His shoulders and his backside are pressed against the stove. Now he tries to press his waist against it too. This he can manage, being relatively thin.

For a short while he is in his mother's womb.

BUT WHO IS THAT IN THE CORRIDOR?

In the womb, maybe, but more specifically?

There is a pocket atlas in the pocket of the rucksack. You can see from it where Finland is, China is, and Germany is.

Germany and Finland are fairly near to one another. There is no dialectic in their proximity. They just happen to have ended up here in Europe. If you really want a dialectic, it is better to take a look at China. For instance, the relationship between China and Germany or China and What's-His-Name or China and Brecht. In ancient Chinese spirituality a plaiting together of some kind of dualism with contradictions can be identified.

Brecht pores for a long time over the map. His family just doesn't seem to turn up and the whole hotel is silent. It isn't very productive to be staring at a map. All atlases are models, but you can't really employ them in real life. You can goggle at a map all you want while still in your room, but once you get outside you nonetheless meet the world as it is, as it was before you started staring at the map. The world and a map of it are similar, isomorphs, but that's about all, and emotionally the sort of information given there lends no support to an emigrant.

But now someone is walking in the corridor.

As if sneaking along, cautiously.

Brecht rushes over to the door and locks it. Luckily the key was already in the lock. But a slight click can be heard nonetheless as he turns it. The Finn clearly hears this, as his footsteps—or whatever they are—stop. Brecht listens for a good while, his ear pressed to the door, the Finn listens for a good while on the other side. Neither dare to make the first move. Brecht is beginning to think that the Finn has gone away. I'm not going mad, Brecht convinces himself. Damn it, the corridor is empty!

Very carefully indeed, and this time without a click, he unlocks the door. Then opens the door an inch or two.

Brecht was wrong. The corridor isn't empty. Quite the opposite—a face fills the whole corridor. The Finn, or someone looking like a Finn, is right here in front of him. Once the door is ajar, he encounters the face of the blond beast, only some thirty centimeters from his own.

The stranger greets him and does so in German, which is, on the one hand, moving. But dialectically speaking it is a very bad thing. Why didn't he give a Finnish greeting? Obviously! He knows that Brecht is German. Looking the informer straight in the face, Brecht is surprised that there is an informer standing at his door. But he greets him back in German—before grunting a "whaddoyou-want?" The man doesn't want anything. He tells Brecht that he shouldn't leave his door unlocked, as there are thieves in the hotel, especially around midday.

"Especially at midday they're suddenly there, at your door, and then you know what will happen."

His tale sounds convincing enough, because the speaker is at his door and the clock is showing midday.

"I can tell you what thieves do," Brecht's new friend tells him.

"By all means, tell me," says Brecht.

The man explains.

"They open the door and step inside." He illustrates this by the corresponding action. The man is now in the room. "Then they look around. Often the occupant is in. But usually it is an American or an Estonian or a Latvian who has been on a long journey and is in need of a little shut-eye. So the uninvited guest looks around and takes something. Picks it up, as if by chance." The guest picks up the atlas, which is still open at the page showing China. The rest of what he says now occurs in sync with his actions. "The uninvited guest looks at China, as if interested in that country. Looks at China, looks a bit longer, then shuts the book and takes it away with him. Like this." The Finn steps, atlas in hand, across the threshold into the corridor.

Brecht's fingers twitch as if he wants to snatch back the atlas, but not a sound comes from his lips. He listens to the Finn's endless chatter, as if mesmerized.

"And they leave, stolen object in hand, walk down the corridor, as if nothing has happened. Walk calmly, like this, watch me. Walk really calmly. Please watch what I'm doing."

The man walks to the end of the corridor, then says:

"Now there is nothing to stop them, and they vanish round the corner."

And he vanishes.

Brecht overcomes his astonishment and runs towards the stairs. He's sure he wants to kill the Finn.

The stairs are deserted, the stairs are silent. Brecht shrugs his shoulders and returns to his room. He has been tricked. The Scandinavian has lured him into a trap. It all happened dialectically. He was alienated from his own actions. But not altogether. When Brecht reaches his room, the atlas is on the floor by the door. The Viking has brought it back. But when? While Brecht was down the corridor looking into the stairwell?

And where is he now?

Brecht gives a shrug. Theoretically this little incident hasn't been without its merits. The thief was a thief and yet he wasn't. Rather, he symbolized a thief. He was playing at being a thief. Did so with epic proportions, coolly, as if it were a "citation."

He was playing the thief, but he was the thief.

Brecht makes a few notes.

BRECHT'S FAMILY FINALLY COMES HOME AFTER ALL

When the women and children finally return home from the unfamiliar outdoor spaces of Helsinki, they seem brisk and harmonious to Brecht. Even to excess. Helene is always clear-headed. But Grete is lively too, even though there are pearls of sweat on her forehead.

Brecht naturally dare not talk about his strange encounter with the corridor man. His alibi is his half-finished manuscript of *The Good Woman of Sechuan*, which is lying on the table. But this isn't really a feint, in fact. Brecht has been thinking about matters Chinese. About Mo Di, for instance. And so, indirectly, about Sechuan.

Helene, however, is describing her adventures.

In a strange way, her good mood is in sync with that of Brecht.

Helene tells how she bumped into a man in the doorway of a store. Helene stepped to her right, the man to his left. Helene to the left, the man to his right. Helene again to the right, the man to his left. It is usual for such confusion to occur three times, then people find their bearings again and continued on their way. But no, here in Finland, things turn out differently, says Helene, triumphantly, we stepped to the left and to the right one more time. After that I went straight into the shop and the man stared after me, a curious look on his face.

"Oh, really?" asks Brecht. "How do you know? Did you look behind you?"

Helene starts thinking. There is quite a long pause. Brecht doesn't like the idea that Helene looked back. Grete comes to the rescue. Little Grete, sweet Grete. She wipes her face and says that it was she who looked behind her. She swells with pride. It's possible. Grete is always looking in every direction, even behind. She is small, with darting movements. Helene is large and slow. Like an elephant? No, not really. Elephants are something else. It's a handy comparison, but it doesn't fit, in the case of Helene. Helene is like a horse or a cow.

"It was, no doubt, a completely ordinary Finn," says Helene, finally.

"Yes, I suppose there are a lot round here," says Brecht, trying to generalize, although he hasn't actually been outside himself and the only strange experience he has had was the man at the door. What is beyond the door is no doubt Finland. But up to the threshold Brecht and his family are on private territory, with diplomatic immunity.

If at all.

The story is at an end, but Stefan feels he has to comment on his mother's tale.

"Actually, mom was quite startled, her face went chalk white."

Grete is flushed and starts coughing. Everyone can hear what pain she's in. They laugh along with her, although by now Grete is no longer laughing, simply coughing. The coughing starts from laughing. And now Grete starts to laugh in order to cover up her coughing. Evidently, the Finnish air is having a bad effect on her. But so did the air in Sweden, in Denmark, maybe even in Germany. In fact, any air affects Grete negatively. Air carries tuberculosis bacilli. If Grete didn't breathe, they'd die off. But Grete is breathing and the germs are doing fine.

Helene has managed to buy a little food. The shops were relatively empty. But at least there was enough bread.

NOW WUOLIJOKI TURNS UP AS WELL

Hella Wuolijoki turns up at lunchtime.

She is relatively rotund. That is the first thing that Brecht notices and registers when he sees her. Right in the doorway.

If Grete is like a fly, and Helene like a horse, then Hella is like a globe. A small globe, but a globe nevertheless.

A ball, at any rate.

As Brecht had suspected, Hella turns out to be intelligent. In the first place, she can speak fluent German, and secondly, she thinks for herself. This is something that Brecht experiences right from the start. Since he is himself a writer, he knows one when he sees one. Admittedly, Brecht himself admits that he once regarded himself as the only writer in the world. He thought the rest were stupid. There is no doubt a germ of truth in this. But the years have gone by and Brecht has been forced to admit that among his colleagues there are also people. Brecht was surprised at this. But he still turned the situation to his advantage. "I am even capable of admiring others," he says as he stands in front of the mirror, alone in the room. "Strange that tolerance has suddenly grown in me. I am arriving at a higher level of humanity, I am reaching a humane maturity."

That was what he thought, even before the war, and now he thinks the same.

Hella Wuolijoki takes a seat. She does not smell of sweat, but of something sweet. She is like a large bon-bon. Unexpectedly, they start talking about the Winter War. Brecht knows hardly anything about the Winter War, but he doesn't want to show it. Brecht has always kept abreast of politics. At least that is what the world thinks. At least those who have read his books. This represents 0.005% of the adult population of the world. Brecht has listened to the radio his whole life. During the Winter War he was in Sweden. Brecht gives her to understand that Finland attacked the Soviet Union first. Since Hella had to be—that was what they said in Sweden—a Russian agent—and so Brecht imagines that this version of events would meet with her approval. Brecht too prefers this version. Finland had to be a sly little bug. Although it is not entirely logical that she would want to swallow Russia, it can be supposed that the local militarists and plutocrats deliberately provoked excesses. So that they could divert attention of the people from the unemployment and low wages. In order to satisfy the demands of the warmongers. And here there is no doubt some collusion with What's-His-Name. What's-His-Name perhaps promised certain things, then pretended he hadn't heard or seen anything.

But so what, if Finland did attack first?

Things have to be seen dialectically.

Russia has great shortcomings if viewed *from one angle*. But from *the other angle* it is not impossible that Russia really did want to liberate the Finnish proletariat.

"From what? From whom?" asks Hella and goggles at Brecht with the whites of her immovable eyes.

"From factory owners, exploiters, landowners, well, I need not say any more on the subject."

"I too am a landowner," Hella points out.

"And a Communist," adds Brecht. "This is a productive contradiction. It proves that . . ."

"I am *not* a Communist, I sympathize with the Socialists!" Hella wags her finger. But too late—Brecht has mounted his hobbyhorse.

"What's the difference, Communist or Socialist or what the hell else, well, something anyway . . . something not in the interests of the working classes . . . which doesn't fit in with the class struggle!"

"Quite the opposite!" cries Hella. "I am very much *for* the class struggle, and the interests of workers are sacred to me!"

Brecht has to think. Of course Hella is right. Matters are reversed, but that doesn't change matters, simply justifies them even more.

"You are a warrior in the class struggle, a defender of the workers and, to an extent, defender of the proletariat out in the countryside, and a landowner at one and the same time! This fascinates me! This is dialectics!"

Brecht decides to become even more candid with her, as Hella smells so sweet. Over sixty and still so fragrant!

With few wrinkles, how taut the skin of her cheeks! No point in concealing anything from her!

"Of course—the Russians are far away, very far away from having the power to be dialectical! They aren't even dialectical in their slogans! Slogans should be dialectical, Hella. Well, I do understand if they're not. All the same, really. Maybe we will never have. What do I know, me being German—yes, a German, unfortunately, in the end we do have dialectics in our blood, we did after all discover dialectics, and we can't force it onto the rest of the world, if it doesn't want to listen—that has its own dialectics, the connectability and separability of German and Russian dialectics, when it comes to the crunch, ultimately—"

Grete has begun to do the stenography. A habit of hers.

Yet another child appears in the doorway. This is not one of Brecht's. Don't know where it came from. Brecht's spiritual energy must have brought it here. Must be a Finnish child.

"I'd got to the point where I was saying that although the Russians are, for some dialectical reason or other, not dialectical right now, they could at least have dialectical slogans on offer. That would help a great deal! The shots at Mainila, in other words gunshots, are one clear example of such a phenomenon.

In principle, the Russians derive support from facts, what they call facts, or the opportunity to name facts, or even a suitable climate for naming them facts, or things that elicit facts, and which we can call facts, and why shouldn't we term them facts, so let us do so—the Russians derive—Hella, are you following me? I'm sorry, but in such important questions, one has to be prestigious, a man of spirit, who should not suborn himself lightly to any old national thought—anyway, let's continue from the word "facts" and let's say that the Russians derive support from the *primitive dramatic aspect* of the facts. This is, to an extent, an oriental phenomenon. Stanislavski was like that. He liked superior beings and gunshots. And maybe blood in the evening snow. Perhaps that links him to Bulgakov. Distantly. And the accordion too.

Brecht is wrong here. Stanislavski did not like gunshots, neither in the light of dawn or dusk. See for instance Mikhail Bulgakov's A Theater Novel. When Bulgakov attributes a scene to the maestro, where there is blood in the snow, distant gunshots and accordion music can be heard and the moon is up, and Stanislavski gets hysterical and demands that the guns are replaced by knives.

This is sheer sentimentality. The treaty with the abovementioned Terijoki government made by the Russian government assumes the variant whereby the Finnish workers and peasants must exchange their *national* freedom for *social* freedom. That is the Russian argument. Yes, I agree it's an argument. It is an argument and it also sounds like an argument that is dialectical, and therefore justified. Hella, what was it you wanted to ask? Whether something dialectical automatically means it is justified? That's what it means, but *not* what it means, at one and the same time. Dialectics itself is dialectical in its rightness or wrongness. You always, always have to say: *it is, yet it isn't!!!*"

Hella, at any rate, gets up. Helene has approached silently and unobserved. Only Grete is stenographing away energetically. She even adds the remarks "shuts his eyes, opens them again" and "balls his fists."

Everything reeks of excess.

But Brecht can read the others' thoughts, as always. He sits down and comments what has gone on before:

"I went outside myself in order to demonstrate the temporary doubts and despair of an intellectual when confronted with great dialectical phenomena. But in order to avoid limiting myself by sheer emotionality, I shall terminate my own thoughts that I had already left in the air some while ago, and which will now serve as a full-stop after all this deliberation. I said that the Russians wanted the Finns to exchange their national freedom for social freedom. This argument is *weak*. And I shall say no more today. I am already well pleased that I have managed to lead my train of thought to its logical conclusion, formulating it in such a way that I cannot be accused of a complete lack of elegance, which is maybe surprising in a man who is spending his first day in a foreign country."

Brecht gives the impression that he no longer wants to say anything. But now the topic has got the women excited.

Brecht seems to doze off for a moment. Then he opens his eyes and seems surprised that somewhere in Sweden they are organizing a voluntary unit in support of Finland, to counter the threat from the east.

"The east, the east! Why not look to the south, where the greatest threat of all is coming from?"

"The south?" Hella is astonished. "What's there in the south?"

"What's there, what's there?" mocks Brecht. "Everyone knows what there is there."

"But what is there in the south?" asks Hella.

"Germany in the south."

Brecht's voice has Wagnerian overtones.

"How far away is this Germany?" asks Hella, mischievously.

Brecht looks at her reproachfully.

"Do not ask a refugee such things. How do I know exactly? When I go outside, and look in a southerly direction, I assume that Germany is down there. Somewhere eighty, or eighty thousand, kilometers away. But you can never be sure at any given moment how far away it is. It is expanding all the while. Pursuing me the whole time. Germany is like an ink stain on blotting paper, or maybe a broken thermometer," complains the emigrant Brecht.

He has still more to say.

The sadness can be heard in Brecht's voice when he says that a new war will strengthen the bonds between the Finnish proletariat and the bourgeoisie. When Russia and Germany divided up Poland the previous September, Brecht was not happy with Russia's boast that now the territory of European Socialism had increased at the expense of the capitalists. Brecht considered such an argument as opportunistic.

"How can it be claimed that the liberation of a couple of million Polish workers strengthens the Socialist bloc, when this strengthening is bought at the price of a pact with the fascists?"

Helene thinks that such difficult political decisions or even mistakes depend on the political situation in Russia. Brecht agrees and regards such approaches as dialectical.

"In fact, the Winter War was a great virtue."

"Excuse me," says Hella drily, "but what kind of a virtue?"

"The Winter War let the world see, or maybe only me, but others through me, gave at least some people, the opportunity to get to know materialism more intimately, *in reality*."

Verbatim—and this is Brecht's argument, brimming with pathos:

"Everywhere in the world, wherever you look, two things are locked in combat, and I, being on this earth, will name them as follows. Listen attentively, Mrs Wuolijoki! In this world, two ideas are vying for supremacy. One of these ideas is: 'The Soviet Union is Socialism.' The other is its opposite: 'The Soviet Union is not Socialism.'"

Brecht forgets himself, looking into Grete's open mouth. Grete is so seized by the rush of words coming from the mouth of this intellectual giant that she has forgotten to continue with the stenography, has put her indelible pencil to her lips and is looking at him. Brecht doesn't like this. A trickle of aniline is running out of the corner of her pale blue mouth. Brecht is a dictator by nature, but still doesn't like being gazed at so submissively.

"What is it?" he asks impatiently.

"Aren't you beginning to have your doubts about the Soviet Union, my dear?" asks Grete, and Brecht sees that his lover could well be about to burst into tears. Helene also opens her eyes wide in a strange sort of way. In her eyes, Brecht sees that the sun is setting. The sun has rounded the corner, is shining in at the window, not over Brecht, but into the corner of Helene's eye and it is there that Brecht sees its reflection. These April days are pretty short. And Brecht no longer expounds at length, but sums up hastily:

"The Soviet Union and Socialism are not one and the same thing. We can maybe find certain elements of Socialism in the Soviet Union and maybe also . . . the corresponding . . . superstructures."

"Let's go there," says Grete. "We're only going to pass through that country. Why only through? Let's stay there. They'd love us there."

Brecht looks Grete in the eye.

"Tired of life?" he asks, as bluntly as you can ask a TB sufferer.

BUT NOW IT'S HELLA'S TURN

The next evening Hella is present again. Brecht was a little befuddled the previous day. It was, after all, his first day in the mists, the North and the night. Brecht has talked so much about this that his senses have become dulled.

The world outside has not managed to impinge, and his inner world is in a flurry, has changed into politics, philosophy and goodness knows what else.

"Hella, I have to admit that I've still not had a walk round your city," admits Brecht. "I've stayed in my room."

"Take it easy," says Hella in a motherly way.

Brecht looks at her and thinks that she has a face, yes, a face like the Moon, but that her body is pretty massive too. For some reason it arouses a measure of unease in Brecht.

"Please sit down, I mean: sit down, would you," he says and sees in his mind's eye how the iron bedstead of the *Hospiz* sinks under Hella's weight. But not all the way. Hella is large, but doesn't weigh an awful lot. The bedsprings creak, but the piece of furniture is far from collapsing. Brecht would like now to ask Hella how much she weighs. Below the hundred kilo mark, at any rate.

Naturally, he doesn't ask.

A long pause ensues. I know, thinks Brecht, that Grete is where she usually is, but where is Helene? She isn't in her room. She's in the communal kitchen making coffee. She has popped out for a moment. As for the weather, it's like it was yesterday. Otherwise, there's very little to be seen in the sky round here. The part he can see is colorless, in other words, gray.

The pause continues for so long that Brecht is tempted to term it the general pause.

In theater terms, this means a long pause, an impossibly long pause. With such a pause, a great artist proves to himself, the audience, and the critics how ridiculous it is to keep silent for so long. He has a thousand little ploys up his sleeve, facial expressions or slight gestures, with which he can surprise his audience. He draws it out as long as he possibly can. He senses when the audience is growing bored. There is no need to even start coughing. A maestro knows by telepathy when to cut the silence and return to the author's text. He starts speaking again. The scene continues as if nothing had happened. This is what Hella is doing right now, someone whose plays, which always have a pause at some point or other, are very popular in Finland.

Hella appears to have laid the golden egg.

"Ich liebte eine Deutsche," she then says, "as a young girl I fell in love with a German."

"Oh yes?" says Brecht cautiously. He is not prepared to enter into intimate relations with Hella. I can't do everything here under the sun, thinks Brecht. And Hella is too rotund for Brecht. Should be bonier, I suppose.

His wife Helene comes in. Grete may soon come and do some stenography, as canonical Brecht treatment demands.

Hella, who is quite healthy and normal, can see that the woman sitting there scribbling under the palm is ill.

When Grete was 17 years old, a gypsy woman foretold that she would live to the age of 33. Strangely enough, that is what happened: 1908 + 33 = 1941.

Hella doesn't know that Grete is busy stenographing. She thinks that the consumptive woman is doodling. Many people do when listening to a lecture or are thinking third thoughts in some second place.

"You haven't asked why I said *Ich liebe eine Deutsche*," says Hella, growing a tad nervous.

"Well, why did you?" says Brecht with the required enthusiasm.

"Our major author Tammsaare wrote a novel with that title."

"Oh did he?"

"He did."

"I understand," says Brecht, suppressing a yawn.

In fact, Brecht doesn't think anything at first. Fine, this "Tammisaari" wrote some novel or other. So what? I suppose those Finns read everything ever written. Something is being written everywhere. This has been caused by the growth of literacy. Literacy pops up all over the place. They all start writing in the end. Once you've mastered the alphabet, you start writing. Why shouldn't "Tammisaari" start writing if he really wants to? It'd enrich culture in general, or some global model or other.

Brecht maybe doesn't know about Whorf and Sapir's theories, which were expounded at about the same time. What can be said about them (in very simplified form) is this: they thought that language determined thought, maybe even behavior. According to this theory, every nation that has its own language has a correspondingly idiosyncratic way of thinking. And it is pleasant to think that in accordance with this theory the Estonians (like the Hopi Indians) are enriching the kaleidoscope of the world.

If it needs enriching, and if this world is necessary in the first place.

If Brecht had known these theories, he would no doubt have found fault with them. But he doesn't know them! So he doesn't find fault with them. He thinks: well, OK. "Tammisaari" fell in love with a German. Many people have fallen in love. And some have even fallen in love with Germans, thinks Brecht. So, love in what way?

Brecht poses this question.

"Tammsaare's novel is about a neurasthenic . . . and masochistic person, but what is happening to me is positively romantic."

"Are neurasthenia and a romantic disposition opposites?" he asks, just in case.

"I dunno," says Hella, casually.

"Do tell," requests Helene.

Hella smooths her dress over her belly and begins:

"Anyway, I was a schoolgirl and read so much that I became anæmic."

HELLA CONTINUES HER TALE

"Yes, I was a schoolgirl and was reading so much that I contracted anæmia. Every night I slept a couple of hours, every night, let's say, from eleven to twelve, then from four to five. I weighed very little, I mean to say that I rapidly grew thin. Then came the fancy dress party. Me and Frieda—yes, Frieda, that was her name—we were dressed up in baby clothes. I was the "blue baby" and Frieda the "pink baby." I weighed very little at the time, around forty kilos. A German student who was dressed up as the Trumpeter of Säckingen, lifted me up onto the lid of the piano. That is to say, I was originally sitting on a chair, then he clasped me and lifted me up onto the lid of the piano. And as I was sitting there on the piano, he began to sing: *die Liebe liebt das Wandern . . . Gott hat sie so gemacht, von einem zu dem Andern . . . Gott nicht glauben . . . ja, glauben . . .* I think that's what he was singing, and I sang back, lying there on my side on the lid of the piano: *ich kann es nicht fassen, nicht glauben . . .* We carried on singing forever. No one would have believed that we were improvising, they all thought we'd arranged it beforehand. The boy was, in fact, a Volga German, a theologist. Oh, what did we do after the singing had ended! We played pantomime . . ."

Tammsaare's novel (1935) tells how an inhibited Estonian country boy, now a student, falls in love with a former (the action takes place during the interwar period of Estonian independence) baron's daughter, but his inferiority complex prevents him from expressing his love for her.

"Thanks to its dialectical qualities, pantomime means quite a lot to me," says Brecht, "because there . . ."

But Hella will not be interrupted.

"Hold on a minute, Bébé," she says, somewhat curtly, "listen to what I'm telling you. We were doing pantomime, then there was a ball, on the street—this was all happening in winter, as you will remember, Bébé, I will have mentioned some time or other that in winter, when fancy dress balls were held, but this was not in the depths of winter, but in the spring. Then we walked in the milky white

31

moonlight. The moonlight lit me up through a veil of thin clouds. Ah, this was happening in April. What kind of winter is that! It was in the middle of spring! Like now. It's April now too. But then it could have been March. Or, maybe, not March, because there was still snow on the fields, though no longer in the city. And we were suddenly walking through fields. What we did was simply smile at one another, and said nothing. And now the *pointlet* of this little tale . . .

"You what?" asks Grete.

"*Pointchen* (the moral, the point)," replies Hella.

The story had to be told right to the end.

"The point is this, that a black dog had been following us, right from the start. It disappeared now and again, then reappeared again. Like a bad conscience. The German tried to shoo it away, but the hound kept getting under my feet and wouldn't let me proceed. I said to the dog: my dear Mephisto, do go home, I'm not on the wrong road."

This theme is from Goethe's Faust. *The Estonian intellectual Linnar Priimägi has pointed out that the Devil in the guise of a dog doesn't appear in the original folk tale version. The satanic dog comes from Agrippa von Nettesheim. (See: "Akadeemia" 2/1990.)*

"But the dog did not go away until I had reached my door. There Schleuning kissed—that was his name—my hand. Yes, I had fallen head over heels in love. But you, Brecht, should know that I, in fact, hated the Germans, who had enslaved us for seven hundred years!"

The seven hundred years of slavery is a colorful image often used by Estonians to describe their history, expressing a certain amount of both masochism and self-pity. At the beginning of the 13th century the Teutonic Knights overran Estonia, bringing with them Catholic monks and the Christian faith. The Estonians made one huge leap from the Viking era into the High Middle Ages. The Teutonic Knights ran the country for about three hundred years, after which confusion arose, where Denmark, Poland and Sweden were all vying for control of Estonia. The last of these three ended up running to show for a while. At the beginning of the 18th century, Russia invaded Estonian territory. (At the same time a layer of Baltic German power was preserved.) Estonia did not manage to become fully independent until 1918. But jumping ahead, it can be told that the Russians were back in Estonia by 1940, and this time vassal status was to last until 1991!

"Or let's put it this way. Europe has held us captive in her cultural bosom for seven hundred years, and for some reason we regard Europe as German and if there is anything we want to escape from anyone, then it is from those that stand closest to us, historically.

"I wanted to fight for freedom, and if we couldn't actually get directly at the Russians, then we could at least fight our beloved Germans. The German's weapon was love. He was so handsome and good. But I couldn't bring myself to love him. No! Can't love a German, that's all there is to it, is what I said to myself. So I didn't. I dropped him. My country was young. His country, your country, Brecht, was old. And then—then I ended up marrying a Finn. I never dreamed that I would end up in Finland. But that's what I've done . . ."

Helene asks, as this is unintelligible to her:

"Ending up here? But weren't you born in Helsinki?"

"No," Hella shakes her head intensively, "I arrived in Finland for the first time in the autumn of 1904, when I was eighteen. I was wearing a blue hat tied with a gray ribbon. I knew nothing of this strange city and strange country and stood there in the rain, until a young cabby spotted me and took me to my lodgings. As I remember, it was on Alexander Street. I couldn't say anything more, because I knew no Finnish at the time."

"How d'you mean?" asks Brecht.

"I came from Estonia."

"What d'you mean, Estonia? Why?"

Brecht is beginning to understand that the world is even more confusing than he could ever have imagined. But he doesn't show his perplexity. He listens politely, as Hella continues.

I'm an Estonian, explains Hella, the Estonians speak the Estonian language and I was born and brought up in Estonia and came to Helsinki to go to the university.

"Didn't what you term Estonia have its own universities?"

"There was one, but I wanted to come here."

HELLA AND THE TELEPHONE

"I was living in Pohjola House, in the *matkustajakoti*, that is, the youth hostel. When I went down in the dark to the refectory I thought that it was me who was that frightened girl in that strange house."

"Yes, yes," says Brecht, to whom this sounds familiar, yet unfamiliar at the same time.

"The biggest surprise of all was when something began to ring in the corridor. Then after that ringing, someone started a monologue in the corridor."

"That was the telephone," guesses Brecht quite rightly and Hella nods.

Brecht himself has never been afraid of the phone, but there weren't any telephones in the Augsburg of his youth.

By the time Brecht ripened and became a youth, then a man, telephones did exist, and they interested him a good deal.

Brecht soon developed his own telephone style. He would say "hello," American-style, into the mouthpiece while shifting his cigar from one corner of his mouth to the other. Sometimes he thought how he had grown up with modern technology and how he and the technical developments of the twentieth century were coevals. But a telephone's a telephone—what is more important is that this round old lady is an emigrant. She has not, admittedly, fled from Germany and What's-His-Name, but she did flee to this same Finland, from somewhere and for some reason.

"Yes, but what were you fleeing from, *Frau* Hella?" Brecht has decided to be candid.

"I didn't flee from anything," explains Hella. "But the university in Saint Petersburg had a lot of applicants and I wanted to study folklore. So I chose Helsinki instead."

"So there weren't so many people trying to get a place here?"

"I suppose not."

A strange reply, but maybe the old lady can't remember everything now in such detail.

"Actually, I'm a *chukhna*," she adds.

"A what?" ask both Brecht and Helene in chorus and Grete drops her pencil on the floor.

"A chookhnaaaaaa!"

Hella is enjoying the sound of this strange word. "That's what the Russians call Estonians and Finns. You can find the root of this word all over the place. In words like *chudi* . . . That's what the Lapps call the Karelians. Our country is bordered by Lake Peipus, or Peipsi as we call it, but the Russians have their own name for it: *Chudskoye ozero*. *Chudo* is the word for *Wunder* in Russian, in other words, a marvel, a wonder."

For some reason, Brecht has a sense of foreboding.

But Hella carries on quietly telling her tale.

"When they call me *chukhna* in Russia or here in Finland, I have always managed to think of some comic insult to throw back at the person who uttered that word. I've said—*russkiy poroshonok*, Russian piglet. You understand? Brecht? Do you get it? They say something convoluted, something which could turn out to be an insult, but something which, at any rate, makes me feel hurt. Yet I reply with a humorous little phrase. Actually, I like Russians."

Suddenly there is a knock at the door.

"Is Ilmanen staying here?" asks someone, whose face remains out of sight.

We can't see their face, because Brecht is blocking the whole crack between door and frame.

"No," says Brecht in German. The person asking the question appears satisfied with the answer, and clearly goes away, as Brecht shuts the door, thinks for a moment, shrugs his shoulders, sits down and turns to Hella with a question on his face. More or less: Sorry, where were we?

Hella tells about her other adventures.

"In 1905, I went to visit my friend Fanny in Saint Petersburg. They were having a ball there. I had nothing to put on except my school dress. But what did we do, me and Fanny? We cut the sleeves off. As for the neck, this is what happened: it started out as pretty small, a little heart-shaped cut-out. It ended up as a huge, square *décolleté*. In the corners of the *décolleté* we stuck orchids. Black ones, not real, as far as I remember, but artificial ones. Maybe some suitor had presented them to Fanny. Anyhow, once I'd pulled on a pair of long black gloves, I was perfectly presentable and even reminded people a little of Yvette Guilbert, or even one of the Three Musketeers. And there were counts, princes, and politicians at that ball, weren't there? But what happened next! The time of the Russian Revolution was drawing near. Lots of people clustered around me and, for some reason, asked me whether it was true that Finland was going to break away from Russia. Is that someone knocking again?"

Grete goes to see, but this time there is no one there, so no one could have knocked.

Hella continues.

"One officer asked me whether . . ."

Then Hella gets up all of a sudden and goes over to the window. Through it one can see a park, the National Theater and the railroad station. In fact, none of them are completely visible. Just the roofs. And since there is nothing interesting to look at, Hella turns round and continues:

"One officer asked me how Obolensky was thought of in Finland."

"And who did you say this damned Obolensky was?" asks Brecht.

Brecht cannot listen to women's tales for very long at a time.

"Obolensky replaced Bobrikov."

"What Bobrikov?" This time it is Helene's turn to ask.

"You know, the one that Schauman went and shot dead," Hella remains on an even keel.

"What Schauman?" It is Brecht who asks now.

"The one who then shot himself?"

"Why?"

Wuolijoki moistens her lips with coffee.

"Bobrikov was a major Russifier."

"And what does that mean?"

"He Russified," says Hella, continuing on her train of thought, because where could she retreat to now? "For instance, he required that all civil servants speak nothing but Russian in their jobs."

"What's bad about that?" Helene isn't understanding a thing.

"Well, he didn't allow other languages to be spoken!"

"So, were people speaking other languages, then, *Frau* Hella—I mean earlier, while this Slobrikov was doing his Russifying?"

"Here, people speak Finnish, Mr Brecht!"

"But why, Hella?"

"Why? Why? What language are Finns supposed to speak? Thanks to Bobrikov, him . . . and everything else . . . the Czar had nearly put an end to Finland's autonomy! And so this Bobrikov was shot by Schauman on the steps of the Senate, then he shot himself and later on Obolensky came, and then, in 1905, there was this ball at Fanny's place in Piteri, as we call the city, where I reminded people of Yvette Guilbert, and then this officer went and asked me how people related to Obolensky in Finland. I replied . . ."

Hella breaks off all at once and stands up.

Her face grows serious, her eyes become slits.

Hella says once again:

"I answered his question. I stood there and replied: not like they did to Bobrikov. So that the Finnish senators might be able to come to terms with him. And then—after all this, the officer said, drily—"

A dryness of tone enters Hella's voice.

"He said drily that Obolenski was not the right man to come to terms with the *chukhnas*. A long pause. About as long as this."

Hella places her hand on an imaginary sword and pauses for a good while.

Then, quite unexpectedly, she looks murderously at Brecht.

"I smacked him," she says at the exact same moment.

Hella's hand flies through the air and comes to rest on the imaginary cheek of her imaginary interlocutor.

And now the voice of the storyteller grows louder.

"And—I said that I was not a *chukhna*! An unspeakable scandal. The officer bowed and replied that *unfortunately* it was not right to hit a woman."

"Soviet officers tended to have good manners and could act like gentlemen when necessary," notes Helene pensively.

"We're not talking here about Soviet officers. They only appeared on the scene some dozen years later. When the Soviets took power, that is. This was a Russian officer, and a very handsome man too. I became the queen of the ball. But do you know what the time is?" says Hella, suddenly getting agitated.

It's nine, and Hella is suddenly in a hurry to leave.

BRECHT TAKES STOCK

About half an hour later, when it is already dark outside, Brecht says:

"I can see a certain measure of dialectics here: on the one hand, a naïve nationalism, on the other, the unskilled use of the tools of epic theater. Hella's epic theater started out in an un-Aristotelian manner. She *showed*, distancing herself, doing so unconsciously, it is true, not taking up arms in a Marxist dialectical way, simply doing something rather childish, with the semi-proletarian spontaneity of a vassal people. *On the other hand*, she did use things she'd really experienced and felt empathy. Stanislavski's influence can be seen in this, which is hardly surprising, because Hella had no doubt played some role in the end of the Winter War and getting the peace treaty with the Soviet Union. For that reason, a Slav kind of theatrical mannerism can flare up in her on occasion."

Grete writes these thoughts down.

Brecht wakes up early for once, with a bad taste in his mouth.

Nothing to be done but to get up.

He climbs out from under the covers. When he put one foot down, his toe touches something cold and slippery.

Brecht cries out instinctively, only then looks to see what is under his foot.

A large frog.

But different to the ones Brecht has encountered before. It's not green, but brown all over. Slimy and bumpy, too. Brecht rubs his eyes, but the frog doesn't go away.

The door to the next room opens cautiously, but no one steps inside.

"Ruth?" asks Brecht for some reason.

"No rat here," replies Helene in a low voice, "so you don't know where it is?"

"Ruth'll be arriving. She's bound to turn up," says Grete comfortingly.

The frog stirs, right there under Brecht's foot.

"Look! Look! Look!" yells Brecht.

"Are you having nightmares?"

"No nightmares, just this creature, this thing, I don't know what to make of it."

"Maybe it's Ruth."

"This isn't any Ruth, it's just that I can't identify it."

The women enter the room and eye the unfamiliar frog. Neither can bring themselves to say anything. Brecht himself takes up the thread of the conversation.

"We now find ourselves on the far plains of the north and we shouldn't therefore draw any precipitate conclusions. All sorts of things can happen up here. I have to admit that when I arrived at the port in Åbo, I thought I saw a fish with red eyes under the surface of the water. Maybe it wasn't a red-eyed fish, but that's what it seemed to be at the time. And now this frog! In a foreign country it's easy to make misjudgements because of unfamiliarity, ones which cannot be rectified. But as Mrs Wuolijoki has been so kind as to look after us, we'll have to ask her. She knows more about local conditions than we do. Even if she's Estonian. After all, she's lived here for a good while."

"I'm sure she doesn't come across frogs every day," says Grete with some hesitation.

"In this way I can manage to understand that Estonia is near to here. It's possible that exactly the same sort of creatures live there as here. No, she must know."

Brecht is being categorical. "Put the creature in a basket and take it to her, as you've got to go to her place anyway to get the food."

"Doesn't matter what kind of creature it is," says Grete analytically, emphatically, her brow creased. "How did it manage to get up here on the sixth floor of a hotel?"

"Either it was here already, or somebody brought it. I wouldn't be surprised if somebody's trying to drive us crazy," says Brecht and opens his map of Helsinki and starts looking.

"Amazing!" he cries.

The women give a start and come closer.

"The whole matter is simpler than I thought! At present, we're in Hotel Hospiz. We're in the center of the city, next to the railroad station. Look how easy it is for Hella to come over to visit us!"

She has to go through the city center, reach the Esplanades. From there along Uudenmaankatu, which is at right angles to it. Along Uudenmaankatu, then left into Telakkakatu and—there you are—Telakkakatu becomes Merikatu where Hella Wuolijoki lives.

Next, Grete puts on her coat and the frog in a basket.

"What's the date today?" asks Brecht.

"The twentieth," replies Helene.

Brecht strikes his forehead with his hands.

"So that's why I was feeling so down: it's What's-His-Name's birthday today! That's why everything makes me want to puke. No, this can't be a coincidence. Brutal secret agents have been sent out to hunt me down. The offspring of primeval soil and primeval moisture, chthonic German beings that crawl under my bed. Teutonic princes transmogrifying themselves into pseudo-frogs."

An hour later Grete is back and, instead of the frog, the basket is now filled with a thermos flask of coffee.

"What have you done with Hitler's emissary?" asks Brecht.

"I let him loose in the park behind the hotel, because it was just an ordinary toad, a *Kröte*.

"Grete?!"

"'ne Kröte!"

"Grete?"

"Of course it's a Kröte."

"Maybe Goethe," suggests Brecht.

"Hella said, what-what-what, oh what a poor, innocent little creature, more useful than harmful, because it eats vermin."

Brecht smiles a wry smile and lights a cigar.

"Yes, maybe I am too, for the Painter, also known as What's-His-Name—

Brecht not only calls the Führer What's-His-Name, but sometimes he calls him the Painter, referring to Hitler's painting and architectural activities in his youth.

—and maybe I also eat vermin for him! How often it is that at night some mosquito gets up my nose, how often do I not eat cattle that destroy all manner of meadows?!"

"Oh! Ah!"

"But why have we still not had our first cup of coffee of the day?"

Brecht doesn't really know much about so-called nature, as mentioned above. He doesn't want to know, either. Brecht treats everything natural with suspicion. What's-His-Name loves the Soil, the Land, and Blood. Brecht pits himself against What's-His-Name as an internationalist, therefore a "rootless" asphalt author. Asphalt is neutral, but soil smells, goes moldy, multiplies and breeds fascism.

DENMARK

Dear Ruth! Where are you?

British troop units make a landing in Norway near Trondheim, then move in a south-easterly direction, in order to help Norwegian forces push back the German advance in the south. The first battle takes place near to Lillehammer. A British vessel is sunk, and all the troops now have are rifles and machine-guns. It is an unequal battle. Lillehammer falls to the Germans. The British forces begin the retreat and the Germans are still pursuing them!

Denmark has been in a sticky situation, right from the start. The invasion caught them unawares. General Kurt Heimer, who was leading operations, arrived anonymously in Denmark on 7th April by train, then at dawn on the 9th the German navy arrived and passed the shore batteries, which did not fire a shot. The ministers proposed that the King capitulate. Only the Army Chief-of-Staff, Prior, wanted to resist, but even he was forced to insist on the resistance only being maintained for a short while. German bombers droned over the roof of the Royal Castle. The Danes decided to capitulate. It was difficult to inform some sections of the population of this fact, because all radio stations were not yet up and running so early in the morning. A German radio sender was helpfully sent by truck to the royal palace to assist. And so losses were kept to a minimum. According to Shirer, the Danes lost thirteen men, and a further twenty-three were wounded. The Germans lost around twenty. At two o'clock, the German general paid a visit to the seventy-year-old King Christian X, who was, by the way, the brother of the King of Norway, Haakon the Seventh. When the Danish King heard that Hitler would allow him to keep his own lifeguard, he became markedly more cheerful and finally said to the German general: "Can I say something to you, as an old soldier? You, the Germans, have begun something unbelievable. I have to admit that it has been done in a grand way!"

The Germans didn't have any major problems with the Danes. The indigenous people were allowed to retain a relatively large measure of freedom. Denmark was proclaimed to be a model protectorate.

This also affects Ruth and her fate.

Ruth is, after all, a Dane.

While Brecht was still in Sweden, Ruth visited him for a while, but then she went back to Denmark in the spring, to act in one of Brecht's plays. Both Brecht and the Communist Party, of which Ruth was a member (as opposed to Brecht, who had never been) asked Ruth to leave Denmark before things got any worse.

Before Brecht fled to Finland, he sent a letter to Ruth in Denmark.

"From now on, I will be expecting you to come, wherever I happen to be, and I will always take you into account." He suggested that Ruth behave calmly, with humor, pragmatically and critically. He gave Ruth Hella's phone number in Helsinki, but suggested she learn it by heart and destroy the note.

PART II

EARLY SPRING

1940

A BILINGUAL GUEST

That evening, a journalist arrives from the main Swedish-language newspaper.

He explains to Brecht that Finland is a bilingual country.

Brecht already knows this, but doesn't let on.

The journalist is a little put out that Brecht is so indifferent towards bilingualism. He of course asks why Brecht came to Finland, and of course Brecht wants to escape to . . .

"The Soviet Union?" the journalist suggests.

Brecht denies this and says that his goal is in fact the USA, but visas take time and he will have to wait for an answer here in Finland and hopes it won't take longer than a month to get the visas.

THE FOLLOWING EVENING

The following evening a journalist turns up from the Finnish-language newspaper.

Now Brecht becomes a little more talkative.

He likes the fact that people know him a little bit here. A refugee can't expect to be popular among a foreign people, in a country he has ended up in on account of the Painter. Only red-eyed fish and frogs know you here. The taxi drivers don't chat with you about your works. And although Brecht suspects that he is being interviewed on the instigation of Hella and her friends, he is happy nonetheless. He becomes quite talkative and tells him that he cannot live without his work. He says he's researching the fall of Roman Empire at present, in order to write a novel about Julius Caesar.

You can get an impression of this work from the Hans Dahlke book. The novel remains a series of fragments. What Brecht did finish was the short-story "The Exploits of Mr Julius Caesar" which is one of his "Calendar Stories." Some people have thought that Rome and Hitler's Germany are comparable and that Brecht has here been influenced by Feuchtwanger. The last Fake Nero *was a striking allegory, but not a historical novel.*

Brecht in fact regards Caesar as a symbol and archetype for all sorts of dictators. Brecht actually remembers Hegel's adage about the business managers of the world spirit. Brecht takes this literally and dialectically. Human beings are, after all, *homo oeconomicus,* and individuality is merely one attribute of businessmen. But the World Spirit? So what if Hegel did mention it? That too is a myth. Some people are very great. Greater than great can be. Mann, for example—

Brecht says somewhere, on the topic of Thomas Mann's neurasthenic and homosexual son, Klaus Mann: "The whole world knows Klaus Mann, Thomas Mann's son. But who, by the way, is this Thomas Mann?" (Klaus Mann, himself a writer, killed himself in exile in 1949.)

"That great Mann, great man that he was, who knows the whole Bible and more, especially the life of Joseph . . . he is very great. Have you heard of Thomas Mann?"

The journalist, who is slightly afraid of Brecht, shakes his head, but changes his head movements into something halfway between shaking and nodding.

Brecht is no fool.

"The movement you just made with your head was dialectical," says Brecht, praising what he has just seen. "Anyway, a certain Thomas Mann is said to have claimed that myth has to be made more human, pulled out of the reach of fascism. That would be our own, humanist myth. Wrong! Myth has to be destroyed! Myth must be replaced by sociology! Caesar is no businessman of the world, but a gangster, influenced by bankers! Bourgeois democracy and fascism are merely different guises of capitalism! Yes, sir!"

Brecht spills his cigar ash, burns his thumb and runs out of the room.

The journalist dare not make a move.

Then Brecht returns, quite calm now.

He sits down, lights his cigar again.

It is growing dark outside.

Brecht complains, with remarkable tranquillity, that he has collected too much material over time, the women bring him more all the time and this mountain of material constitutes a threat causing the whole plan to founder. There is always present this insane idea of writing "The Biography of Caesar"! What could be more damaging, less dialectical! Let that "great name," that Mann, write the biographies of Joseph and Potiphar's wife!

Mann, whom Brecht hated, later regrets that he had not in fact chosen a completely unknown figure instead of Joseph to write about, even a nameless pharaoh.

"It took a good deal of effort on my part to simplify the history so necessary for my project," says Brecht, heartily rounding off his speech, "clearly I'm growing old."

The journalist says farewell, leaves then later on sums up things as follows, once he has arrived home:

"How many of the best minds in Europe are now shut up in such little rooms! A hotel room in France: Lion Feuchtwanger. A hotel room in New York: Thomas Mann. A hotel room in Hollywood . . . And between them fronts, mined stretches of sea, peoples driven from their homelands. I can do nothing about it that an ancient image has taken me over: and darkness was upon the face of the deep and the Spirit of God moved upon the face of the waters."

BUT SOMETHING HAD TO BE HAPPENING IN THE SOUTH TOO

Hella comes up at lunchtime and says:

"There's something happening all over the place, even south of the Gulf of Finland, so it would seem."

She says nothing more.

But what is it that is happening over there, on the southern shores of the Gulf of Finland? It's only eighty kilometers away. That is, after all, where Hella was born!

Russia has asked Estonia to accept a further 1,150 troops, who would be stationed in the port of Paldiski.

How many Russian troops are already stationed in Estonia?

They are 31,647 in number. But they are not very visible, because they stay inside the Soviet military bases that were built in 1939. In that year, a treaty was signed, so that 25,000 soldiers could enter Estonia. Now there has been another demand, this time to expand the bases. The Soviet Union points out that the presence of several thousand troops on Estonian soil in no way constitutes the Sovietization of the country. To avoid giving this impression, the soldiers have been forbidden to mix with Estonians. They are not allowed to speak to them. When, on 7th November, Estonian Leftists want to celebrate the Great October Revolution, Molotov forbids this, sending word via the Soviet Ambassador Nikitin. Nor do they want the Estonian Foreign Minister Piip to give a pro-Soviet speech.

All the while, the troops continue to flow in.

And at this very time the Estonian literary specialist Eduard Päll is in Leningrad, putting the final touches to his translation of the Short Course on the Inter-Republic Communist Party (Bolsheviks). *This work—according to rumor—was written by Stalin himself! By the autumn, the Estonian language version is already in print.*

Then Helene rushes into the room, saying she has finally found an apartment.

"In the workers' district."

Hella does not know this part of Helsinki.

But when Helene goes into more detail, Hella realizes that this is Töölö, which is rather a nice district and quite near to the center.

"So what," says Brecht, "it is where it is, and in the end it doesn't make any difference. And as I have always supported the rights of workers, there is nothing to stop me from calling the part of town where I happen to live a workers' district."

This story about the workers' district is repeated in several biographies, especially in Schumacher, but also in Hayman. The address of the apartment was Linnankoskenkatu 20A, in a noble, centrally situated apartment building. According to some reports, Brecht received furniture from Finnish Socialists. Brecht later wrote a poem about this help, terming it altruism on the part of the Finnish workers.

THE WORKERS PROVIDE MORE ASSISTANCE

The apartment has four rooms. The kitchen has all modern conveniences, even a refrigerator filled with food.

All Brecht's things remained in Sweden.

But now he has again found the essentials in life.

The worst thing for a writer is not, Brecht thinks, having to keep your mouth shut. It's a lot worse when you have nothing to say via that mouth.

Terboven is appointed Reichskommissar for Norway. Up to now, Vidkun Quisling has thought of himself as the leader of the people there. From 1922–26 he was Nansen's assistant in the Soviet Union and Asia Minor. In 1933 he became Minister of the Interior. Some people have called Quisling's National Unity Party a pro-fascist organization. Now that Norway has finally been conquered by the Germans, they no longer allow him to run the country. He has too little authority among ordinary people. So the top job goes to Terboven who is a principled young Nazi.

That evening Goebbels meets the film star Jenny Jugo in Berlin. She is 35 years old and already made her début in silent films. Once a star, she was sent to Bulgaria to represent the German Reich there. Goebbels thinks that Jenny is sharp and sly. The minister has already trained her before, read the riot act to her, as he puts it. Principally on account of mannerisms. This last trait does not appeal to Goebbels. The three of them often watch films together (Hitler being the third party present) that can teach Jugo something. In Goebbels's opinion, she suffers from delusions of grandeur. But now Goebbels thinks that she could do something for the German cause in the Balkans. Jugo's request for a rise in salary leaves the minister relatively cold. Instead, he teaches Jugo how to behave in a foreign country. "The truth must be used as often as possible," explains Goebbels, "otherwise the source will lose its credibility. Lies are only useful when they are impossible to expose. Under certain circumstances the truth can appear to be an untruth, and then you have to abandon it. And smile, whatever else you do."

When Jugo leaves, Goebbels remembers the comedian Heinz Rühmann. He has become too insolent. He should be given another warning, decides Goebbels.

And lo and behold: a miracle! When Brecht moves in, the furniture is already in place. The apartment is of course very small: only eighty meters square in total floor area, but under war conditions many people live much worse.

Brecht does not know which of the two rooms that face the sun to occupy and use as his study. He draws lots.

The first night in the new apartment, Brecht feels that there are two moons.

This thought bothers Brecht. It has something irrational about it. But—is it not so that people are unable to think of circumstances and objects that cannot be altered by way of thought, ones which are not dependent on our thought processes? Should you think of such things, your thinking equipment breaks down, anomalous and asocial ideas are generated. Even causality should only be posited when it can be demonstrated. If some crazy piece of material evidence should come along, then it should be cast aside, or be ignored. If something is without contradictions, you should pay no attention to it.

But there are still two moons in the sky: one low, the other above it.

Yes, this may well be dialectical, though it's still very strange.

But then, in the darkness, two Finns pass by. They are speaking in low voices.

"Ilma," says one of them and laughs.

"Ilmasilma," replies the other and laughs the same warm, pithy laugh as the first.

Brecht is sure that they are workers. The middle classes and capitalists would not be out and about at night. They do not laugh in such a common way. Only the laughter of ordinary folks is warm.

Finnish workers laughing in the spring night, thinks Brecht, and there's two of them, which is of significance as only two can have a dialogue. When you're on your own, you wander around gloomily, in silence.

Brecht is now relieved, and looks up into the sky just to be sure. There is, of course, only one moon. Brecht goes to bed.

TANGO

On the Friday, Brecht is sitting in the railroad station restaurant with the Finland-Swedish poet Elmer Diktonius.

Diktonius is a proletarian author. At least that's what Brecht has thought since he found out that Diktonius had been the music teacher of the head of the Terijoki government, Otto Ville Kuusinen. What Brecht and Diktonius do not of course know is that Kuusinen's wife is right now wading through the icy River Ussa, in the direction of the labor camp at Vorkuta in deepest Russia. Thirty women prisoners have arrived from Kochmes and some are walking barefoot through the freezing water. Nor are these two men the only ones who don't know. No one knows this. Kuusinen's wife has disappeared without trace. And not even Kuusinen knows where his wife is, and presumably doesn't want to know, as it is better not to have any connection with an enemy of the people. Brecht regards Kuusinen as the true leader of the Finnish proletariat.

As they carry on their conversation, it emerges that Diktonius fought in the recent Winter War on the side of the Finnish bourgeois government.

This is curious, although it may conceal some dialectical deed or other.

"OK, war is war, but what now?" asks Brecht.

Diktonius explains that Finland's prospects have improved and now there is a hope that she will manage to keep out of the *big* war.

Brecht understands Diktonius' point of view to a certain extent. Nothing to be done if the un-dialectical tactics of the interim Soviet government have caused more enlightened minds to move to the right.

Then Diktonius stresses the fact that the Finns do have big worries. Virtually all imports to Finland have dried up. And war refugees are arriving from Karelia people who have to be housed somewhere.

Over one half of Karelia (24,748 km²) was handed over to the Soviet Union. Its southern part now belongs to Russia, to the Leningrad (nowadays: Saint Petersburg) oblast, while the northern part belongs to the so-called Karelian Soviet Autonomous Republic. This is all according to the treaty signed on 13th March 1940. That is how the Winter War was ended. (In this war, around 23,000 Finns perished and between 200,000 and 270,000 Russians.) The very next day almost every vehicle in Finland was requisitioned to evacuate those Karelian Finns remaining in Russia. Around 400,000 people fled.

By the way, Karelian refugees have even come to Hella's manor house. They begun working on the land. And Hella is trying to find accommodation for them.

"Thucydides: the strong do what they wish, the weak agree to what they can." (Citation by the diplomat Y. Kvitsinski in the newspaper Literaturnaya Gazeta *12.08.1992.)*

Brecht doesn't think that Finnish beer is real beer—which balances out the fact that local cigars here aren't real cigars.

Someone is playing a quiet tango on violins and the piano.

Tango music has reached Brecht's ears on occasions in this country.

Brecht asks Diktonius why you hear tango music so often here in Finland, when it in fact comes from a southern country, Argentina.

It is reckoned that the tango came from Africa to Argentina, not however from Spain like the similar dance the fandango, as popular thinking would have it. In the Bantu language, the word "tangu" means "to dance." Another theory is that the tango is connected to Sango, the Woruba god of thunder.

Diktonius tells that if you play tango music slowly it becomes very melancholy. In the case of the quick Argentinian tango, it is simply a matter of passion. But if you slow down a record of an Argentinian tango with your hand, you will immediately hear mournful music. The slow tango has become the Finnish national dance. This reflects the boundless melancholy of a primeval arctic people, which is awoken when, in the Polar night, people see the glow of the sunset on the horizon of the tundra. In it is reflected the hungry and dulled yellow eyes of wolves.

The Finns are in second place when it comes to global suicide statistics . . .

A good friend of the author of this novel, the suicide researcher or suicidologist, Airi Värnik, stayed for a couple of months in the year 1989 in the "Hospiz" hotel, in the very same room where Brecht had lived, prior to his move to Linnankoskenkatu.

This century, the tango has certainly affected cases of suicide in Finland, as it engenders such emotion in Finno-Ugrian peoples. The Hungarians are in first place when it comes to suicide, are they not? The national mood was affected a great deal there by the tango hit "Sad Sunday." After listening to it, many Hungarians went and committed suicide.

The slightly unpolished and, in Brecht's estimation, proletarian Diktonius now really gets going.

"Tango rhythms enter directly into the bloodstream of a Finn. They rush through his veins like a boiling wave, especially if he's drunk. The blood rushes to his head, and his hand automatically seizes his *puukko* knife, which he always has on him. He thinks all the world, singly and severally, and all its elements individually, such as rocks and cattle or snow are swinging to one rhythm, including himself, his lymph nodes and even his toes. Then he hears the inner voice of the wolf within him, a voice urging him on to committing orgiastic murder. He rushes blindly through the thick undergrowth and thrusts the knife into the back of his rival, who has just been innocently having a pee at the edge of the clearing."

Brecht shakes his head in disbelief.

He errs on the side of caution. Yes, he has read that in Nordic countries, people are easily seized by arctic hysteria. You never can tell when the fetters will fail.

Can't fully trust this Diktonius either. But he now starts reading a poem. In it, he describes himself as a huge block of granite, which has always of course been solid and cold, but within which something is seething and raging.

While filling his pipe, Diktonius warns poetically:

"... jag har lust att rusa fram, / bli grön skog, / Jag ville flamma som norrsken, / vridas I blixtparoxysmer";

("... I have the the urge to rush forth, / become a green forest. I want to burst into flame like the Northern Lights, / writhe in paroxysms!").

In Brecht's ears, this sounds quite appalling. He wouldn't want anyone to be writhing in paroxysms. It's just not elegant. Let the Painter do so. Diktonius is, admittedly, a proletarian soul, but Brecht is not afraid of him. Diktonius' hands are delicate and musical. Brecht knows that a barking dog does not bite, and he has seen before how proletarian writers flirt with decadence.

Dialectics are concealed in this, and Brecht continues to embroider on his beloved theme.

"Ah yes, paroxysms, they too . . . But no thoughts are identical. Thoughts are insubstantial, ephemeral and without responsibility. Thoughts are like Finnish drunks: they curse one another and stab while dancing the tango . . ."

"Finns do not stab people while dancing the tango," says Diktonius, inviting Brecht to re-enter reality. "They dance first, stab later."

But you just try to slow Brecht down!

"This is dialectical," he agrees immediately. "They dance and stab after dancing. Dance and knife belong together, influence one another. These concepts are in a sexual relationship. Their family quarrels are stormy and unpredictable—especially when you can't get a grip on the events in hand. The higher you are, the further you see. From above, you notice that one pair forms a pair of pairs with another. And so on. What at first glance appears to be a random babble and bustle ultimately turns out to be cemented together in a unity of contradictions. When alone, separate, nothing happens. There has to be something outside of yourself, like, for instance, a country that is alien to you. An emigrant's clash with his environment is very intensive, and for that reason exile is the best school for dialectics. You can ask for a dance in a foreign country and never be sure that you won't suddenly be stabbed, quite unexpectedly . . . And you . . ."

Brecht ponders for a moment and lights another cigar.

"But in being a synthesis, this does entail yet further changes! Refugees are refugees on account of change! They know nothing but change. They scan the sky, the land and the behavior of the oppressed classes. They scan the expressions on the faces of the oppressors in their castles and the slightest sign reveals the greatest passage of events. The likes of us have a good eye for contradictions."

Brecht raises his glass.

"To change," he says softly.

"To change," echoes Diktonius.

They chink glasses.

ON THE STEPS OF THE BOURGEOIS THEATER

When they have gone their separate ways, Brecht automatically makes for the Hospiz.

The city is fumbling along in semi-darkness as usual. This, on account of war and spring. The war, recently ended, and the spring.

Large dark clouds move across a yellow sky. The tower of the black railroad station building stands tainted by romantic inklings. The wind wafts up the dust. A war veteran is mumbling words of mendicancy in a foreign language.

Brecht goes up onto the rise by the theater entrance and looks at the advertisements. He doesn't understand the language, simply knows that the National Theater—

The Finnish National Theater was first constructed on the initiative of Kaarlo Berg-bom in the year 1872. Its present building and name are from 1902. After Berg-bom, the theater was run on a more serious basis by Eino Kalima (1917–50), Arvi Kivimaa (1950–74) and Kai Savola (1973–1992).

—well, that the Finnish National Theater is staging one of Kersti Bergroth's plays, *Anu and Mikko*! Some drawing-room farce, no doubt! Brecht looks at the theater program for a good while. It seems nice enough, thinks Brecht, that the theater, being a cultural institution, has started up again so soon after the war has ended. But on the other hand, he is convinced that here (as in Sweden where he has just come from) what could be termed realistic theater dominates the scene. Behind this granite façade, the action of the play is played with inner sympathy (Einfühlung). Here, the audience is made to believe that they can detect the fragrance of the cherry orchard located behind the building . . .

AT HOME

Brecht goes home to see what is going on in his rooms. He carefully opens one or two doors. The children are sleeping. Helene is sleeping.

There is light in the kitchen.

There sits Grete cutting the more important items of news out of the newspaper, in order to acquaint Brecht with them in the morning. Below the ceiling burns an unshaded lightbulb. The text of the China play is also spread out on the table. Grete always deals with it in the morning, sometimes recopying muddled parts, sometimes correcting the more blatant faults in the logic. Grete follows the development of the plot closely, as the work is getting longer and longer and Brecht is beginning to lose track of where it began and where it is going. In broad terms, he does of course know where he is heading, but there are the inevitable repetitions and places where the plot goes off the rails.

Brecht doesn't like the fact that Grete's consumption is entering its final phase.

The "little revolutionary" is on her way out. Everything points to this. Small droplets of sweat glisten on her forehead, and her cheeks are flushed. But her scissors cut nimbly. The pile of material on the life and exploits of the Painter grows apace. Grete is wearing a chintz dress over her thin body.

Importunate desire seizes hold of Brecht. He lights a cigar.

He makes a suitable movement. Grete rises and turns her back on him. Brecht presses Grete against the table, lifts the chintz dress, pulls down her warm woollen briefs and takes her from behind.

Neither Wuolijoki nor Weigel are afraid of Margarete. Margarete is small, in Hella's opinion deathly pale and puny. Granted, she does know many languages. (Although she never learned Finnish, as she thought it was too complex. And Hella did, after all, speak fluent German.)

None the less, she was crazy about Brecht, and although she was not jealous of Weigel, who was masculine and bony, Grete did see a threat in the reappearance of proud, sparkling and tall Ruth.

Brecht has written in his eighth sonnet that Margarete and him made love behind a hedge one night, in a wooden bed, in a study, between a closet and the window, on the slope of a hill, in a hotel, in the homeland of the proletariat, in the Fourth Reich, and at all seasons of the year. For Brecht, Steffin was an expert on the language of ordinary folks, someone who corrected with application Brecht's intellectual use of language.

It has been said that Margarete's blue eyes had an "angry fire" about them.

A couple of pages of the China play have been crumpled up and Grete smooths them out.

Brecht strokes the head of the little revolutionary, blows on her forehead which is now bathed in sweat and goes to his room.

It is dark in there.

Suddenly Brecht's hand touches something cold. He cries out and quickly switches on the light.

It is, of course, not a frog, but the copper coffee pot, which is now cold.

Brecht writes a poem:

> *By the whitewashed wall*
> *lies a black soldier's suitcase filled with manuscripts.*
> *On it are smoking materials and a brass ashtray.*
> *A Chinese tapestry, depicting a doubter,*
> *is hanging on the wall above it. There are also masks. And next to the shelf is a*
> *small six-valve wireless set.*
> *In the early morning*
> *I turn the knob and listen*
> *to the victory broadcasts of my enemy.*

It has been pointed out that when describing the room, Brecht is selective about which objects he mentions. This gives the impression that the room is empty, that all there is in there is a suitcase, the tapestry, the shelf and the wireless set. In actual fact, there were many other things in this furnished room.

Eighty kilometers further south, in Estonia, in the Gloria Palace movie theater, the film The Women of Niskavuori, *based on a play by Hella Wuolijoki, is being shown. This is Hella's best known play. She wrote a whole series of plays about the people living on the farm called Niskavuori, a whole family saga, over several generations. Strong, pragmatic yet sensitive women dominate the scene. The men are taken on and discarded.*

OH, THAT COUNTRY CHINA

He can hardly have seen this play!

Shall we try to explain what it's about? Will we be able to explain the problem even to those who don't want to know, even to those who want no closer acquaintance with Brecht as a person, and—even to those who don't even believe that Brecht ever existed?

Anyway, let's try, since if we have gone to all the trouble of inventing Brecht, then we can also invent his play about China and the series of issues involved.

Brecht has had this *idée fixe* for quite some while that the bourgeois dialectical contradiction involving "morality *versus* pleasure" simply does not exist.

Morality and pleasure are one and the same thing.

Both are opposed to reality. Being a moralist is pleasant. But life demands sadness and badness, so you have to exert yourself. Amorality requires effort.

It's not easy to be bad.

Brecht has been wanting to depict this idea for a while, and now he is getting down to work.

His protagonist is Li Gung, who appears to be coming from the side of goodness.

Why Li Gung?

Why shouldn't it be Li Gung, when the play is set in China? This achieves the alienation effect.

You always view someone from China differently than you would a German, and some things immediately strike you more forcibly. If a German slips on a banana skin, this causes no surprise in anyone. If someone from China were to do the same, then we, the Germans, see this action as if for the first time, and we begin to think about what a banana is, what a human being is, and what falling is.

Setting a play in China allows you to use a variety of Chinese theatrical effects.

But Brecht still has problems with his play because he doesn't like the prevalent fashion of *chinoiserie* among the ruling classes. Flirting with China is something the rich do in large numbers, but with quite a different aim in mind to that of Brecht.

Silk and rickshaws, pagodas and parasols.

Brecht sees in his mind's eye a half-finished (and failed) large Europeanized industrial city, where the trees are gray with dust and smoke covers the soul and the city, so that it becomes almost impossible to live there.

This is where Li Gung lives, and earns her living as a prostitute.

In Brecht's opinion, a prostitute is womanly, spontaneous and close to nature. At the same time, she is the product of capitalist relations. This is where the dialectic emerges.

Li Gung reacts in a no-nonsense way. In this she resembles Ruth for Brecht.

Ruth sometimes does wild things. She yells. All or nothing! Ruth is beautiful, tall and terrifying. She has attacks of rage and passion. Both types of attacks could affect Li Gung too.

Now a larger-than-life character is born: wild, lovable, good, giving, free and tender.

Li Gung is in love with a pilot.

Brecht has always liked pilots. His thoughts are revolving around pilots.

Brecht once wrote a play about pilots, where airplanes and pilots were the embodiment of all sorts of philosophical categories. Then he wrote another play on the topic of flying. Both of the premières caused a major scandal in 1929. The first one was The Lindbergh Flight, *and Pilot Hope vied with Pilot Self, and harnesses technology with the help of God. Since, however, Lindbergh later turned out to be a Nazi, and Brecht felt insulted and changed the name of the play to* The Ocean Flight. *The second play was* The Baden-Baden Lesson on Consent, *which depicted dying pilots, who wanted to change the world at any cost. In a positive direction, of course!*

Li Gung is in love with a pilot. This pilot is unemployed at present, as they often are in the capitalist world. Li Gung meets the pilot in the park where he wants to hang himself. He had been struck by a fit of despair. But otherwise he's a manly enough type. Brecht decides to portray the pilot as himself. The pilot, whose name is Sun, decides to exploit Li Gung. He blackmails the girl into giving him money which she borrowed. The pilot intends to buy out the owner of a garage or hangar in Peking and in so doing get to fly again. The corrupt boss then ousts an honest pilot and gives Sun the job. The immoral actions of the pilot do not worry the prostitute Li Gung. She devotes herself to the pilot, gives him money and Sun promises to marry her. They decide to go to Peking together. Brecht thought that Sun was only able to buy one plane ticket. (After a series of adventures the one ticket can be turned into two after all.)

Brecht has Li Gung look up into the sky at a plane flying there. This is a positive experience. Li Gung looks into the sky and declaims:

A pilot
is braver than others. Among the clouds
flying into great storms
he moves across the sky bringing
his friends in distant countries
friendly mail.

Li Gung is good, the pilot is good, the pilot brings good mail.

But then dialectics enter the scene. Three gods arrive at the city. They are neither Chinese nor Christian gods. They are simply gods. Three men, who arrive. They have a moral dilemma. They are looking for a good person. The only person giving the impression of being good is Li Gung. They give her money to start a tobacconist's shop.

But Li Gung is good!

She gives away almost all the money. Both honest, needy people and scoundrels receive money.

And also the very manly pilot Sun in his leather trousers, someone who is neither good nor bad, just simply himself, terrorizes Li Gung, he does not however wish to do any harm.

So there is nothing else left for Li Gung to do but split in half.

This is dialectics.

She splits in half.

Li Gung continues to represent goodness and pleasure, but her other guise, her nephew Lao Go, is very bad.

Li Gung is Lao Go, and Lao Go is Li Gung. They are antitheses, but they together form a synthesis, all the more as they are played by the same actor.

Nephew Lao Go is very far removed from goodness and pleasure. He is rational, calculating and cruel, does business without feeling. He is a reality in the class society. He makes the tobacco industry profitable. Soon he has a big factory. He ruthlessly exploits people. That makes him a lot of money.

And so, bad Lao Go exploits people, and living in the same body is Li Gung, who is good, and by way of this money can help the poor more effectively.

This is dialectical alright, but at the same time Brecht thinks that he is beginning to lose track of the plot.

He looks out of the window, and the sky is getting light. Morning! And I'm still awake! Brecht gets into a mild panic. How many fruitless hours has he spent on a couple of Chinese. What a waste of time! Brecht gets up and walks over to Grete.

The little revolutionary soldier is sleeping, and in the pale light of dawn he can see a string of saliva running onto her pillow from the corner of her mouth.

Brecht is moved and touches her bony shoulder.

Grete opens her eyes immediately.

"Sleep, sleep," whispers Brecht, "I'll bring you that Chinese pillow, I can't stand the sight of it anymore, we'll see tomorrow what you can do with it. Haven't the time to be messing around with it today."

When writing down such sentences it is good to have Yuri Lotman's article along-side "Doing Justice to Biography." Here you can find interesting ideas about this whole problem complex when you use a concrete person as a literary "hero." This is not as easy as it seems. What it boils down to is that I would not wish anyone else to write a novel about my wife—using my wife's name. On the other hand, I have no complaints about anyone writing a play about Richard III. These two extremes have a complicated set of intermediate stages.

"Of course," agrees Grete. "Do you want to get under the blankets with me?"

"I don't, look what the time is," says Brecht, hurt, and strokes Grete's cheek and goes back to his own room.

He gets the feeling that a large snake has slithered under the bed, just as he enters the room.

That's impossible!

Quite likely, the result of a sleepless night or tired eyes.

But Brecht no longer wants to get back into bed nor to look under the bed.

He sits down in an armchair and shuts his eyes.

He is surrounded by Finnish silence.

He sleeps for a few hours.

Tromsø is declared to be the temporary capital of Norway.

But as for Mexico, at the very same time, Trotsky can hear shouts through the window: "Down with Trotsky! Trotsky out!" These are not Mexican workers. The workers are celebrating their May Day holiday as usual, and their slogans are the usual Communist ones. Trotsky knows full well who is chanting slogans against him. They are not many in number, but there are enough of them. They have pursued Trotsky all the way to Mexico.

In a completely different country, much nearer to where Brecht is now, and only some eighty kilometers from Helsinki, in Hella's native land, that same Hella who has recently been attacking Brecht behind his back—in the capital of her native land President Päts is holding a speech and raising his glass to make a toast to Stalin, the Great Leader.

IN THE NIGHT

In the night, Brecht imagines that someone is walking under his window. Walking. And throwing sand up at his window! Sand? Yes, there's something rustling and scraping! The North? Loafers? Witches? Hitler's agents? Small boys?

Brecht doesn't ask anyone.

Then silence returns.

ON THE SUBJECT OF THREE POETS

It is Saturday lunchtime and three people have just stumbled upon the memorial statue to Aleksis Kivi. This statue is right in front of the National Theater.

The weather today is fine, it is a quiet, sunny day and this almost forces people to joke and chat a little.

The three people are a Finn, Hella, and Brecht.

Hella has met this Finn before, but she cannot remember his name. At any rate, this man gives the impression of being very Finnish. Finns are usually very introverted. But this man is afraid of nothing and takes up the subject of the biography of Finland's maybe greatest writer, Aleksis Kivi.

Aleksis Kivi is always thought of as having been impetuous and slightly agitated, by nature. He also drank a lot, but later (1870) he started becoming a little peculiar. He had hallucinations. His fear of losing his mind became so great that this classical poet would sometimes bound naked through the village like a lion. Although he was well known (in literary circles) as a great poet, it did happen that he was refused entry to a theater because of his appearance and clothing, when one of his own plays was being staged. Then came treatment in a madhouse (1871). After that he lived in the country in his brother's barn. There anxiety tormented him and he would shout loudly in the night. When his sanity improved, he would swear at the village children in Latin. He then died (1872).

The sun is shining onto the cheeks of the listeners, making them aware of the continuous presence of spring, encouraging conversation, talk and tales.

Hella is holding her face obligingly towards the sun, her head cocked to one side, and her eyes closed as she listens to the Finn's story, and they stay closed even as she picks up the thread:

"The Estonians have such a writer as well, that is to say Juhan Liiv. I met him in my youth, we had the same landlady and he wrote me many letters, but I couldn't be bothered to read them all, nor did I know at the time that he was a classic writer, and now they are lost. His decline began (around 1893) when he began to hear voices and suspect he was being followed—by both the police and some shady types and suspect individuals. Then he disappeared from town. For seven years (1895–1902) no one in Estonia knew if he was alive or dead. He was then discovered living in the forest at his parents' house, where he had been hiding all this while, and the person who discovered him was a cultured peripatetic psychiatrist. From then on, attention was paid to the madman, and he became a classic. He too used to run around naked in the woods like the Finn, Kivi."

"But how long was this madman of yours actually insane?" asks the envious Finn.

"Oh, a couple of decades," says Hella with her classic tranquillity.

"Regressive behavior is widespread among the Finno-Ugrian peoples," generalizes Brecht. "As far as I can see, you people try to strip naked during times of excess. In northern climes with their cold weather this can be pretty effective, they must be tough, thinking dialectically, because what would be the point of stripping naked in an Equatorial climate?"

"Our classic author thought he was the King of Poland and made a couple of attempts at visit his people in Poland, but was thrown off the train as a perfectly ordinary loafer," adds Hella.

Now, the Finn is getting impatient. He has so much to tell about Kivi, but Brecht coughs significantly and now the Finno-Ugrians both hold their peace.

"Naturally, I won't omit to mention our Hölderlin in this context," says Brecht, picking up on the theme of deviant geniuses. "Ours was a classic author who lived in the shade of insanity for the whole of *forty* years! (1803–1843.) He died mentally when he was in his thirties, having by that time written his life's work. After that, he lived a dark animalistic life in a tiny room, tinkling away at the keys of his piano and muttering incomprehensible tales. If he heard his own name mentioned, he would become very angry, since he imagined he was someone called Scardanelli. It is true that even in this period he wrote some poetry, wash-baskets full of them in fact, but *no one* could be bothered to decipher them because—as I have said—his life's work as a classic was already *complete*.

The Finn nods.

"Yes, that's how it was," he says thoughtfully, as if he was there at the time, "I too remember one of his poems. The one which goes—when I was a boy—"

Brecht cuts him off. He now declaims in his loud, shrill voice:

> *When I was still a boy,*
> *A god often saved me*
> *From the shouts and blows of people,*
> *I played there safe and well*
> *With the blooms of the meadow,*
> *And the zephyrs of heaven*
> *Played with me . . .*
> *Oh all you trusty*
> *Friendly gods . . .*

Brecht lights a cigar.

"Yes indeed, Hölderlin does pontificate rather, and is on nodding terms with the gods, although he didn't actually understand much of the world around him."

Triumphantly, Brecht looks the Finn in the eye. The latter has no other choice but to hang his comments on the peg just driven in.

"Hölderlin died (1843) when Kivi was born (1834) . . . Kivi was a little more skeptical—not only in his life on Earth, but with regard to heaven . . . Our Finnish classic wrote like this about his childhood:

> *Down from a rock rushes a child*
> *eagerly into its mother's arms.*
> *Shouts with shining eyes:*
> *I've seen heaven . . .*
> *Stood for long in drumlin country,*
> *surveying the map of the heavens.*
> *In the end I saw a blueing meadow,*
> *saw a distant fir.*
> *Saw, with pain in my breast,*
> *my cheek flowing with tears.*
> *Even I did not understand*
> *that I was crying. I have seen heaven!*

The mother, however, tells the child that it has not seen any heaven. Heaven is always *above you*, the horizon consists of an ordinary strip of land. This has led to our classic confusion as to whether God is above us or somewhere in between."

By now, naturally, Hella has taken the bull by the horns.

"If we are to continue these ruminations broached by our Finnish brother here, let us add the name of our own classic author, Liiv, who was also born roughly at the same time (1864), as Kivi died (1872), and no longer looked upwards, not even across to the horizon."

"Why?" asks the Finn. "Had societal oppression grown to such an extent?"

"Maybe that had something to do with it," sighs Hella, "but maybe Estonians in general tend to be materialist and pantheist, and spiritually more unpretentious. One of the characters of our classic author did indeed want to see a great, shimmering lake, but he simply *did not get to see it* as the *woods* grew in front of it. If only that stretch of forest wasn't blocking my view! is what our classic author sighed, but he didn't make any attempt to cross the forest. He stayed where he was, where he was cut off from the horizon. His gaze grew calm at the soughing, quivering, monotonous ornament that the woods became. And this is how he described it in a poem:

> *The woods murmured darkly, truly . . .*
> *I heard them with fear.*
> *That dark murmur stayed in my breast,*
> *it is still there now—*
> *it is as if I am longing for it,*
> *will never be happy again . . ."*

Silence reigns for a short moment. The church bells begin to ring in the distance. And Brecht begins to trace something with the toe of his shoe in the gravel. From one point, he draws three lines all curved in a bow.

"Line A," he says, "is Hölderlin—*die Lüftchen des Himmels spielen mit mir!* This is a vertical line, aimed at the heavens above. B is a Finn, aimed at forty-five degrees, vacillating between heaven and earth, in dialectical terms even forming a synthesis. And Line C is your crazy Estonian, Hella—a horizontal line, aimed along the surface of the earth and becoming entangled in thickets of nature in the nether distance."

Brecht would like to continue talking.

But it now happens that a drunken Finn taps him on the shoulder. Brecht whips round like lightning. It would come as no surprise if the Painter's men had already caught up with him!

But the man bothering him now is simply drunk. Brecht has seen plenty of these types in the postwar Germany of his youth.

The man asks something.

Brecht doesn't understand.

The Finnish writer, the Kivi expert, interprets for Brecht, saying that the man wants to tell him a dream he had.

Brecht isn't interested in dreams, especially those of this man, but he's in a foreign land and dare not begin to argue.

He looks up, with measured interest.

The man claims that he has seen himself in a dream along with Brecht (he didn't, of course, know his name, and simply called him "you") sitting on the edge of a cloud in heaven. But from there both of them had fallen straight down to hell, straight into barrels. Each their own barrel! In one was shit, the other treacle.

Brecht considers this a tale for common people, and this gladdens him. Why not speak with a Finnish worker? And as can be expected, the man immediately poses a rhetorical question:

"And which barrel do you think I fell in?"

Brecht naturally lets it be known via the interpreter that the man disturbing him fell into the barrel of shit.

The man continues telling his tale. There is clearly a point he wants to make. And here it is! The Devil appears forthwith. Sees what has happened and grabs both men—both him and Brecht—by the scruff of the neck, hauls them out of their barrels and bawls: lads, now lick one another clean!

The tale is at an end, the point has been made, the proletarian raises his hat and staggers away.

The tale is an epic one, presented as a street scene (*Strassenszene*). Brecht could have been enthused.

But all he does is yawn.

Can't get enthusiastic about everything all the time.

THE DOUBTER

Brecht shows Hella a small papier mâché donkey that is standing next to the typewriter. Round the donkey's neck is a sign: "I too want to understand!"

"I write a sentence, then look at Him," explains Brecht, "and if the donkey shakes his head, I cross out the sentence and write it again, so that He will understand."

He touches the donkey and it nods.

"You see," says Brecht triumphantly, "simple workers love me more than intellectuals do."

MAY DAY

In Finland, the First of May is a particularly important holiday. It is quite true that May Day, Walpurgis Night and Workers' Day are celebrated in other countries too, but nowhere so passionately as in Finland.

Brecht is sitting along with the others on the slope of a hill, drinking champagne.

On one side sits Helene, the other Grete.

In front of them some Finnish Social Democrats are sitting.

"Where are my children?" Brecht suddenly asks. The Social Democrats cannot tell him. How should they know where Brecht's children have got to? Silently they transfer the question to Helene who is, after all, the mother of Brecht's children.

"What?!" says the tall, bony Helene, giving a start, after having dozed off in the warm spring sunshine.

"Where are my children?" shouts Brecht in a shrill voice.

"Must be somewhere," says Helene, trying to calm him down.

"Are you sure?" Brecht is not assured.

"Yes, I am."

Brecht turns his back. He is hurt and now looks at the red flags that are flying, held in the tanned hands of the workers. Everywhere, cloths have been spread out and on the cloths there is champagne, or at least lemonade, and sandwiches. The Social Democrats indicate a man standing on the rise opposite, holding a yellow balloon.

"An informer," whispers one Social Democrat to another.

"Whose?" asks Brecht, on his guard, suddenly managing to understand the Finnish language in some mysterious way. Actually, the Social Democrats are not speaking Finnish. They are using the Swedish language, which resembles German somewhat. That is how Brecht manages to understand.

The Social Democrats—there are two of them, a man and a woman—shrug their shoulders. They have no idea whose spy this informer might be, even if he is spying. But presumably he is. This man has drawn attention to himself before, in clubs and study circles.

But right now, he is standing on the opposite slope, holding a yellow balloon.

He could be spying for the Painter or the Man of Steel.

But he could just as well be working for Sweden, Bulgaria, Norway, Britain, Albania, or the United States of America.

"Look, here come the children, and you didn't believe they'd ever come back," repeats Helene in an accusing bass voice.

The children arrive, carrying blue balloons. A fresh breeze is blowing. Even here in the North summer has arrived. Brief, pitiful, cold, but summer nevertheless. On all sides there is some kind of summer. There is nowhere that summer is completely absent.

But not only summer. The children arrive.

Someone else as well.

SHE LOVES A GERMAN

Brecht senses there is something behind him. Or someone.

He turns round rapidly. Hella is just stretching out her hand to touch him. Damn her, thinks Brecht, sneaking up on me quietly like that . . .

"I was thinking of putting my hands over your eyes," Hella is not in the slightest abashed, "didn't you know, Brecht, it's a habit, putting your hands over someone's eyes from behind and asking: guess who? A surprise. Don't you know the trick?"

"Yes, I do," says Brecht in spite of himself.

"I once loved a German," says Hella, the politician and author.

"You've said that at least twice before," says Brecht, the refugee, writer and politician.

Hella's neck and wrists grow red.

The blood collects under her white skin, and the flush does not fade for at least a minute.

This, can be seen clearly in the spring sunshine (or in fact, already the summer sun).

Several workers—Brecht likes to call them workers—are playing the accordion.

MUCK'S PROBLEM

The May Day celebrations continue and Hella goes for a stroll with Helene.

"What's actually wrong with this Grete?" asks Hella in her blunt manner.

Grete is a stonemason's daughter. She actually fell ill with tuberculosis before she met Brecht in 1932. Neither her stay in Russia nor the Crimea helped. And after her appendix was removed the dangers increased several times over.

Helene explains that Grete is very ill, dying, in fact. Helene was worried about the children to start with, that they would be infected, but she no longer worries about that.

"Do what you like with her, but we can't just shrug her off. She'll always be with us," Helene confesses.

They draw attention to themselves, as Hella is round and Helene angular.

Everyone on the political left knows Hella. Who Helene is remains an enigma to many.

Hella accepts a bottle of champagne presented by a friendly worker—that is how Helene thinks of the people they are walking among and this fine spring day. Hella looks at the half-empty bottle holding it against the spring light, then gulps down the lot.

"That's how you have to behave on *Vappu*," she says, and tosses the empty bottle over her shoulder.

Helene is thinking that although Hella's views are Socialist, this recent gesture is more redolent of the lady of the manor, someone who only flirts with a love of the working classes.

"So this Grete is like a third child to you?" the lady of the manor continues her First of May Audience.

"For me she is, well, sure, a third child, but she's something more for Brecht," Helene explains. "Brecht is in fact in love with her. He never calls her Grete, but Muck. He likes it when she squeals."

"When does she squeal, then?"

Helene, the actress in exile, who is strolling alongside Hella, suddenly looks Hella in the eye.

Her face is very close to that of Hella.

And although Helene looks twice as old as she actually is, Hella is thinking: in Estonia, we would say that her eyes are as deep as mine shafts.

"You can tell *me* everything," she laughs encouragingly.

Helene sighs.

"It's like this, for instance. They're always working together. Grete reads through everything Brecht has written. He no longer has the time to read through all his own works. As he wants to know everything, but he can't know everything. Grete knows for him. Isn't that the right division of labor when you're dealing with a genius? Grete has worked her way through Hegel, Wieland and Upton Sinclair. And now we've arrived at our little Muck or Squealie (*mucken* = to squeal). When Grete is writing down what Brecht is dictating, she writes and writes and writes. Brecht talks and talks but at the same time, his hand slips under the table and between Grete's legs."

"Well, and then?" Hella finds this interesting.

"Then Grete, or Muck, starts squealing."

"Have you seen this with your own eyes?" Hella cannot stop herself asking out of sheer curiosity.

Helene raises her eyebrows, thinks for a moment, recollecting.

"No, I don't think so," she says finally, "but Brecht has written about it in a sonnet of his. By the way, he has a habit of writing sonnets to Grete, and then I, my dear Hella, have to draw his attention to the form of a sonnet and such things. While it was me who forced Brecht to side with the proletariat and the idealization of the class struggle, it was principally Grete who persuaded him to use sonnet form. Brecht really did give a new lease on life to the refined 12-line form, born of the collapse of feudalism and the rise of capitalism, and if that is thanks to anyone, it is thanks to Grete. No one drew his attention to the classical perfection of form, apart from Grete. She is ready to analyze every word, every letter. And I'm telling you, Hella—there is no better secretary than Grete. Even I wanted to be Brecht's secretary, once upon a time."

Helene tried to learn to type, because she didn't like all those secretaries and female assistants (*Mitarbeiterinnen*) that Brecht always surrounded himself with. But this act of self-sacrifice ended up with an badly inflamed tendon of the wrist.

Helene shrugs her shoulders.

"Let's go back now," is Hella's suggestion.

"Let's," agrees Helene, gladly.

They make their way between the workers to their spot of the slope of the hill where they had left Brecht, Grete, the children and a couple of Finnish Social-Democrats.

Meanwhile, a large white balloon has appeared in Hella's hand.

Some admirer no doubt gave it to her.

She now lets go and it sails into the air.

THE ROMAN EMPEROR AND THE FANDANGO

One evening, full of the whispers of nature, the Finnish stage-producer, Eino Salmelainen comes to visit Brecht.

The major Finnish theater director Salmelainen (who is important for us here principally as the producer of Brecht's Threepenny Opera) *appears in Brecht's thoughts right at the beginning of the novel, when Brecht is on the deck of the ferry looking out over Turku harbor (Ilmalainen, kylmalainen . . .).*

He crosses the Sibelius Park, where children, tired by the winter of war but who are now reawakened, are playing eagerly, and he enters the apartment of the famous emigrant.

He has never seen Brecht in living life before, but has come across his work.

The first thing he says to Brecht is:

"I get the feeling you're a Roman Emperor."

Brecht is pleasantly surprised.

"Where do you get that from?"

"Mr Brecht, I can hardly err in my opinion, because when I look at your skin, your Roman nose, your hair combed forward over your pate, completely black, despite the hard years of exile . . ."

"Yes?" asks Brecht with feigned indifference.

"Yes, that's how I've always imagined Julius Caesar."

This really is a dainty morsel for Brecht. He cursorily presents all his theories on the subject of Caesar for Salmelainen, including those where Caesar emerges as the archetype of a dictator.

"But one shouldn't exaggerate the freedom of will and choice of dictators," pronounces the dramatist.

"The economy is the base, ideology the superstructure . . ." says Salmelainen.

"Quite," replies Brecht looking Salmelainen keenly in the eye, "have you by chance been reading some popular Russian introduction to political economy?"

"Shouldn't I be reading them?" asks Salmelainen, surprised, as he had thought that Brecht likes Marxism a lot.

Brecht is at a loss for words.

The room is growing dark.

The arctic spring night washes over the two men.

All of a sudden, Brecht gets to his feet and opens the curtain.

This—a donation by Hella—is only held up by press studs and can easily be taken down.

"I don't need curtains across my window," says Brecht, in explanation of his abrupt action, "I have nothing to hide from the Finnish workers that live across from me in the block opposite."

Brecht shrouds himself in the curtain in one proud movement, and shouts: "Olé!"

Then he dances the fandango.

And when he has described several dance steps, he also starts singing.

He sings in a penetrating metallic voice, which sends shivers down Salmelainen's spine.

Brecht's eyes are burning in the darkening room like those of a cat.

He sings of the faraway island of Tahiti and of the Moon, which is beginning to sink beyond the sea, and about the tired whores who have stretched out on the sandy beach in the moonlight.

He repeats the same *pas* several times, whirling the curtain in such a wide arc that it almost hits Salmelainen in the face.

The subject of the theater is no longer discussed that evening. Instead it is acted out in epic, citatory form. Soon, Hella and Grete and the children arrive.

They too start dancing. They dance briefly, for a minute, perhaps.

Brecht stops dancing first.

Soon, a shaken Salmelainen leaves for home.

It is drizzling.

"Olé," mutters Salmelainen to himself.

The drizzle turns into rain.

A LARGE BLACK OBJECT

One day, Brecht steps into the corridor.

A large black object darts past him.

It could have had four legs, but it could have had two.

Two-legged creatures have risen onto their hind legs, and their forelegs are therefore termed arms.

Three-legged animals never show themselves.

Always either two or four.

Pairs of limbs are important for living creatures.

Creatures with one or three limbs are termed invalids. In some cases, monsters. But two! How antinomian! How binary! Two comes immediately after one. That too is important!

Why didn't I observe that large black creature more attentively as it darted past, thinks Brecht regretfully.

SCHILLER

It is evening. The trees are in full leaf. Hella remembers that when trees are in leaf a woman can start wearing open shoes. To be more exact: when the leaves grow so large that they cast a shadow, your toes can be exposed. That is what her headmistress once said. There is a grain of truth in this adage. While it is still April and the streets are dusty and there are no leaves, there is no point in exposing your toes.

And so, Hella has bare toes, the leaves cast shadows and Brecht, not we, has chosen Schiller as his theme.

"In this author we find a dialectical relationship between drama and epic."

Brecht is sorry that he can't remember where.

"Don't remember where?" asks Hella and her face is very close to that of Brecht—Grete and Helene are away somewhere, a couple of meters away, and the children are playing outside.

Brecht does not allow himself to be intimidated by the Estonian woman.

He has met women before who want to get him for themselves at any price. He has always refused them.

But Hella smells of milk.

Hella is the Cow, he thinks, for no apparent reason.

Thinking in this way, he automatically frees himself from responsibility.

"Schiller said you have to add epic elements to a drama."

"Yes, but I do seem to remember how our literature teacher dealt with Schiller. This teacher's name was Heinrich Bauer. The conflict arose between us because of the play *Maria Stuart*. I researched the history, as well! Let the real historical facts be as they may, but the important thing is that I managed, by way of her, to say what I really thought. In my school essay, I praised Elizabeth, who had been entirely by-passed, and pointed out that she was the first to fight for women's rights, a feminist to use an anachronistic term, while Mary Stuart was simply a flibbertigibbet who did nothing but *dance* and *make love*. And do you know, you Brecht, that I also wrote about how that stupid Schiller didn't understand how great Elizabeth really was, simply got schoolgirls to go all weepy, while at the same time, along with the other teachers . . ."

Brecht doesn't consider this story particularly interesting.

Naturally Estonians have thoughts and these can on occasions be ones worthy of taking seriously, but Brecht remembers very clearly what happened between Schiller and himself in the native land common to them both.

"I too," Brecht begins in quite an epic manner, "I too was ordered to write an essay at school, and what's more, about Schiller, as well. To be more exact, the topic of the essay was the 'Wallenstein's Camp.' Personally, I felt that this play was about as innocuous as a feast in a beer hall. Especially once you started to compare Schiller's war with the ones going on today, especially those instigated by the Painter, by Ni-En and others. I got a bad grade for that essay, four out of ten. But I didn't leave it there. I went to the headmaster and demanded justice. I asked that I should not be judged on my thoughts, but on my use of the German language, as you couldn't assess the former, as he knew nothing about them, but that he should at least know something about the latter, being a philologist. In a language essay it should be the language that counts, not the thoughts! I didn't give up, but in the end I got a three."

Brecht enjoys the fact that this tale has made a deep impression on Hella.

He continues, and remembers that he once wrote a distortion of Schiller by the name of *The Battle of the Fishwives*.

Brecht thought that classic plays were only staged in order to be "emotionally uplifting" for the people. In such plays there are always well-known passages or scenes that are supposed to played with shouts and feelings, so much so that it begins to go black before your eyes. In order to alienate the players from such immoderate and pointless emotionality, Brecht wrote a scene depicting Elizabeth and Marie Stuart as two "fishwives," with the women, two from the common people, the proletariat, in Brecht's estimation, were fighting over a few cents or grams of something or other. Such a scene was intended to bring the queens down to earth. They were no longer "queens" as such—people we rarely encounter in real life—but this had now become a quarrel between two women, viewed dialectically, as when a meeting between two people is unavoidable.

When this scene comes before his eyes in all its alienation, he gets to his feet and starts acting.

He plays both fishwives.

Depicts them.

Not plays, depicts.

He speaks in dialect, in a loud, shrill voice.

Suddenly he yells for Grete to come in.

"Grete!!!" he bawls and tears off his collar.

Grete appears in the doorway and Brecht insists on dictating it to her. Grete only takes a few minutes, then the text is ready.

"I ought to scratch your eyes out!" Grete prompts.

"I ought to scratch your eyes out," shrieks Brecht like a fishwife.

Brecht covers the imaginary fish crate with his body.

This is the height of alienation, as Brecht is not a fishwife and the crate of fish does not exist. Everything is imaginary and is not, at one and the same time. But Hella also remembers Brecht's peculiar comment: "*Zitieren! Wir zitieren, nur zitieren! Wir sind keine Fischfrauen! Wir sind Brecht der Erste und Brecht der Zweite.*"

Hella really likes all this. She understands that this small, smelly, scurfy little man is what is termed a genius. In the German cultural space, geniuses are important figures. Goethe is a genius and Kleist, and . . . others too. Not to mention the Manns, especially Thomas, whom Brecht hates like no one else. Even the Russians had many geniuses. The first to spring to mind are Dostoyevsky and Tolstoy.

Brecht is really getting into his part.

He empathizes.

But he is also capable of stopping abruptly.

Halfway through a word, he promptly forgets this spectacle of his, and suddenly begins to take an interest in the other people around him.

Hella has already understood that Brecht likes only himself.

Hella too loves herself above anything else in the world, so she is strangely moved when Brecht says, with genuine interest:

"But how did your Schiller tale end, Hella?"

"Bauer left me an hour later," Hella explained happily, "and asked—one hand in front of his eyes—whatever was he to do with me. I wanted to reply like a woman. I had to rise to a new, unexpected level. I then said as that new person, transformed, alternative: if you admire Maria, I will no longer dance with you.

'Where and when won't you dance?' asked Bauer relatively innocently.—'I will not dance with you at the school dance,' I replied and Bauer raised both arms in horror indicating with them both that I should vanish, and quickly. I curtsied, thanked him and left."

THE FOLLOWING NIGHT

The following night it grows cooler.

British and French forces withdraw from southern Norway. The battles only continue around Narvik.

The nights are white and wild. Now and again, distant elk crash through the undergrowth—if they are not elk then they are wolves. Or lions?

The Russian government sends the Lithuanian government a diplomatic note. It claims that Russian soldiers living in Lithuania have been kidnaped.
   Indeed, a certain Babayev had certainly been leaping around, and later killed himself.
   Belgium has already formed its government in exile.

"Who is Ilmanainen?" Brecht asks Hella.
   "Ilmarainen?" Hella doesn't understand.
   "Well, something like that. Ilman . . ."
   Hella laughs.
   "*Ilma* means *ohne* . . . But Ilmarinen created the firmament, he was that kind of god."
   Brecht is satisfied with the explanation and wishes her a good night.
   The window is open and Brecht wakes up early. The wind is blowing into his face from the open window. With cramp-like movements, Brecht wriggles back under the covers, knowing that sooner or later the window will have to be shut.
   I think that I'll soon close the window, Brecht is thinking, and I think, that this thought is the right thought. There is a point in thinking only such thoughts that make you actually do something, bring activity, let's say—and act (*Tat*).
   Thought can only work in practice when closely linked within a certain axiomatic field.

Beyond that field (*Feld*) axiomatic arguments are of no importance.

Arguments do not arise in a vacuum.

There is not point in thinking that there is no point in closing the window.

That is not a thought, but something else, something vague.

Brecht is repeating to himself, as always, that causality only pays off if the knowledge concerned is necessary and productive. There is no point in thinking about things that do not depend on us. We cannot change this northern climate so that it becomes warmer, we cannot twist and turn the axes of the Earth. For that reason, I cannot sympathize too much regarding Finnish nights. Thinking too much about Finnish nights, feeling empathy for them, is decadent and counter-productive. Mental anomalies arise, disturbances of the apparatus of thought, and I will become asocial. Everything I do after that will be nothing but a shameless reflection of its reality. That is lyricism!

Rudolf Höss becomes the commandant of Auschwitz. The Finns go to the Estonian Embassy and the Finns expect them to criticize their native land, i.e., the way the Estonians are reacting and behaving, but this does not happen. The Estonians, for their part, think that the Finns are coddled too much with praise, and that there ought to be a small pause in all this praise of Finland. As for Russian prisoners-of-war in Finland, their daily ration is: 300 gm bread, 300 gm milk, 20 gm margarine, 115 gm flour or potatoes, 100 gm meat, 125 gm herring, 10 gm sugar, 0.5 gm tea, 15 gm salt.

It is touching to know that during those very times there is an advert in the window of the office equipment store "Konttorityö" at 25B Esplanaadit, Helsinki, for a typewriter by the name of "Pikku-Continental"—Little Continental. Yes, it is with that very typewriter (which still exists, though it is slightly in need of repair, and stands on my writing desk) that the first draft of this novel was written.

Brecht switches on the light and is shocked when he sees his own face in the black mirror of the window pane.

He takes a sheet of paper and starts writing:

"Liberal thought collides with its own class boundaries, for that reason, consistent conclusions are out of the question."

Brecht stares for a long time at the sentence he has just written, but at the same moment late spring mist wafts in from the window, and soon begins to pearl on Brecht's forehead.

Then Brecht smiles a relatively convincing wry smile and adds:

"Reactionary thought should be avoided only by the revolutionary proletariat."

Yes, best to put it that way. Sounds pretty convincing. Brecht shuts the window, wraps himself in the bedclothes—a thin soldier's blanket, but a warm one—and falls face down onto the mattress Hella brought him.

Around him is an alien country, an alien city, an alien Ultima Thule.

PART III

LATE SPRING

1940

THE IDEA OF A TUNNEL

The government of the Estonian Republic decides to start building a tunnel at the bottom of Toompea.

Toompea is a hill in the Estonian capital Tallinn near the sea.

This tunnel was to link Lühike jalg with the Baltic Railroad Station.

Lühike jalg (Short Leg) is a narrow medieval street which rises up to the top of Toompea.

When you get to the top of that hill, you can see the Baltic Railroad Station down below.

From there trains come both from the east (Russia) and the south (Latvia, Lithuania, Poland, Germany).

This tunnel would have cost the Estonian government around 100,000 Estonian *krooni* to build.

And if anything bad happened, then this tunnel could double up as an air raid shelter.

This idea became public on 6th May 1940.

But no one took the idea particularly seriously.

On 9th May, German troops invade the Netherlands and Belgium. Observers found it difficult to assess whether it all happened on the 9th or 10th May.

But at any rate, it was all accomplished by 10th May.

Hella thinks she has used up all her good connections on Brecht here in Finland. She plans, something crafty in her own estimation—being Estonian, she knows that the profession of an Estonian is to be crafty—that she will invite everyone, i.e., Brecht, his lawful wife Helene, his lover Grete, his son Stefan . . . in a word, everyone to the ELANTO cooperative party.

But oh dear, what actually happens!

Hella and others have no doubt thought this through well. Klaus Salin and Orvokki Siponen do a dance from *The Threepenny Opera*. They do so by applying Salmelainen's choreography.

But what Brecht doesn't know is that Väinö Tanner is also coming to the party. Hella wants to introduce them.

Tanner is without a doubt one of the most important Finnish politicians of the 20th century. He was a Social-Democrat and his political career began during the first decade of that century. He took part in the negotiations in Moscow prior to the Winter War and during that war he was in the cabinet.

Brecht only knows Tanner slightly. But his name has stuck in his mind.

Brecht does not yet know anything of Hella's so well-laid plan. He goes to the party suspecting nothing.

"Isn't it nice here?" says Hella to Brecht.

People are already dancing the tango, as can be imagined. Vodka is flowing, not in streams, but in rivers.

Hella is staring into space. Who knows, maybe she's tired. She's under strain, thinks Brecht. Hella is just too—

But Brecht has no time to think this through, about what it is that Hella is too . . . Hella comes up to him, looks at him from head to foot, and her gaze is not at all weary. Who knows how she's managed to liven up meanwhile. You can always liven up if you really want to. It's a question of auto-suggestion. Nothing is impossible, certainly not for Hella.

"Let's dance," says Hella.

She takes hold of Brecht's hand in her own sweaty palm.

Now a waltz can be heard. Hella grabs Brecht's left hand with her right. All at once, Brecht is in Hella's embrace and is forced to start whirling around. In a waltz you have to whirl. At first, they rotate clockwise, then anti-clockwise. Hella presses against Brecht. She has a protruding stomach, a round one. This presses against Brecht's stomach. Brecht's stomach is concave, if anything. He is an emigrant, and starving. He isn't a lord of the manor. He is living in penury. Brecht's hand is on Hella's back. Her back is warm and moist under her silk dress. Brecht feels his hand slip involuntarily under the underclothes that cover the lower part of Hella's body. Hella is over sixty, but Brecht gets a hard-on. Even he doesn't know why, but that's what happens. But now a political theme interferes.

"I'm going to introduce you to a particular gentleman," says Hella in Brecht's ear.

Why is she saying this? Brecht grows really nervous. Our stomachs are touching, can't she feel my hard-on? And if she does, why is she talking about introducing me to some man, as if I were a homosexual. Haven't been for ages!

Some claim that in his youth Brecht had such experiences. Brecht is decadent, after all, and Oscar Wilde and Arthur Rimbaud could have been his models for romance to a certain extent. Even in his plays such motifs occur. The ecstatic friendship between Caspar Neher and Arnolt Bronnen has forced biographers to bring up the subject and make veiled, guarded hints.

At any rate, at that particular moment, Brecht wasn't homosexual, and so he asks Hella, with irritation:

"What gentleman do you want to introduce me to, and why?"

"Just a gentleman," says Hella slyly.

"Why the fuck can't I know which gentleman you're pairing me off with?" Brecht grows positively angry, the waltz just flows and flows above and around them.

"Väinö Tanner," replies Hella, all innocence.

Brecht's face grows pale and he begins to bawl:

"No! No! No! He's responsible for the fucking Winter War! He's against the Soviet Union! He is . . . he's a fascist! I'm leaving! I'm getting out of here! I'm . . ."

He make a run for the door, but then begins to grow afraid, turns back and asks (now in a whisper), where the back door is. They show him and Brecht runs outside.

That day is Helene's fortieth birthday. Brecht married her in 1929, having just divorced Marianne Zoff. In fact, Brecht and Helene's first child was born back in 1924. This is Stefan, who is now sharing their refugee Odyssey.

Jenny Jugo gets back from her Balkan trip and tells Goebbels what there was and what she did there. Goebbels is pleased with Jugo.

The new French Prime Minister, Paul Reynaud, forms a new government and its Minister of the Interior, George Mandel, gives the order to intern all Germans resident in France under the age of sixty-five. This affects Brecht's friend and fellow writer Lion Feuchtwanger, who is living in Savary in the South of France. The news arrives after sunset. Feuchtwanger listens to the silence. He is being given forty-eight hours to take a maximum of 30 kilograms of luggage with him.

In Finland, all stocks of grain and flour are requisitioned.

And the German invasion of the Low Countries? That very same day, Molotov praises this aggression that very same day. Molotov says that he "understands that Germany must defend herself from Franco-British attacks" and that he "is in no doubt that Germany will achieve victory." It can be imagined that the Kremlin was hoping for a tough, protracted war. But to the surprise of even the Germans themselves, everything goes remarkably smoothly.

Schulenberg tells Molotov, right at the beginning of the operation.

Or who knows, maybe even before it started.

MOTHER'S DAY

The next day is Mother's Day, but I am not recording this here for sentimental reasons (the boys are doing the conquering and it was their mothers who gave birth to them), only in order to register the course of events.

Let's scroll forward a couple of days.

A couple of days later, the Estonian Ambassador in Moscow, A. Rei, sends this letter to the Foreign Minister A. Piip:

"Moscow. (. . .) Although the tone of the negotiations has been correct and friendly till now, we have been defending our point of view up to the hilt, and cannot push things any further. For some while (between roughly 1st and 10th May) the Russians did not seem to be in any hurry to round off the talks with us, but we were then invited to meet Molotov at the Kremlin, where in the space of two hours all matters outstanding were dealt with. (. . .) Molotov said (. . .) that all these questions were relatively unimportant and it would take them some time to deal with them, but in the West right now great and significant events were taking place and that they cannot delay any longer. (. . .) He demanded that the agreement be ready for signing by the 13th May. We are in no doubt as to the fact that the events in Holland and Belgium have influenced the talks and that the Kremlin now wants the delay to be over. We also agreed that the draft would be gone through that same evening with Dekanozov. Having gone through tactics and standpoints at home *earlier on, we went to the Commissar for Foreign Affairs at eleven o'clock in the evening. Negotiations lasted a total of three hours [until three o'clock] and were very tough. We managed to negotiate improvements regarding a number of minor matters, but when it came to the few important ones, the Russians were rock firm in their determination not to give an inch. (. . .) Our opposite numbers were pretty knowledgeable and skillful men, with whom it was hard to argue, as we had no firm ground under our own feet. (. . .) You know very well that we cannot just get up from the negotiating table and say: we can't sign such an agreement. We do not want to break off negotiations as did Tanner and Paasikivi, and leave Moscow. We must sign the agreement and the only thing to do in such circumstances is—"Make the best of a bad job." What cannot be saved will inevitably have to be agreed on. (. . .)*

I am not in the position to write anything further at this juncture."

CHURCHILL'S FAMOUS PHRASE AND WHAT HAPPENED NEXT

Churchill says: "I have nothing to offer but blood, toil, tears and sweat." And the Germans break through the Allied front at Sedan. On 14th May there is a truce with the Netherlands, and this is in force from midday. In the afternoon, at around three o'clock, Rotterdam is attacked from the air and surrenders.

Churchill says later that [the Soviet Union] "had to occupy the Baltic states and a large part of Poland by force of arms or stealth before they themselves were attacked. Although their policy was callous, it was most realistic at the time."

The Netherlands capitulates. The Maginot Line is also breached.

A treaty, which states that Russia will expand its bases in Estonia is signed.

To the treaty a list is attached giving the forty-two places in Estonia where Russian troops will be stationed.

Here in our novel, it is only worth mentioning the places nearest to where our good friend Brecht is staying.

Let's mention a couple. Where do Russian forces go to?

For instance the Pakri peninsula (4,200 hectares), Little Pakri island (1,070 ha), Great Pakri (1,200 ha), Osmussaar (436 ha), Klooga railroad station and Lake Klooga (500 ha) . . .

Major-General A. Traksmaa writes the following to the Estonian Foreign Minister A. Piip:

"(. . .) Up to then, everything had remained confused and unclear. (. . .) The unclear situation allowed us to entertain a number of hopes for a good outcome, when interpreting our thoughts on our interests as delineated in the pact, where there is room for different interpretations. For instance, we entertained the hopes that the stationing of troops as mentioned in the confidential protocol would only apply in the case of war and would lapse thereafter . . . (. . .) These hopes came to an end during the talks with Molotov on 11th May (. . .) We have to come to terms with the fact that the troops and air support are permanent. (. . .) . . . these are principles where we made no progress whatsoever during the talks with Molotov. 'It is militarily necessary and everyone will have to make their sacrifices. In our own country we demand, under such circumstances, much greater zones to be out of bounds and under much stricter conditions,' was Molotov's opinion. (. . .) I imagine that the real reason is that Soviet Russia now feels she has a free hand."

IZVESTIYA SAYS IT STRAIGHT OUT

The major national Russian newspaper writes as follows:

"Recent events, such as the occupation of Belgium, Holland and Luxembourg again prove that the neutrality of small countries is sheer fantasy, as they are in no position to defend their own neutrality. Small nations have very few chances of maintaining their sovereignty. All negotiations they enter into with large countries regarding rights and wrongs are simply naïve, since the latter make the decisions in war as to whether small countries will survive or not."

Churchill flies to Paris to find out what is happening there.

He no doubt learns something, but there is a lot that remains incomprehensible to him.

THE BALTIC GERMANS LEAVE ESTONIA

As we know, Hitler called Germans home to the Reich before the *big* war started, even from such places as Estonia.

The last of the *Umsiedler* are now boarding the "Der Deutsche" (there are about four hundred people on board).

THE ESTONIAN PRESIDENT PRESENTS LITERARY AWARDS

President Konstantin Päts presents literary awards to authors.

August Jakobson, a realist, even naturalistic perhaps, gets one for his play *Phantoms*. (As you can see from the title, the play covers more or less the same material as Ibsen's *Ghosts*). Between the years 1950 and 1958, this writer occupied more or less the same post as the President of the Estonian Republic who is now presenting him with the award. During those years he had become the First Secretary of the Estonian Soviet Socialist Republic, and, in name, its President as well.

The second prize goes to someone considered as one of Estonia's greatest writers, Tammsaare, whom Hella was alluding to when saying she loved a German; his famous novel is entitled *I Loved a German*. But this time the prize is awarded for another of Tammsaare's novels, one depicting the arrival of the Devil on Earth. The Devil wants to say to Peter that even the Devil can find bliss and salvation. In Estonia, the depiction of the Devil (also known as *Vanapagan*—i.e., the Old Pagan) is so fundamentally different in that of Christian tradition that there is no point in starting to describe it here. By the time Tammsaare receives the award he has already been dead for two months and he thus remains oblivious, at least in mortal guise, of all the things that happen to Estonia and the rest of the world.

Another prizewinner is Mait Metsanurk, who does not die until 1957, doesn't do anything remarkable or bad during the rest of his life, simply rewrites and carefully polishes his previous works and keeps out of politics.

This can't be said, however, about the following two men.

Johannes Semper, whose subtle psychological novel is being rewarded this time round, becomes the Minister of Education a couple of months later under the Communists. He is an expert on André Gide and is the head of the PEN Center, but after the war he falls from grace. During the "Thaw" he manages to start publishing again. But he's lost his touch, and publishes little of value before his death (1970). He sits there in silence, his face distinguished. He may be saying something privately, among friends, but we can't hear what it is.

Johannes Vares-Barbarus also receives a prize. His case is a special one. We will only say here that at the time the award was presented, President Päts didn't know that this provincial doctor and anarcho-futurist poet had already been chalked up by the Russians as the next prime minister in the forthcoming government. It is even disputed whether he himself knew. Maybe he thought that people would pay attention to him because he was a good poet.

And the others?

Each fate is no doubt interesting in itself, but we can't list them all here.

Of the prizewinners that year, August Mälk and Pedro Krusten managed to flee abroad in 1944. The former to Sweden, the latter to the USA. They saved their lives and their honor.

After the war, the poet Jaan Kärner, one of those who was receiving an award (and who was someone that collaborated with the new régime), went insane and could no longer be taken seriously.

And there was one more poet that got a prize. This is Johannes Sütiste, whose health was broken by German captivity, but found no approval either from the Russians when they returned, and died in 1945.

Those are the ones who were receiving the awards.

Brecht never got to know all of this because he was very much taken up with the German nation and with himself.

Columns of German tanks reach the English Channel.

Brecht is leafing through an old 1907 edition of Meyer's encyclopedia, which Hella has on the shelf. He wants to know who these Estonians really are. And this is what he learns:

The Estonians are a nation living in the European part of Russia and are of the Mongol race and the Finnish family of nations. E-s live in Estonia proper, on the island of Saaremaa [Ösel] and neighboring islands of Hiiumaa [Dagö], Muhu [Moon], etc., in the northern part of Livonia and in the gubernias of Pihkva [Pskov], Vitebsk and Saint Petersburg. During the Middle Ages, the areas popu-lated by the E-s extended much further to the south, areas also occupied by the now extinct Courlanders and Livonians, but were gradually pushed northwards by the Letts. The territory is 38.5 square kilometers in size, and the population around 750,000. The Russians call them "chukhnaa" or "chukhontsi," which means "foreigners," the Letts "igauni," which means "to go into the enclosure." The Finns call them "virolaiset" ("inhabitant of the border marches"). They call themselves "tallopoeg" ("farmers").

E-s are neither handsome nor strong. The exception to this rule is the coastal dwellers. Inland, the people are short in stature. Their heads are small, their faces broad and pressed together. The Mongoloid features are pronounced. Their cheek-bones are broad, their mouths small. Thick brows cover deep-set eyes with gray irises. They have straight fair or brown hair that hangs loose. Their shoulders are undeveloped in proportion to their height, and their arms are long, their hands are, however, broad and their fingers short. Their broad calves flatten out at the back of their short legs, which are supported by small feet. For this reason, the posture of E-s is loose-limbed, their gait sluggish.

E-s dress in a uniform way. The menfolk wear long black coats with no collars or lapels, the material for which is termed "vatman." Under this, they wear jerkins made out of blue broadcloth. They wear short trousers made of linen or leather, woolen socks and, instead of boots, they wear shoes made of untreated leather, termed "pastels." On their heads they wear round hats. In the winter they wear sheepskin coats and caps made out of fox fur.

The women wear brightly colored pleated skirts and tightly clinging black underskirts. Married women wear a tightly fitting black cap ("tanu"). In the area around Reval and on the islands, on the other hand, they wear a broad headband ("pärg").

The dwelling houses of the E-s are robust, and are without chimneys. The bedchamber is heated by the foot of the threshing stove, from which the smoke, used to dry grain, issues freely and leaves by way of the door.

The majority of the population are Estonians, people who do not understand a word of the German language. Once an E-n has received an education, he will become a member of the German, more rarely Russian, nation.

E-s have a noticeable tendency to produce poetry. When congregating they always declaim improvised poems and verse, sung in a minor key. Women especially sing when performing most tasks (in the fields, on the threshing floor, when spinning, etc.).

When the Finnish national epic the "Kalevala" became known in Europe as a whole, the E-s began to collect their own national folk material, which Kreutzwald published in 1858 as Kalevipoeg.

Originally, the E-s were a warlike people and were also pirates. They were much feared in the Baltic Sea. Their nature is Fenno-Ugrian, both introverted and distrustful.

During recent times they have mixed more with Russian elements. For this reason, E-s have grown more able to communicate and more hard-working and cleverer than Russians as regards many household activities.

PART IV

EARLY SUMMER

1940

20th May

Today, in 1940, Lai-Tu has finally arrived as well. She telephones Helsinki and asks whether she can come to their lodgings.

Hella greets Lai-Tu joyously but lies when she says she has to go out. She gives Brecht's address.

Lai-Tu rings the doorbell. She has a red rose in her hand and is wearing a Bailman costume.

Why Lai-Tu?

Brecht loved the idea of cloaking his ideas in oriental guise. He has written a whole book that paraphrases the philosophy of Mo Di. Ruth features it under the name of Lai-Tu. But others feature there too under various names.

Here is a short key to his "Chinese work."

Engels—Eh-fu, Lenin—Mi-en-leh, Marx—Ka-meh, Hegel—Hü-jeh or He-leh, Rosa Luxemburg—Sa, Stalin—Ni-en, Trotsky—To-tsi. Brecht himself—Kin-jeh or Kin-leh. Russia is Tsen, the Soviet Union is Su, Germany Ga or Ge-el or Ger. Hitler is Hi-jeh or Hui-jeh, Plekhanov—Le-peh, Anatole France—Fan-tse, Feuchtwanger—Fe-hu-wang, Emil Ludwig—Lu, and Berlau's pseudonym has already been mentioned.

Mo Di lived during the period before the birth of Christ (from 479 to 400 B.C.). Brecht has palmed off all kinds of thoughts on him, including his own problems of dialectics and Hegel.

At the level of everyday politics, there is of course a clash between Mi-en-leh (whom Brecht likes) and Ni-en, whom he likes less, but whom Brecht dare not criticize in public. Not only for fear of Ni-en. Brecht likes Hi-jeh even less.

The covert theme of the book is, of course, dialectics, Brecht's greatest love.

"Where did *you* come from?" asks Brecht.

"You did after all invite me," replies Ruth. The other women do not come out into the corridor.

Quite true, Brecht had invited Ruth. Earlier on, Ruth had left her husband and three children for him, and what is more she became left-wing too. (When they applied for a visa for her, they tried to reduce this to being an "armchair Communist.") Brecht really was expecting Ruth. He had asked her to share his life in exile. Brecht had written the following:

"Dear Ruth, come quickly. Nothing has changed, everything is secure. *J.e.d.* [this is short for, *Jeg elsker dig,* the Danish for "I love you"]. And the situation will remain the same however long we are parted. Whether for ten or even twenty years. (. . .) Take care of yourself and make sure you avoid danger, because our time will come soon, and you have to be ready for it. My darling Ruth *epep* Bertolt." [*Epep* is another of Brecht's the abbreviations that he had engraved into a ring he gave Ruth and is the Latin expression *et prope et procul* (so near and yet so far).]

Helene and Grete are shocked. Brecht is astonished. But he thinks that the event is the beginning of something unexpected.

Grete doesn't say a word. In fact, she says nothing for several days.

"She's not staying here," says Helene. "Take her to a hotel."

The door swings open and Ruth announces with shining eyes:

"A hotel, of course, where else? Let's go!"

Brecht picks a Fridhäll boarding house nearby.

They walk in the darkness, which is already rustling. The leaves have grown larger. Brecht puts his arm around Ruth's waist. Ruth says that she barely escaped from Denmark with her life. She had been doing a performance when the Nazis broke into her apartment. Ruth had been playing Brecht's "The Fear and Misery of the Third Reich." When she arrived home that evening, the Nazis had thrown stones through her windows, broken down her door, and smashed up everything inside.

Brecht is pointing out features in the night sky through the window of the boarding house.

"See that constellation that looks like a W? That's Cassiopeia. It's our constellation. Wherever we are in the world, our glances will meet at that constellation."

"You have brought the heavens down to Earth," replies Ruth, from the bed, "not only these five stars, but the whole of the heavens."

"Is everything all right?" asks Brecht still gazing out at the sky. (What he means is: have you been faithful to me?)

"Yes," replies Ruth.

She always replies like this with a clear conscience, if she leaves aside when she got back from the Spanish Civil War. Brecht was very jealous of her then, but with the help of the influential parliamentary secretary Georg Branting they later managed to get a visa for Sweden. And it was Brecht's own fault. He was afraid of going to Spain himself and hoped that Ruth would tell him all about it.

So they again had an affair. Brecht recites: "Dark times . . . in a strange city . . . but the tread is light as before . . . forehead smooth . . ."

Berlau later went to live back in Germany, but Brecht no longer bothered with her, except for making countless phone calls, drawings, writing letters and proposals to get together sometime. She said in a letter in 1951 that Brecht was now hunting "fresh flesh." For his part, Brecht accused her of making him age by five years. Nevertheless, she made attempts to meet Brecht before his death. But she was no longer allowed into the theater. When Brecht and Weigel finally went to live separately in 1953 (so what if they still lived near to one another?), this was her last chance. But nothing came of it. In the 1960s, she began walking with a stick. In 1974 she received a place in an old people's home as a victim of the Nazi régime. Alcoholic as she was, she drank several glasses of wine one evening and lit a cigarette. She obviously fell asleep while lighting it. She was asphyxiated by the smoke of the ensuing fire. The 15th January 1974 was decided on as the date of her death. Berlau had wished for her ashes to be strewn out over the sea. But nothing came of it. The urn was placed in the Dorothea Cemetery in Berlin. (Dorotheenstätische Friedhof in Berlin). There too Brecht is buried.

One day, Brecht is at Wuolijoki's place. Hella is glowing as usual, and talking with great intensity. About herself. About Estonia. About comedies. About Finland. About horses. About birds. About capitalism. About Cinderellas.

Then the telephone rings. Ruth Berlau is on the line and she asks whether she can come over. Hella is suspicious and says no: she's busy. This occurs on 21st May. Hella hopes that Berlau will not come over.

Hella goes on glowing and talking. More about herself, Estonia, Comedies, Finland, Horses, Birds, Capitalism and Cinderellas.

Hella is eating all this while in the kitchen. Brecht never has anything to do with kitchens. He has a bottle of beer in front of him and is drumming his fingers on the tabletop. He looks Hella in the eye and wonders whether Hella could betray him if the need arose. Not to What's-His-Name. Much more likely to Russia. He would feel more secure in America. But he can't get there without crossing Russia.

In the far north, in Petsamo, there is still a way out. But this is likely to be shut off soon. So the only way is through Moscow, and as quickly as possible. Without stopping anywhere on the way.

Then the doorbell rings. Despite being put off, she has arrived anyway. (Hella has not told Brecht who was on the phone.) Hella sees a tall, beautiful woman leaning against the front door and how the short Brecht pounces on her. They kiss for a long time.

Hella is already prepared to think that they would have sex right there in the lobby.

Hella's daughter, Vappu Tuomioja, to whom I am grateful to a certain extent for the development of this novel and to whose home on Merikatu street I was cordially invited, remembers that Ruth was a real beauty, had a gorgeous body, and that her love for Brecht was more than obvious.

Berlau was without a doubt a feminist and ahead of her time. Unfortunately, she was also a Communist. She did, after all, become famous by cycling to Moscow in the 1930s to do reportage there.

Some people have called her "Red Ruth," but this is hardly surprising when you consider how popular Communism was between the two wars among the young intelligentsia of the West.

Sylvi-Kylliki Kilpi thought that Ruth was bouncing with health and a jolly sort of person, but in sexual and ethical matters she embodied that type of female that Kilpi dreaded. She lived life according to "her own rules."

The boarding house (some ten minutes' walk from Brecht's apartment) serves coffee to guests. Coffee was rare in wartime.

Berlau reveals in one curious sentence of her memoirs that Hella had coffee nonetheless. She had obtained it from the superpower next door (aus dem grossen Nachbarland).

But Ruth wants to bring Brecht coffee herself. At seven o'clock in the morning she rushes out with a copper coffee jug wrapped in newspaper to outside Brecht's window, knocks on the window pane and hands over the coffee.

25th May

Towards the end of April 1938, 842 Germans were arrested in Russia. Among them were, for example, Fritz Schultke, Hermann Schuberg, Hans Kannenberger, Hans Neumann, Heinrich Susskind, Hugo Eberlein, Werner Hirsch and many others.

Stanislavski's *An Actor Prepares* appeared in 1938 in German translation in Zurich under the title *Das Geheimnis des schauspielerischen Erfolgs*. In the German language, realism and Nazism coincided for a short while.

Brecht had always regarded Stanislavski as a child of the old, naturalistic times. He compared the method with those clods of earth that botanists bring to their tables when doing research. The main focus of the work is describing situations and examining the mental life of individuals.

His theater, still eighty years later, can be seen sometimes looking like something from a bygone era, like a museum exhibit.

Brecht wanted to promote that type of theater where you didn't live the role. He regarded living your role as a marginal phenomenon, which didn't do any harm. Brecht thought that you had to cut off any empathy you had as an actor and that showing feeling in certain places in the play should only be used very, very sparingly and even then mixed in with other activities.

What's-His-Name lived his role to the full. In the end, he started believing that he was the person he wanted to be.

Brecht wanted an actor (and an individual) to see himself from the outside. Brecht was a proponent of estrangement and alienation.

At any given moment you should be able to ask yourself: what is going on? What is happening now?

Estrangement and alienation are, in actual fact, separate things.

Estrangement (Entfremdung) comes originally from the young Karl Marx. This term has to do with the early phase of capitalism. People are totally estranged from their work.

Alienation (Verfremdung), which Brecht spoke a good deal about during his lifetime, is not a sociological term. Brecht was thinking of something relatively simple.

You have arrived at the stage in your life where you are so used to a particular phenomenon, in thought and deed, and that is how it should be. All of a sudden, Brecht shows you that not everything is so self-evident. What is natural suddenly appears strange, alienation is invoked. It is if you have just been born and do not quite understand phenomena. Why doesn't the Sun fall on our heads? Do we exist? What is natural about the fact that a woman sells her own body and mucous membranes? Why do we eat the dead bodies of animals? Where did Hitler come from, could our small child become another Hitler, and when will it become evident that it is no longer a child but has become a Hitler?

To describe Brecht's "alienation effect" you would need a whole novel. It is also called estrangement. The relationship between the terms Verfremdung and Entfremdung is an interesting chapter in history of the mind. But we aren't going to start down that road here. Brecht has described it thoroughly enough in his own works, the most important of which being Theoretical Works *and* Little Organum for the Theater *(both available in Estonian, published in 1972). It ought to be mentioned here that "alienation" is a term that stems from the 1920s Russian "formalist" theory of Viktor Shklovsky, who used the term "ostranneniye," which, loosely translated, means "being pulled aside," or, why not, "inducing wonder." The idea from Brecht's point of view was to depict a relationship that we all regard as normal, e.g., that between a capitalist and a worker, in such a style that we look at it as if seeing it for the first time.*

Lion Feuchtwanger, the major novelist and once a friend of Brecht's, was at this time traveling to the concentration camp at Les Milles. He traveled to the prison voluntarily, by taxi as far as I know, and paid for his stay himself. He was an alien from a French point of view and therefore had to be interned.

In Finland, a peace and friendship agreement between that country and the Soviet Union.

The Russian news agency TASS considers it difficult to make agreements with the British. German troops conquer both the Netherlands and Belgium. Blücher tells Berlin that these victories have made a deep impression on the Finns. On 23rd May the head of the British fascists, Oswald Mosley, is arrested. And Trotsky's villa in Mexico is attacked for the first time. This attack is carried out in the name of the well-known painter David Siqueiros. Siqueiros (like Diego Rivera) was no doubt a very good monumental painter, but he was also very left-wing—like many intellectuals between the wars. Siqueiros announced publicly that he did not wish to make an attempt on Trotsky's life, the action was merely a protest at Trotsky's residence in Mexico.

On 24th May, the Allies gave up the battle for Narvik. German forces came to a standstill near Dunkirk.

26th May

In Finland, twenty-six people in a bus plunge into a river. Seventeen of them are already dead when help arrives. In Flanders, battles are taking place. In Italy it is, for no apparent reason, no longer permitted to drive private vehicles. Here in Estonia, there are fires. A sawmill is burnt down and some of the farm buildings at Alatskivi also burn down, with the loss of three cattle and three pigs. In the borough of Avanduse, it is a haystack. In Tartu some boy or other goes to a barracks and is killed by a stray bullet.

27th–28th May

The famous newspaper Pravda *accuses Estonian intellectuals of being pro-British. The paper thinks that those going around cracking anti-Hitler jokes should be arrested by the secret police. This is far from a joke, because at the same time, Russian troops are amassing on the Estonian border. In the world of culture, things are, however, a little different. Or is this synchronicity? On 28th May, in the Museum of Modern Western Art in Moscow, an exhibition of Estonian and Latvian books is opened.*

Mercader (who has also been played by Alain Delon) meets Trotsky for the first time.

He presents Trotsky's grandchildren with a toy plane and teaches them how to set it going and fly it.

At the same time, the disaster at Dunkirk is, of course, taking place: that day, 17,804 soldiers are evacuated.

It is rumored that foreign planes of unknown origin are flying through Swiss air space. In the royal palace in Oslo, Terboven is holding a speech and promises to extend the hand of friendship to the Norwegians.

That is how the war is developing. It begins with random incidents, which then accumulate and ultimately move toward closure. Why? Let's say simply: people are relatively stupid.

29th May

TASS announces that Lithuania is behaving in a provocative manner. Lithuania has indeed set up a commission to investigate, but whatever it achieves, it's too little, too late.

In Lithuania, it's rumored that Russian soldiers have been killed. They're supposed to have been tortured at unspecified places where they were taken blindfolded. This makes Urbšys telegraph all his ambassadors: in case of a disaster, Lozoraitis becomes the head of all diplomatic activity.

1st June

Brecht is wondering what to do next. He's alone in the room. The weather is fairly cool, no point in opening the window. The dust swirls, the sun is shining, but summer hasn't yet arrived. So what is it now? Don't know. Is thinking about summer a productive activity to indulge in? In summer the most horrible things happen, and because in summer the weather is warm and bad people find themselves outdoors. In winter, they hide away in their rooms, shivering and waiting. But in summer! Oh dear! In summer such an interest is aroused! Interest in doing what? In going outside, shouting, conquering, emancipation, occupation.

Today, Brecht is ruminating as follows:

There are rumors everywhere of a German spirit of resistance among the German troops. This makes Brecht think about the name Frederick Winslow Taylor. Taylor, in turn, makes Brecht think about a Taylorized society: Taylorism tends to talk about the fact that care and diligence are things that can be put on a conveyor belt. But a conveyor belt renders personal gallantry meaningless. Gallantry and diligence are no longer private matters. German soldiers, Brecht is thinking, at the same time as it is getting light—yes, thinks Brecht, as German soldiers don't receive instruction in any form of personal ethics, they are suborned to a group spirit (*Geist der Truppe*). A soldier is like a weapon or tool for victory. Soldiers are like bombs. But bombs don't have a soul, or are not reckoned as having one. Do bombs and cats have a moral code, Brecht is asking himself? He doesn't know the answer. Surely not. But if they do, then it's better, perhaps, not to know.

I am indeed an individual, thinks Brecht, gets up and goes over to the mirror. Yes, he is an individual—in as much as anyone in the unifying circumstances of today can ever be. Does he differ a great deal from other people— that is something he doesn't know. But he does differ in some things from other people.

I am not *ilmaton* (Finnish for "without character"), thinks Brecht, remembering Hella's claim, based on Hella's claim, that both Brecht's and her company are *ilmiö* (i.e., a phenomenon).

The German Luftwaffe is already bombing Paris. People think that Dunkirk has just been conquered. In actual fact, it is not conquered until the following night.

4th June

Yes, Dunkirk has already been conquered. The flags fly for three days in Germany, and the church bells ring. Hitler is convinced that the war will be over within six weeks. Churchill lets it be known that even if Britain itself is conquered, the war will go on at sea and all over the globe. The Allies begin to retreat from Narvik.

Grete dies exactly one year later.

At the same time, the Lühike eesti-vene-eesti sõjaväeline vestmik *(Short Estonian-Russian-Estonian Military Phrasebook) comes into print. Here phrases can be found such as "Isn't there any more?" and "Give it here!" and "I'm going to shoot!"*

Brecht sees how swiftly warfare develops in modern times. Nowadays, it's only the pace that counts. Fronts, maneuvers and strongholds are no longer of any consequence.

The Finnish sky is empty and sad. But from it, at any moment, can come *ilmavaara*, i.e., the threat of an air raid. And the building opposite is bathed in a semi-transparent light and Brecht himself is white and *ilman rusketusta* (the Finnish for "untanned").

A few days later, Italy declares war on France and Britain. The French government leaves Paris, the embassies are evacuated to Bordeaux, including the Estonian Em-

bassy. André Malraux leaves for London, from there he travels to the USA. Norway has no other choice but to capitulate. In Estonia, it is said that the Russian bases are moving up to a state of alert and the Lithuanian Ambassador is summoned to Moscow by Molotov.

One evening, Brecht collects all the women around him and starts talking. "The French are finished. This stems from the fact that they are too patriotic. Over there, practicing the art of patriotism is not only a benefit but also a bane. They are not married to their own country, it has become their mistress. *La patrie*! The Danes, however, have fallen victim to their own humor. They only see the funny side of war. They were convinced that fascism didn't suit them, as they had too good a sense of humor. They more or less make a living from pigs and for that reason they should have got on well with the Germans, as the Germans need pigs. Fascism was not unfortunately something that the Danes took seriously so one morning a dozen or so planes arrived from the sky and occupied the whole country. The Danes have always claimed that their humor is untranslatable, as it consists of small linguistic nuances that have their own comic logic, and this, in turn, meant that the Germans didn't notice that they were not being taken seriously."

When the women have gone out to look at the sunset, Brecht is alone. Should I take off my trousers? he is thinking. No sooner said than done. And why not? Brecht takes them off and throws them onto the floor. Trousers are plural! Always plural! Why? Maybe because there are two trouser legs. How many should there then be? Four? That's an animal! A hundred? That's a centipede! Who am I? thinks Brecht. A two-legged, even a half-three-legged one. All nonsense. That which hangs between a man's legs, is no leg of mine. It's all the same really. Don't know what it is. The only thing that Brecht knows for sure is: he is a man from the black woods, Brecht.

10th June

That morning Brecht has drunk the coffee brought to him by Ruth, had sex with the consumptive Grete, and is now thinking, along with Grete about his new play. Some of it is ready, and yet isn't. When will he be thinking about the parts? Maybe before lunch. Before noon Brecht hardly lets anyone into his room, not only not into his bed but anywhere near him. The only thing that feels right is—no, not Helene, but the wireless. It tells him so many bad things. If he were to believe what they say on the wireless, he should go and drown himself immediately. The world seems so bad.

Nevertheless, the thought that mankind is good germinates in his mind. He cultivates the idea that people become bad when they have the brakes on. The market economy and all those other things.

When they take off the brakes, people grow good again. What sort of good? Loving one's neighbor or member of the same species, to put it in concrete terms. Because it's good to love others. Those who kill everyone else are maybe not bad, simply murderers. The civilized world is not merciful toward murderers. Killing, at least killing a member of the same sex, is not the thing to do.

This author has killed no one either. Murder is always such a blatant business. Have to torment people to the end. On the other hand: I have eaten pigs. But on one occasion, when my old father was bedridden and asked if I would kill a rooster—N.B., a rooster and not a pig, I refused categorically. "Son, can't you go and kill the rooster so Mother doesn't have to do it alone?" said Father in his hospital pyjamas. "No," I said. I had up to then imagined myself to be a carnivore. But let those people that like killing kill animals for me. Extinguishing life is their privilege. I will eat what they kill for me. Everyone has their roles in society, let everyone stick to them. If you're sensitive, you do sensitive work. If you're cruel, you do cruel work. The two types don't get in the way of one another, they have more of a complementary function.

Brecht thought that human beings were intrinsically good. It's hard to know whether he "really" thought so. Maybe this idea of goodness is linked to his struggle against the market economy. Capitalism is cruel, just as cruel as Communism. Goodness is rare. It occurs mostly in utopias or in the form of flattery.

How someone changes for the better, or doesn't, this is what we see in dreams or moralist works. Urbšys is arriving in Moscow today. He says what he says, but nothing affects Molotov. Promises by the Smetona government to have a reshuffle don't impress Moscow either.

14th June

That same day, Nikitin arrives in Tallinn. Brecht does not of course know about this, and it would in any case hardly interest him. Ants Oras, our famous Anglophile and renowned literary expert, is traveling to Tartu, Estonia's second largest city known for its university. This city is called the Athens of the River

Emajõgi—i.e., the Mother River. Why the Mother River? Through the city flows a relatively large river, whose name is Emajõgi or Embach, or more exactly Mutterbach. In the 1970s, when we were only allowed to make subtle hints, one pop singer sang a song about how the Emajõgi takes its waters secretly from under the willows on the riverbank, and that is no cowardice. God knows what it was all about, but perhaps instructions on how to tack and change course under the mysterious willow trees on the bank.

But why was Oras traveling to Tartu, as he is not the hero of our novel and Brecht never met him in his life (in the same way as AO never met Brecht), to the university there?

A Baltic conference was to be held.

What did they discuss there?

Baltic issues, no doubt.

But it was already too late.

The occupation of Lithuania had begun. On the night of the 16th President Smetona fled Lithuania. Russian ships tried to intercept a motor boat in the Gulf of Finland that belonged to our President (the President wasn't on it) and take him to Kronstadt.

What else happened? History is a fairy tale!

Roosevelt gave orders to build an atomic weapon, and a flag with a swastika on it was hoisted up the Eiffel Tower.

A few more remarks about Urbšys. He was summoned to the Kremlin, and Molotov read him out the ultimatum. Reply by ten o'clock. The Lithuanian government received the ultimatum at two o'clock. Smetona proposed resistance, but the rest wanted to go along with the terms of the ultimatum. Smetona crossed the East-Prussian border. It was said that the Russian emissary Dekanozov sent another delegation to Smetona, but that it did not achieve anything.

The Lithuanians will know more about this than me.

Brecht wakes up suddenly in the night. The concept and nature of protective coloring are driving him crazy. Cocteau is supposed to have said somewhere—I don't quite know where—that the idea of painting tanks was one of Picasso's. He had suggested the colors. Like protective coloring. So as not to be seen. They should be painted in quite a wild manner. Savages paint themselves much more than we do, if we paint ourselves at all. A savage and a present-day arbiter of fashion can shake one another's hand. And why shouldn't they do so? Who can ban a cuckoo from crowing?

Fateful times for our nation are getting closer every minute.

In 1988, on Prangli island in the Gulf of Finland, one inhabitant, Oskar Mets-väli described an incident:

"In early the morning of 14th June 1940 I went out to sea. I was fourteen years old at the time.

Our boat was in the usual fishing zone, around three to four km south-east of Keri island where we were doing deep sea angling for cod. There were four or five other boats from Prangli in the same area. The weather was fine, visibility was good, the sea was as smooth as a mirror.

Between two and three, a passenger plane came from the direction of Tallinn, traveling its usual route. It was a white, single-winged aircraft. Suddenly I saw two Russian fighters following it. They were flying at the same altitude and fired shots at the passenger plane in turns from behind in short bursts. At first, I didn't understand what was happening. The volleys of shots could be heard two or three hundred meters away. All three planes flew low over our heads. Then I saw the passenger plane fall. It fell into the sea a couple of kilometers from our boats, there was neither smoke nor fire. When it fell on its left-hand side into the sea, only then was an there explosion and we heard the rumbling. The Russian fighters turned back towards the Estonian mainland.

A little later a gray submarine rose from the water, at about the same spot where the plane had fallen. I wanted to go nearer, but the man I was with was more afraid and suggested we got back to the island as quickly as possible. As I was young, I wasn't afraid. The submarine went up to the nearest boat. I later heard that the submariners had sent a boat hook through the porthole of the cabin of the boat, smashing the glass. The boat was drawn nearer. There were no threats, they just wanted to have a look that they hadn't fished anything exciting out of the water.

Later, I heard that foreign money was scattered over the surface of the water, plus pieces of the aircraft, the bodies of the passengers, other trash. A couple of fishermen had managed to get hold of some of the foreign money. They later gave it to the Estonian coastguard. Stupid thing to do; they should have kept it for themselves.

The submarine stayed above the surface for quite some while. At the same time, a very fast plane came from the direction of Finland in the direction of the scene of the incident. It flew at about the same height and was no doubt a fighter too. The plane that had been shot down had presumably had time to send a radio signal. The plane flew quickly out of the scene and disappeared back to Finland. Those in the other fishing boats watched all of this. No Estonian coastguard vessel approached the scene.

On Prangli, people later said that there had been some VIP aboard that plane, someone who wanted to flee Estonia and for that reason the Russian fighter shot the plane down."

(Noted down by Küllo Arjakas)

The plane took off at 13:54 hours. It only managed to fly a couple of kilometers. On board were the German businessmen Rudolf Coellen and Friedrich Offermann, the American Henry William Antheil (historian Arjakas reckons him to be the first American victim of the war), the Estonian of Finnish woman Gunvor Maria Luts, married to an Estonian, and the French diplomatic couriers Paul Longuet and Frédéric Marty. These two were carrying diplomatic mail, which the submarine subsequently picked up. It is strange that the submarine rose out of the water at the exact spot and managed to find the suitcases. Arjakas suggests that the plane was shot down because of the mail. It could have been, at any rate Estonia was now under an air blockade.

No doubt nothing more will ever be found out about this incident, as Arjakas stressed in his notes back in 1983, the year the Korean airliner was shot down, about which not much was revealed either. It was shot down. Period. What difference do a few hundred people make, one way or the other?

This incident didn't affect Brecht. I've tried to investigate whether he knew anyone on the plane. Unfortunately, I'm not a very good researcher. George Antheil was a student of Ernst Bloch's; Antheil lived peacefully until his death in 1959. I have written a note with the title "Transatlantic Flight" in connection with him (1927, when he must have been 27) but what has that to do with the shooting down of the Kaleva? In Finland he was busy with the life of a Chinese pilot and his exploits. He didn't want to spend time on the problems surrounding him. Flying is loneliness (too close to heaven) and can end badly, as we have seen in the case of Saint-Exupéry.

15th June

Exactly halfway through June. Brecht has not left Helsinki. Other Germans, however, are constantly in motion. They are like quicksilver. Now they are only twenty kilometers from Paris. Albert Camus (in his diary): "Finished the first part of the Absurd. Human beings are wiping their own dwelling houses off the face of the earth, set their own fields on fire and sprinkle salt over them so that they are rendered unusable by others." Why are the Germans twenty kilometers from Paris? Or why would the French—for the sake of argument—be twenty kilometers from Berlin? All because of the lunacy of national leaders. The masses carry out what they are ordered to do. Then people write about these crazy people in the history books. A man with one leg and his belly ripped open who is thrown into a ditch at the side of the road doesn't get into the history books. That's what the spirit of history is like. Hegel once saw Napoleon mounted on a white horse and he thought he'd not seen Napoleon but the *Zeitgeist*.

Does this mean that everything that lives or, under certain circumstances, gives the impression of doing so, or can be interpreted as being alive or is involved in some similar activity, has to expand at the expense of others?

But perhaps, in actuality—the Earth, our Earth is so sated with organic life that no one can live freely and comfortably.

Unfortunately, everything happens because of others, and it is the most restless and fidgety people who get to be the greatest.

How proud does a cat get when it crushes a mouse?

The mouse can never answer.

It is said that a rat does get a little proud.

16th June

(Ruth Berlau dies exactly thirty-four years later.)

Brecht would like to buy Steffin some oranges, but there aren't any. Once he bought one in London for Margarete and wrote a poem about it. He remembered the yellowish nighttime fog under the streetlamps of Southampton, and the even yellower orange peel! This happened in 1934 and Brecht had to eat the orange himself, as Grete was far away.

17th June

At midday, Russian troops reach Tallinn from Klooga. They are stationed in Estonian barracks. There is a ban on the sale of alcohol for three days. It looks as if this is usual when a coup d'état takes place. The common people tend not to understand what is going on. When a state has begun to rot from the inside, such things soon happen. It cannot offer any resistance. You can say about it that it is like an overripe fruit that falls into the picker's lap.

Schulenburg does go to see Molotov (really don't really know what they have to talk about), but their talks lack substance: Russian forces have already arrived at the Lithuanian border. There is nothing more to be done. Soon, a new government is formed under Justas Paleckis. As for Germany, its government there bans all involvement and opinions on the subject.

18th June

M. Unt (not me, the author of this work, but a jovial Social-Democrat who is no relation of mine, but lived in the small town of Pärnu) is summoned to Tallinn, the capital. He is to meet the Secretary of the Communist Party Säre and the Russian Ambassador Bochkaryov. Säre can't make it that quickly. He's in Altsla for some reason. He is also summoned to meet M. Unt.

At the same time, Hitler meets Mussolini in Munich. The latter is not happy that a treaty was signed in Bordeaux and that a part of France has not been occupied. Mussolini now understands that the whole business is not important for Hitler, as Italy has not taken any practical part in this war, and the Führer doesn't want to share any victories with anyone.

De Gaulle is already in London forming the National Committee there.

In Estonia, on the other hand, a series of less romantic events is taking place. A decree is issued whereby weapons are to be confiscated from individuals. Who are these "individuals"? The people? Arms taken from the people! On whose orders? The annual Song Festival is cancelled. Between eleven o'clock (at night) and five o'clock (in the morning) you're not allowed to go out on the street. (This is supposedly the time of day that there is the greatest risk for revolt and resistance.) Prime Minister Uluots holds a speech on the wireless, where he appeals for calm. That's all very well, but the Reds are already occupying the railroad stations, post offices and ports.

You're not allowed to take photographs outdoors—something which nowadays, in the age of satellites, is something that can't fully be appreciated.

The time is at hand.

Rise up or die on your knees?

Does pride pay off or is it a mere verbal fiction? What is better: not to be usurped and dead or usurped and alive? But why bother to live if you don't know what you're living for? Is not such a life an unnecessary luxury? It consumes the world's resources of electricity, keys and love, which run out, or disappear off into the blue or at least to places where we never get to know what really happened, if anything did happen.

Estonian merchant vessels are already being confiscated. They are towed to the port of Paldiski, where there's no way out.

Brecht reckons that the comparison between painting savages and painting tanks is in some way linked with "alienation." Disguises are alienation, individuality disappears. When trendy young people paint one another, their basic aim is of a different order. They usually achieve it.

Something is stirring at the military bases!

For some while there hovers the real threat of war. Jokipii has angered General Huhtala. As is his wont, Schulenburg meets Molotov as if nothing has happened. What can they be talking about? Whether to start killing millions of people right away, and jointly or severally? Our one million souls have already been sold down the river. Later it emerges that some have scattered throughout the world at large so that the whole nation is not wiped out.

At four o'clock Nikitin visits Rei again. Again at eight o'clock. At midnight Nikitin is to meet with the head of the Estonian armed forces Laidoner. At 23:00 hours the ultimatum runs out. At the same time, Marshal Pétain is forming a new government in France.

In the shadow of this all, the world takes no notice of the fact that Russian vessels are trying to board the Estonian cruise liner the *Estonia* and tow it to Paldiski, that town already being in their hands.

Already at midday, Russian forces arrive in Riga. Andrei Vyshinski arrives too. An ultimatum has also been presented to Latvia.

Margarete is looking at an elephant. Oh, how clever the elephant is! The Indian god of writing, Ganea, has the head of an elephant. Some people think that this symbolizes the unity between the little human world of mortality and cosmic laws that don't usually fit into the heads of mere mortals. A big head has a big memory! But it can only thrive if it eats the root of the mandrake. Brecht needs no roots. How does an elephant kill a snake? It's weakened by the bite of the snake, loses consciousness, falls over and in so doing crushes the unsuspecting snake. In the olden days, people used to think that an elephant is like an elk—it sleeps standing up. A gray elephant is as gray as the cloudy Finnish sky. Sainte-Beuve is the one who first spoke of an "ivory tower" (in connection with Vigny). A writer who does not care for society lives in an ivory tower. But on occasions, elephants charge into china shops and cause havoc.

19th June

Well, now the game is in full swing and there is no going back. The Russian Ambassador Bochkaryov meets Maksim Unt twice. Zhdanov has already arrived at twelve in the morning. At about the same time Karl Säre meets Herman Arbon, who is a well-known underground Communist figure. At one o'clock Zhdanov is said to already be in President Päts' office. What could they be talking about? In Latvia, Vyshinski has already presented the new list of cabinet appointees. The Minister of the Interior is to be the writer Vilis Lācis, a national author, whose works about life at sea and as a fisherman have been particularly popular in Estonia as well.

Rei, by some miracle, arrives back from Moscow before Zhdanov arrives.

Did they perhaps take the same train?

On maybe the same day, the play There Shall Be No Night *by Robert Sherwood is being staged in Britain with Lynn Montana and Alfred Lynch. The characters are an American woman and her husband, and their son. The father is usually a pacifist, but he wants to be no longer. But he gets killed in the Karelian Isthmus. The woman and the uncle, Walden, burn down their house and prepare to join the fight.*

Sweden allows German trains to pass through her territory so they can get to Norway, and the Polish exile government decides to move from Paris to London.

20th June

M. Unt meets twice that day with Ambassador Bochkaryov. Twice! Aren't things obvious enough to everyone, or do people have to put on a brave face during a disastrous situation?

The Latvian government has already resigned.

Arbon, Säre, Lauristin, Ruus and M. Unt meet once again.

Some people have said that Unt received the order to stage an uprising. He no doubt didn't want to announce this, the whole thing had been decided in any case, and an "uprising" would have looked suspicious. At the same time the Minister of the Interior is receiving a lecture at the Russian Embassy that demonstrations must not be prevented from taking place. It is said that Vares-Barbarus was at this same time holding talks with Hans Kruus and Zhdanov. In case readers don't know already, it ought to be mentioned here that Vares was a poet of anarchist tendencies, who had been brought in especially from a small town in order to act as prime minister. The successful gynecologist fell for the bait. (Later, in times we are not dealing with here, he killed himself, or was killed. No one will ever know what really happened. A logical end for an anarchist and futurist.)

Brecht has three women. Hella likes Margarete, who is sick and serious. She is happy to tolerate her. Weigel just isn't like a woman at all, she is like a wife or comrade-in-arms. Hella, Helene and Grete do not like Ruth, who appears to be emancipated. She is a very erotic person and doesn't hide the fact. She also shares a view of the world with Brecht. Brecht has written: "Me-Ti said that the relationship between two people is good when they have a third thing in common, something that interests them both. While Me-Ti expects good to come from the two hands involved when a man and a woman share work, for instance touching as they carry a bucket, Mien-Leh (Lenin) expects that young people's hands will meet when they are shouldering the wheel of history."

In 1944, Ruth gave birth to a son called Michel, who died at the hospital. Jumping ahead, we should mention that because of this misfortune, Brecht promised to adopt a child immediately after the war had ended.

Grete nevertheless tries to look after the ecstatic and chaotic Ruth and even translated Ruth's novel into German. Helene was already worried by Ruth's natural ability for social play acting and tried to push her in the direction of the alienation effect. Ruth had once played Marta in Wuolijoki's play *The Women of Niskavuori*.

In 1958, Ruth sums up Brecht:

His everyday language: *A) Words of praise: normal, friendly, necessary, helpful, gifted, amusing, genuine. B) Words of censure: corrupt, venal, blackmailer, un-dialectic, un-Marxist. C) In the theater: show, try out, contradictions, speaking drily, fable, why?, again and again—why?* Favorite animal: *His dog Rolf.* Favorite color: *Gray.* Favorite materials: *leather, wood.* Requirements: *A) Food: new potatoes in spring, asparagus with vinegar and oil, carp, beef soup, Spätzle, dumplings, horseradish, every sort of cheese, raspberries and raspberries and raspberries. B) Drink: lemon juice in the morning, at midday and in the evening, beer during the evening break and finally, when alone, whisky—but only in the fogs of London, when drinking tea with friends, a dram against the cold—would screw up his face and only when necessary, champagne made him sleepy.* What he liked most of all: *Old brass objects, old clocks, beautiful pipes, peasant crockery, old knives, ancient Chinese rugs.* What he needed: *A lot of tables, a typewriter, a reading lamp, white, pretty typing paper, scissors for cutting out pictures, glue for pasting them in.* Other necessities: *Pupils, gifted actresses, composers, conversations, experts, detective novels, peace and quiet.*

21st June

At nine o'clock in the morning the factory sirens begin to wail. Someone obviously has had to switch them on, otherwise they won't sound. Things proceed along their normal course. At ten o'clock in the morning there is a demonstration on Vabuduse plats (Freedom Square). Many of the people taking part look unfamiliar to most locals. Some historians have claimed that many foreign workers had been brought in from the military bases. Maybe this was true, or maybe it was Estonians who were sufficiently disgruntled to form a group of a few hundred people. The same group later moves in the direction of the Presidential Palace at Kadriorg in order to demonstrate there. President Päts appears on the balcony, but he doesn't get a chance to speak, as the more active members of the crowd begin immediately to chant slogans. At 16:00 hours, political prisoners are released from prison with a good deal of pathos. There are no more than ten of them, because Päts had had an amnesty for the rest back in 1938. At six o'clock the crowd is back on Toompea hill. Twenty minutes later, red flags are already flying from the balcony of the parliament building. The name of the daily newspaper "Uus Eesti" (New Estonia) is immediately changed to "Rahva Hääl" (The

Voice of the People). In the evening, after Ruus, Vares and the others have just left the Russian Embassy, the new government is proclaimed. At 22:20 the anarchist and gynecologist Vares-Barbarus has sworn the oath before this very same President Päts. Let us not forget that Päts is sixty-six years old and on his desk there is a bust of Stalin with a dedication that says roughly as follows: *Dorogomu Konstantinu—Josif Vissarionovich* (Russian for: To my dear Konstantin—Joseph Vissarionovich). But what this dedication looked like exactly is something that no one will ever know. At 18:45 the Red Flag is hoisted from the Pikk Hermann tower next to the parliament building. Someone must have done this, presumably some Estonian or other. That evening it is the Estonian Chief-of-Staff, General Laidoner, who broadcasts on the wireless and appeals for calm amongst the Estonian population.

Viktor Suvorov is someone you cannot always believe under all circumstances, but he knows a great deal, and says that on that same day the Russians decided to create yet another army, the 17th.

In the "Bi-Ba-Bo" movie theater, a première is taking place of the film *Dramatic School* with Luise Rainer, Alan Marshal and Paulette Goddard.

Chaplin met Paulette Goddard. By that time, Chaplin was already in America. Paulette was, according to Chaplin's memoirs, roguish and amusing. What they had in common was loneliness. Paulette played a role in The Great Dictator *where Chaplin was Hitler in another guise. The film was released in 1940. When the world war was still raging in 1941, Paulette played in the films* North West Mounted Police *and* Nothing But the Truth.

Her fourth husband was Erich Maria Remarque. An author who has greatly influenced my development as a writer. In the 1960s you could get hold of works (mostly in Russian language versions—other channels were closed to us) by him and by Hemingway. Both wrote watered-down versions of existentialism, but they were better than nothing. Paulette's real name was Pauline Marion Goddard Levy and she was born in 1911. (Whether she is still alive is something I haven't been able to find out, despite all my efforts.) Remarque himself was born in 1898, the same year as my father, and died in Hollywood in 1970, leaving Paulette alone. They had married in 1958, when she was 48 and he 60.

When describing the tragic days in the history of our nation, I was obligated to write so much about Paulette by the fact that Remarque wrote with great feeling about people who had ended up under the wheels of war. And I was more indirectly affected by the fact that by the day I have been describing, Paulette's birthday had passed eighteen days previously. She was a girl from the beginning of June.

In Brecht's opinion, Paulette's *ilmaisukeinot*, i.e., her powers of expression, were not Aristotelian. Paulette tried to empathize, not depict. Paulette doesn't play her characters so it would be possible for you to expect them to behave differently than they actually do.

22nd June

Yesterday, France capitulated.

Brecht is looking at photos, where Hitler is dancing. Hitler is happy that he has conquered France. It must also be added that maybe the French are in some way satisfied with this conquest—otherwise such a large country could not be conquered so easily.

With regard to Hitler's dancing, many have thought that this series of photos was an anti-Hitler forgery. Hitler is stamping around with such fervor so this moment has been cut loose in order to compromise him.

He needed to be compromised, but did it have to be done so rationally?

And what would be left over of the world of insanity if people acted rationally?

Insanity can only be countered by sense—if at all. Brecht—he calculates in coldly rational terms that Hitler would have no mercy on him. Why not? You'd have to ask dead people about that. He no doubt had judgments of his own. And isn't even a maniac human? He does at least look like a human being.

Hitler is proud, because he has conquered a neighboring country, his old enemy. This has been the case since the German Empire capitulated in the woods at Compiègne back in 1918. A former restaurant car was brought together with another carriage in a forest clearing. Shirer remembers that it was a bright summer's day.

Brecht thinks that if the fivefold Maginot Line collapses, there will be no escape. He too is someone who no longer has an escape route. Germany regards him as a Communist. But Russia thinks of him as a revisionist and, above all, as a Formalist, since before his death, the old lord of the manor and aristocrat Stanislavski managed to enjoy exceptional popularity among the political leaders of the Soviet Union.

In one country, getting into the spirit of things becomes an official doctrine, which may not be betrayed on any account. Otherwise you end up in Siberia. In the other country not getting into the spirit of things becomes an even greater sin.

For making public his views on theater Brecht would no doubt be shot. In totalitarian régimes frankness pays. That is what I have begun to think these in recent times. Kill frankly, send frankly to Siberia or Auschwitz.

Verfremdung better suits democracies. Pity that Brecht understands this so late in life.

Our own home-grown author, Aadu Hint, holds a speech on Raekoja plats, the square right in the center of the Estonian capital, Tallinn. From what the papers say you can conjecture that he supports the new régime. The assistant to the Minister of the Interior, August Tuulse (45) and his wife (37) take poison. For a brief while, the old blue-black-white flag of Estonia flutters from Pikk Hermann tower. But the new government has been sworn in. The declaration pronounced by the new government has been written by Zhdanov. It promises to preserve Estonian sovereignty and defend the country.

General Laidoner is removed from his post.

On that same day, Mahatma Gandhi writes an article that I have only seen in the Russian language version. (I do not know Hindi.) The article is entitled "How to Struggle Against Hitlerism." The following is written there:

"Hitlerism will never be defeated by counter-Hitlerism. It can only breed superior Hitlerism raised to the nth degree. What is going on before our eyes is the demonstration of the futility of violence, which is also Hitlerism.

What will Hitler do with his victory? Can he digest so much power? Personally he will go as empty-handed as his not very remote predecessor Alexander. For the Germans he will have left the pleasure of owning a mighty empire but the burden of sustaining its crushing weight. For they will not be able to hold all the conquered nations in perpetual subjection. And I doubt if the Germans of future generations will entertain unadulterated pride in the deeds for which Hitlerism will be deemed responsible. They will honor Herr Hitler as a genius, as a brave man, a matchless organizer and much more. But I should hope that the Germans of the future will have learnt the art of discrimination even about their heroes. Anyway I think it will be allowed that all the blood that has been spilled by Hitler has added not a millionth part of an inch to the world's moral stature.

As against this, imagine the state of Europe today if the Czechs, the Poles, the Norwegians, the French and the English had all said to Hitler: "You need not make your scientific preparation for destruction. We will meet your violence with non-violence. You will therefore be able to destroy our non-violent army without tanks, battleships and airships." It may be retorted that the only difference would be that Hitler would have got without fighting what he has gained after a bloody fight. Exactly. The history of Europe would then have been written differently. Possession might (but only might) have been taken under non-violent resistance, as it has been taken now after perpetration of untold barbarities. Under non-violence, only those would have been killed who had trained themselves to be killed, if need be, but without killing anyone and without bearing malice towards anybody. I dare say that in that case Europe would have added several inches to its moral stature. And in the end I expect it is moral worth that will count. All else is dross."

The erudite psychiatrist Viktor Hion gave a speech to the masses (or whatever they were), which is said to have gone like this: "Whose flags are they?—The workers' flags!—Who will start to rule beneath them?—The workers!—Will they be able to rule?—They will!"

23rd June

Hitler is said to be inspecting sites in Paris. He has with him the artist and sculptor Arno Breker in uniform, the well-known architect Albert Speer, and someone who is less well-known to me, Hermann Gießler. They ride from one site to the next in an open Mercedes. In Montmartre, on seeing Hitler, one newspaper vendor shouts: "Look, there goes the Devil!" Hitler's dream was once to be in Paris. Hitler regarded himself as an artist and Paris is the capital of art. The three of them criss-cross the city for three hours. That night, Hitler tells Speer that Berlin ought to be made more beautiful than Paris. When Berlin is beautiful, there will no longer be any point in razing Paris to the ground.

24th June

Brecht is given an art magazine by the critic Hagar Olsson, in which he sees a reproduction of Picasso's *Guernica*. This makes an impression on him. He takes the decision to do something similar himself, as Picasso's work expresses his

116

epoch in artistic form. In this work he of course sees his beloved alienation (*Verfremdung*).

M. Unt is in Pärnu. The beach hotel there has suddenly become a holiday home for workers. The President's residence in Oru has already become a children's home.

But does life exist, does nature work in some way, what is a cold summer, a warm one? It is fairly hot. The temperature in the shade is 29 degrees, in the sun it is of course more—43 degrees.

Arnold Veimer (who later on became one of the Chairmen of the Soviet of Ministers) tells the people of the Tallinn slum on the Kopli peninsula, at a workers' meeting, that Soviet rule will never be established in Estonia.

25th June

Zhdanov travels back to Moscow, his work is complete.

The famous mythologist and later emigrant Ivar Paulson publishes a poem, where the following lines welcoming the new régime can be found:

"Over a pile of suffering, a righteous finger found us at the door standing."

Sympathy for the new régime is also expressed by the writers August Gailit, August Jakobson, Mait Metsanurk, August Mälk, Aleksander Antson, Juhan Sütiste, Evald Tammlaan and Henrik Visnapuu.

The Socialist aesthete Nigol Andresen says that Estonia will not become some kind of dictatorship of the proletariat and that the Soviet Union does not intend interfering in the internal affairs of the country.

Brecht is pleased that the weather has become a little warmer. But still—that eternal winter! "Do not fight injustice all too hard / it'll freeze anyway, because it is cold, / Just think about the darkness and great frost / here in this our vale of tears" (From the finale of *The Threepenny Opera*). The Meat King in *Saint Joan of the Stockyards* says: ". . . every hour / go to the window, see whether snow is falling and if / snow is falling then / it is falling on him." Joan feels the cold and is dying in the cold, of pneumonia. In *Song of the Playwright* there is a blizzard, with a hat on its head. In the play *Drums in the Night* Murk's feet grow cold. In Sechuan there is a lot of cold. Švejk and Hitler meet towards the end of the play in a snowstorm. Galy Gay is ready to step across the eternally frozen frontier of Tibet. Some people have thought that Brecht did not want to be born and wanted to remain in the Oedipal phase. This is termed productive regression.

But now it's warm! Brecht has been to the Finnish sauna and has had sex there on a number of occasions.

But now it is warm! Brecht rolls in the hay. His naked leg brushes against something rough. A toad? No simply a thistle, the type of flower that is common during this short summer.

"The political naivety that was prevalent in some quarters concerning the events of the time is a significant factor. This is also the case with regard to a number of members of J. Vares's government. Nigol Andresen has confirmed on many occasions: 'Who the hell knew that things would turn out the way they did!'

From what has been said it is logical to think that among members of J. Vares's cabinet, and people connected with it, the hope was entertained that Estonia would become a so-called people's democracy, with close ties to the Soviet Union, agreed on by way of treaties, but would retain a certain measure of sovereignty in its internal affairs. The Mongolian model was often referred to.

Mongolia was a satellite republic of the Soviet Union. Soviet-Mongolian relations began in 1921 when an agreement was signed on the development of friendly relations plus the mutual assistance treaty of 1934 and the protocol on the same subject of 12th March 1936. Until the year 1940, there was no talk in Mongolia of the development of Socialism, only of a revolution against imperialism and feudalism.

The fact that in the summer of 1939, the Soviet military attaché let drop the utterance that the relations between the Soviet Union and Mongolia would be a model for ones between the Soviet Union and the Baltic states, may have been a coincidence. But the fact that the Mongolian road was, in 1940, being discussed not only in Tallinn, but in Kaunas and possibly in Riga, is harder to regard as a coincidence. Especially as in the fall of 1939, when J. Stalin and V. Molotov were negotiating with the Baltic states, their status was compared with that of Mongolia. What was actually said to the Estonian delegates when the treaty was signed will never be known. The U.S. Ambassador for Estonia and Latvia, J. C. Wiley, telegraphed Washington on 6th October, citing the words of a high-up official in the Estonian Foreign Ministry: 'In order to try allay Estonian fears, Molotov talked about Mongolia in Moscow, where there were Soviet forces, but the "sovereignty" of the country was not threatened. My informant thought that it was this that was particularly alarming.'

The Latvian Foreign Minister, V. Munters, made notes of the meeting on 2nd October with J. Stalin and V. Molotov, and wrote down, with regard to the Soviet leaders' comments on a mutual assistance treaty: 'We give you our word, look at Mongolia. After the agreement is signed everyone will know that there are now two masters here—the Latvians and the Russians.'

(. . .)

When J. Vares swore his oath of office as prime minister on 21st June, the Head of the Chancery, E. Tambek, says in his memoirs that Vares added: 'I, for my part, did everything in my power to save the Estonian people and their country!' According to Tambek, Vares was not pretending. It is said that he even had tears in his eyes.

During a chance meeting towards the end of June, J. Vares's old friend H. Tulnola asked: 'Did you actually think up yourself what you announced at some meeting, i.e. that now the Estonian nation has become truly sovereign?!' The answer came: 'Shut your mouth and stop whining! The gist of my speeches was written by the Russians and even the speeches themselves were censored by them. I regret the fact that I was brought in to preach sermons against our own people, when there is no hope of saving them. But I don't mean the Estonian nation any harm.'

It is known how painful it was for J. Vares that, despite his high office, he was unable to do anything even for friends of his that were arrested. A few weeks after the meeting where Estonia was annexed by the Soviet Union, J. Vares's wife said to a good friend: 'I was the only one to see the tears that Barbarus shed onto his pillow at night. But there's no way out.'"

(Heino Arumäe, in the cultural magazine *Looming* 10/1991)

Someone once said somewhere that during one of Barbarus's speeches in 1941, somebody released a crow (*vares* is the Estonian for *crow*) with clipped wings in the hall, one wearing red trousers. Vares-Barbarus was a futurist poet.

> My contempt crushes to death
> a hundred thousand soldiers, a hundred thousand guns,
> a hundred thousand pikes!
> Crushes to splinters, will push
> fifty kings, fifty realms
> to destruction. My anger is greater than
> shells spewed forth by high caliber howitzers,
> thunderous lightning, the revolutionary mass, that
> has raised on high the placards of revolt
> in the hail of bullets . . . Just wait! My curses
> will stand erect and roar like lions (. . .)

(Fragment of a poem written in 1918 by Johannes Vares-Barbarus)

In the early 1990s, the former assistant head of the Estonian Soviet Socialist Republican branch of the KGB, Vladimir Pool, describes what happened six years later, after the war, on 29th November 1946:

"... *pushed the man lying on the floor slightly aside (. . .) as I was the first to enter the bathroom.*

. . . Vares was lying on his left side. His left arm was near his head, his right arm was stretched out. There, next to him on the floor, lay a 7.65 caliber Walther pistol. The pistol raised the body slightly. Underneath was a pool of blood.

The commission stated that the cause of Vares's death was a shot that had entered the right ventricle and the pulmonary artery, causing a blockage to the heart and hemorrhaging of the left pleura. The shot was more or less point blank. The bullet entered the left-hand side of the rib cage between the third and fourth rib and lodged in tissue between the fifth and sixth vertebrae of the spine. Death was instantaneous.

The Estonian nation wanted to know what really happened to Vares. The fact that he did not die of natural causes was already public knowledge that same day. The signatures of the doctors, assistants and guards binding them in no uncertain terms to a vow of silence did not prevent leaks. All kinds of rumors spread through the city. The fact that the authorities remained silent added fuel to the flames: Vares had been murdered, had been shot dead.

It is said that a document was found in Vares's safe that demonstrated his negative attitude to Stalinist politics and his depressed state of mind. I can say nothing about this. All I know is that the safe was opened by the Chief Public Prosecutor, Paas, the Assistant Chairman of the Presidium of the Estonian Supreme Soviet, Andresen, and the Minister of Security, Kumm. The three of them collected the documents there and signed a paper that no material relating to Vares's suicide had been found in the safe. In Vares's briefcase there was material evidence relating to the deed: an empty pistol holster, a Reinhold 615 fountain pen, and a diary, out of which pages had been ripped. On one loose page Vares had written a suicide note in pencil. I have the Russian translation before me. I shall try to translate it back into Estonian. (. . .)

'"*The avalanche of sickness in which I am submerged has strained, exhausted my organism to such an extent that I can no longer (given my age) recover and become fit for work again.*

'*Now that Soviet efforts require vigorous workers, I feel, because of my heart problems, my high blood pressure and my weak nerves that I am not up to the task.*

'*This feels burdensome and depressing, and I have reached the conclusion that there is no other way out.*

'At the present moment the illness has taken on unpredictable proportions.

'I fear the worst—utter confusion, mental collapse.

'May everyone who understands what I have done forgive me.'

(Initials.)

Vares wrote a postscript in red pencil:

'Forgive me, dear Siuts. You heroic comforter. I know that my act will shatter your life too. I can't go on any longer.'"

(Initials.)

Johannes Vares was buried, as has been said, on 3rd December 1946. But his widow Emilia did not survive him by long. Exactly three months later she too took her own life. On 3rd March 1947 the following note, signed by Boris Kumm, was sent to the Ministry of Security of the Estonian Soviet Socialist Republic Abukamov:

"Today at around 10:30 the body of Emilia Ivanovna Vares was found, the widow of the former Chairman of the Supreme Soviet of the Estonian S.S.R. E. Vares had left the following note: 'Dear Relatives and Friends! I cannot go on living alone, without my dear husband, so I have taken this step. All my belongings, clothes and books I give to my brother and sister. Please bury me next to my late husband.

E. Vares.'"

26th June

It now emerges that the drawing-room poet Valmar Adams, during period of independence between the wars (what are termed "Estonian times"), when he was in mid-life of life (the title of one of his poetry collections refers to Dante), underwent some sort of interrogation by the secret police, and that he was said to have been an underground operative. Author Albert Kivikas thinks that in the new Communist ideas, he saw something of the ideas and ideals of his old literary movement *Tarapita*. The mythologist Ivar Paulson was quick to write as an obituary: "to the unknown worker hero, fallen in the struggle."

Sugar, of which you can have three more kilos than was to be expected, can be collected up to 1st August . . . The Isamaaliit (League of the Nation) political party is being shut down, and for some reason also Fisheries House, as if it ever did anyone any harm.

The Finnish Soviet Society sends its greetings to the new Estonian government.

M. Unt goes again to visit President Päts. They clearly have something to talk about.

Today the Soviet Union has also occupied Bessarabia and Northern Bukovina.

What does all this mean? Has there been a coup d'état and do the people agree with it? The people are silent, *bezmolvstuyet,* as they say in Russian. Pushkin ends his "Boris Godunov" with the following well-known remark: the people are silent, a whole square full of people is silent. They remain silent until the curtain falls. Then comes the applause, in the theater of course, sure to come and justified, in a safe space.

From there you can go home, you can even order a taxi.

Wasn't it at the end of the 1960s, in Warsaw, that a woman sued a theater for soiling her clothing? Wasn't this during some performance of Suzuki in Warsaw? The audience shouldn't be harmed physically in any way. It didn't deserve it. Environmental theater is dangerous. In *La Fura dels Bau* huge wheels are rolled around during in performance, and you can hardly get away from them. Run for your life. This often happens on the street. There too you sometimes have to run for your life so that you'll get home in one piece.

But why is this called theater, why not call it real life, or even crime?

And if the woman sued Suzuki for damages, it shows that the audience does not necessarily have to remain silent.

But now I suddenly feel that I am being unfair to Suzuki—wasn't it in fact the Terayama troupe? It happened to someone, and someone in the audience protested. On the other hand, our nation was so paralyzed on that occasion, in such a state of shock, that it hardly uttered a word of protest.

27th June

M. Unt shuts down the Kaitseliit (Home Guard Association), the Educational Association, the Choirs Society, the Scouts, the YMCA, the Estonian Sports Clubs' Association.

Lion Feuchtwanger has arrived at the end of his spectral journey—the internment camp in Nîmes, where he is told that is not a prisoner, and he tells himself that he is not a German.

The Soviet Union now turns its attention again to Finland. Someone suggests that the Åland archipelago be demilitarized, otherwise that country will be incorporated into the Soviet Union.

28th June

Brecht receives a message from Feuchtwanger's secretary stating that he is in a camp where there are men from the age of sixteen to fifty-six. Feuchtwanger will be fifty-six, that July. But the papers also mention that France will hand over any German, should Germany require it.

Brecht looks outside. A Finn passes, bag in hand. It's a woman. She's clearly going to the shops. It's evening. The sky is clear. The shadows of the trees are lengthening before your eyes. Helene and Grete have gone for a walk in the park. I wonder whether they're talking about me, thinks Brecht. Are they exchanging impressions? Or are they indulging in some women's chatter, and don't even mention me? Are they talking about things that don't concern men? Or maybe they are walking in silence. Digging their way through the grass with the toes of their shoes, picking a leaf within reach, pursing their lips, squinting with their eyes.

There's a rumbling sound coming from somewhere. Thunder? Brecht thinks that if things get serious, the Finns will hand him over, most likely to the Germans, because who else would want him?

Brecht is discontented with himself. For some reason, he suddenly wants to be taller. Nordic people are taller. When they wade through deep snowdrifts, their heads still protrude. It's better for people in the theater to be taller. They can be seen from further away when on stage. In the ancient world, they used cothurns and masks. This made the actors taller and simpler at the same time. That too is dialectical.

Sir Winston Churchill understands the motives and actions of the Russians: "They have had to occupy the Baltic states and a large part Poland by stealth and force of arms, before they are themselves attacked. Maybe their policy is hard-hearted, but at the time it was realistic." (From: "The Gathering Storm.")

On 26th June 1942, after a long period of torment in Russian labor camps, Carola Neher dies of typhus. She was a famous German actress and lover of Brecht's, whom she met in 1922. She once played Polly in The Threepenny Opera, *the leading role in* Happy End, *the title role in* Saint Joan of the Stockyards. *When the Nazis came to power she fled with her Communist husband, and Brecht saw her for the last time in Moscow in 1935. Carola was arrested in July 1936. Testifying against her were the future leading SDV leaders Walter Ulbricht and Wilhelm Pieck. In 1938, a German emigrant in Paris wrote an open letter to Brecht, but*

Brecht remained silent. He accused Brecht of betrayal: "Clearly fascism can't find better allies than its opponents. If you didn't exist, Goebbels would have invented you." Brecht didn't reply. The issue cost the lives of the emigrant (Walter Held) and his family (wife and child). When they (during this same year, 1940—and by the same route) tried to cross the Soviet Union, they were arrested on the Trans-Siberian Express and ultimately shot. Brecht never found out what happened to Carola. One letter to Feuchtwanger, where he makes timid attempts to find out something, was never sent. In February 1940, the great opponent of introducing method acting into theater was shot. (It isn't known whether Brecht and Meyerhold ever met. Both had been in Moscow in 1935 to watch the great Chinese actor Mei Lan-Fang, and their mutual friend Tretyakov [who was also shot] was there, so it's possible that they met.)

Brecht writes a poem to the memory of Tretyakov, and also writes a poem about what he imagines Carola's captivity to be like, where he posits: "I cannot do anything for you . . ." Brecht asks the world: "I won't start saying: these were hard times / will instead ask: why did the poets keep silent?"

M. Unt liquidates the Kaitseliit and the Minister of Economics Nichtig testifies his name to Narma. This is witnessed by the author Rudolf Sirge and the translator Jüri Šumakov. By the evening, M. Unt has managed to close down all the ethnic societies (e.g., the Russian, Ukrainian and Polish ones).

Red Army soldiers are given unlimited credit by the Estonian Bank—one Estonian *kroon* is worth seventy-five copecks. The normal rate of exchange is, by the way: one Estonian *kroon* equals ten roubles.

29th June

Brecht sees that one famous country has collapsed and that another (Finland, where he is right now) is tottering. He writes a new play called *The Good Person of Sechuan*. Not a murmur about his American visa. He only gets coffee from Ruth, sugar is not always available in the stores, and it takes some effort to find cigars.

The Finnish parliament approves of the retention of censorship, while in Estonia, M. Unt approves the law whereby all private persons must hand in their weapons.

The new Estonian Minister of Agriculture, Jõeäär, states that farmers will not have their land confiscated.

30th June

Brecht understands how difficult it is to be without a theater where he can stage scenes and write plays. He is now in difficulties with the sixth scene of the *Sechuan*. It's easy to imagine anything you like when sitting at your desk, but not until it is staged do you really know whether something will work or not.

M. Unt now allows the purchase of beer and wine, but spirits remain prohibited. Estonian diplomats abroad are given the order to return home. The majority ignore the order, and a good thing too.

In Lithuania, the Foreign Minister, Vincas Krėvė-Mickevičius, is in Moscow meeting with Molotov. The latter says something like this: you ought to be more realistic and understand that small nations will disappear in the future, in any case. Right now, your Lithuania—like Latvia and Estonia—are joining the revered family of the Soviet Union, in other words, the system which will, in future, rule the whole of Europe. And you will see for yourself how, within four months, all the Baltic states will be voting for the Soviet Union. That evening, Krėvė meets with Dekanozov, who is back home again. Dekanozov, for his part, says roughly the following to Krėvė: the Second World War will make all of Europe fall into our hands like a ripe fruit. And after the Third World War we will have conquered the whole world.

1st July

It strikes Brecht that the world is changing by the minute. Initially, there were still newspapers. The German-language newspapers from Austria, Czechoslovakia, Switzerland and the Saarland fell away one by one. Initially, radio still broadcast, but one fine day broadcasts from Vienna went dead, the next day, from Prague. The Copenhagen and Oslo ones only broadcast German propaganda. All that is left is London, but you never know how long that will last. Even the map of Europe keeps changing, no map is quite the same the next day as it was the day before.

Ruth Berlau writes bitterly in her memoirs that Brecht despised all women except Luxemburg, Krupskaya and his own Weigel. "He treated me like a turd and would call my smile your whore's smile (dein Hurenlächeln)."

2nd July

A lot of gnats appear from somewhere. Some are larger than others. The small ones whine nastily. They bite. The large ones are silent and do not bite. They're harmless, but unpleasant. They feel more threatening. But they aren't! Fingers crossed! But they're still in the room with you. Yes, like the anachronisms in my plays—like the fact there was a contemporary pilot plus archaic gods on stage at the same time in the Sechuan play. Brecht considers this dialectical. In the same way that a small and a large gnat together form some kind of synthesis (leaving aside the fact that it is hard to term them antitheses), when they're in the same room together. And on stage are the pilot and the god—they *are* thesis and antithesis. They synthesize in the play, in the space formed by the stage, where the performance is no longer a synthesis, but a new thesis, and its antithesis is the audience. Then, very murkily, a new synthesis is created. Is this always ideological and can it always be expressed in words? No it isn't!

The dialectics of a whore's smile is that it doesn't originate with the whore. And yet if it's not the smile of a whore, can you still call it a smile?

Wuolijoki seems to be worried about Estonia. Brecht can't understand this. He compares a small nation (e.g., Estonia, but Finland too) to a small businessman, that a large trust (fascism) wants to swallow up, but who is unable in any case to preserve its sovereignty and should hand over authority to the proletariat (the Soviet Union). There it will prosper. An acquaintance of his, the Finnish Socialist Erkki Vala, who praised the fact that Estonia joined the great family of Soviet nations, thinks the same in his book written under the pseudonym of A. R. Torni. The book is called *De baltiska Sovjetrepubliken*, Stockholm, 1945. This book only appeared five years after it was written, and in Sweden. (A pity I don't have a copy.)

Explanation of the above:
On 8th April 1941, Brecht writes in his diary the meaningful sentence, in which we recognize something of ourselves: Merkwürdig, wie die Tragödie des kleinen Geschäftmanns gegenüber den Trusts widerholt in der Tragödie der kleinen nationen, Völker, halb so gross wie die Einwohnerschaft Berlins, führen ein Politik, ausgehend von der Gleichberechtigung aller Völker! *(It is surprising how the tragedy of the small businessman in his struggle against the large trust repeats*

itself in the tragedy of small nations—nations whose populations are about half that of Berlin, who conduct politics with the point of departure that all nations are equal!)

Ruth is walking around in a dress, which could be described as *ilmava* (airy). When Brecht sees her out on the grass, it somehow reminds him of his first sexual urge (*ilmaus*). This was for Black Marie, a servant girl in Augsburg, his home town.

Brecht thinks that dialectics occur as follows: elements that are unclear stack up. That's the quantity. At a given moment there occurs a qualitative leap: clarity ensues. A feeling becomes another, i.e., its opposite, and an individual occurrence now proves to be typical, and vice-versa. The change of quantity into quality is, by its very nature, a leap (*saltus*).

Still on the subject of dialectics, Brecht says that the best school for dialectics is emigration and that the sharpest dialecticians are refugees. "They are refugees on account of change, and the cannot learn to feel anything but change."

In August 1991 I happened to be in Finland. My wife and I set off on the morning of the 19th. We didn't listen to the radio that morning, and did not know what had happened. We arrived at the port in a taxi. The harbor was closed. No ships were sailing. There were a lot of people in the departure hall. No one knew what was happening. The situation reminded you of the film Casablanca *or why not, of Remarque's novel* The Night in Lisbon. *Or the British serial* Bangkok Hilton, *or Joffé's* The Killing Fields. *I remember thinking that I didn't want to go into exile. I was on a working trip, but it seemed to have coincided with a putsch. A short while later, a man shouted: let's go, and let's be quick about it! One small vessel left! The Russian border guard asked us, as he returned our passports: What's the hurry? There were warships in the sea roads, with a wake around them although they were stationary. Our little vessel sailed between them all. No one fired a shot (maybe we didn't have diplomatic posts on board). Three dreamlike days passed in Finland, which were time enough for everything that happened: Yeltsin climbed up on the tank; there were radio reports round the clock from the radio journalist Harri Ti-ido. Lii (my wife) thought that I shouldn't return to Estonia, but the idea was raised that she could travel round the Gulf of Leningrad via Vyborg and bring over our car and the cats. Maybe she'd be let through. One night—it was the 20th—a good friend of mine phoned me up, the actress Maija-Liisa Marton (she was the head of the Finnish national drama school). She said she knew that I was over in Finland and wondered whether I was having problems. At that point I burst into tears. I was already experiencing what it was like to be a hypothetical emigrant. And suddenly a Finnish friend is helping me out!*

PART V

MIDSUMMER

M. UNT'S JOTTINGS

JULY–AUGUST
1940

Midsummer, ah, midsummer, now you are here! I'd like to talk and talk, about anything at all—maturity, preparedness, blue skies, fields of crops, heads of corn, the white country road disappearing beyond the woods, the dust raised by the bare feet of a young girl in the last ray of sunshine before sunset.

But is it worth speaking about all this? I don't know! Who does? Maybe we will one day, whatever that knowledge turns out to be.

Just for a change, I'll tell something about myself.

When I was asked to write the story of my life, this is what I wrote:

"I was born in Pärnu, but the fact that I was good at all subjects at school, except for scripture, meant that scripture didn't really become a stumbling block either. I attended Pärnu Grammar School. During the summer vacation, I also worked. When the Great War broke out and when Pärnu was bombed in 1915, the grammar school was evacuated to Murom in Russia. I too traveled to Murom that summer, to continue my studies. In the spring of 1916, I returned from Murom. My brother and I were taught by Latvian revolutionaries who, as a result of the events of 1905, were in the house of arrest in Pärnu (we spent days at a time in their rooms) so when the Revolution broke out it was welcomed. The grammar school got going again. During the German advance in 1917 and the never-ending bombing of the hinterland the grammar school and all other organizations and institutions were evacuated once again. I left Pärnu with my mother and father. As Father had a sister in the Caucasus, he decided to go there. We lived with Father's sister near to the town of Telavi, where my aunt's husband worked in the Czar's wine cellars. Now and again, major events occurred. The Civil War began. I lost contact with my parents and decided to travel home. But this did not prove easy. I fell ill. I was suffering from typhus, jaundice and other illnesses. My life was saved by good people. When I had recovered, I tried again to travel west, to nearer my home. Some people think that I was mobilized in 1918 and joined the Red Guard and that I changed sides and joined Denikin's White Guard. I don't remember so clearly myself, and who would manage to remember everything, anyway? Complex times, complex ways, the holes and vortices of history! But I do remember by some miracle getting on board ship in Sevastopol. The ship sailed—you wouldn't believe it—for Bulgaria! Well, I went on from there to Italy, didn't I? Then to Austria, and from there on to Germany, then to Latvia and home. I've destroyed all my service papers! A strange business, if ever there was one!

I got in touch with the Soviet consulate in 1932, or maybe 1933. From there I received underground literature from Comrade Klyavin, which I distributed. I have disseminated underground Communist literature. By way of Comrade Klyavin and others, I provided the Soviet Embassy with various pieces of information: for instance, about Päts's coup d'état, about military forces and other matters. I also sent information via Comrade Ismestiyev (the TASS correspondent in Estonia). On the evening of 18th June 1940, I received a telephonic and telegraphic order to come to Tallinn, which I promptly did. In Tallinn, I met with Comrade Säre. I knew him from before. I have also had dealings with Comrade Lauristin. I was invited by Comrades Ruus and Ismestiyev. In the evening of 18th June I met with Comrade Bochkaryov of the Soviet Embassy who asked me if I would agree to become the Minister of the Interior. I replied that if entrusted with such a post, I would accept. On 19th June I met with Comrade Zhdanov on two occasions and after that with Comrade Bochkaryov. And on 20th June, Comrade Zhdanov gave me the assignment of a meeting during the night, and a demonstration for 21st June. Having received this order, I set to work immediately and informed the Secretary of the Communist Party Säre. During the night, the plans were put into action, both in Tallinn and the provinces and on 21st June there was a mass rally and power was seized. On the night of 21st June, things I had organized were also put into operation. After that, I met with Comrade Zhdanov. From that time onwards, I have been occupied with the tasks the Party has allotted me."

My name is Unt! Like Hunt—which means "wolf" in Estonian—but with one letter missing! I sometimes tell people that I'm a wolf from the woods around Pärnu. I am the first Minister of the Interior of Soviet Estonia!

The beginning of July 1940. I was traveling over to Finland now and again. I met with Brecht there. He talked and talked! He was complaining that the wireless stayed silent, so he began thinking about anachronisms in plays, presumably his own. You can have gods together with modern industry. In his exotic plays he has tried to show how European customs have penetrated exotic parts of the world.

I'm not exactly in such a place myself, right now, but I have an extraordinary ability to harness doubles for my needs as well as telepathic information and have a certain ability to double or triple myself. So I can be over there (in Finland) and over here (in Estonia) at one and the same time.

Well, I was compelled, here in Estonia where I was born, to shut down all the ethnic clubs and to punish criminal prattlers, wasn't I? And in some way I did manage to punish such foolish prattlers. If someone was shooting his mouth off, say on the street corner, then a member of the people's militia would slap him across the cheek. If someone were doing so in a room, then water would be poured down from the apartment above, causing a flood below.

Brecht told me for some reason or other that he can't identify any stable train of thought in Mallarmé. Although unstable thoughts are supposed to be there in his work. And Mallarmé's fear of being banal often ended up in further banalities.

Well, on 4th July, I declared the EKS—the Estonian Literary Association—to be a legal organization, didn't I? I greeted them all on the occasion of this declaration. On the other hand—the Salvation Army had to be shut down. Parliament was also dissolved.

And then, a big event: the island of Naissaar was leased out to the Soviet Union.

Brecht says that he gets up at three in the morning. Mostly because of the flies. In Germany, there are not reckoned to be as many flies. Some of them are probably gnats. In the dark, you can't tell the difference between a gnat and a fly.

What else did I do? On 6th July I was compelled to liquidate all associations and societies that had survived up to now. I didn't manage to get rid of 100% of these. Some of them slipped my mind, but I'll close them down next time round, won't I? I'll manage somehow.

Brecht and all his women are now somewhere in the countryside, at Hella's manor house. In Marlebäck!

The smells of the Finnish summer irritate Brecht, but he holds back and doesn't get all confused.

As for me, I announced in the new Soviet Estonian daily "Rahva Hääl"—The People's Voice—that unemployment will disappear completely. If there are to be any shortages in society, it'll be a shortage of workers.

Then, on 10th July, at 15:00 hours, I announced that all weapons had to be handed in.

I went and held speeches in small country towns.

Some people tell me that the price of vodka has risen.

I was talking to Brecht about why he was so keen to go to America. Better to go to the Soviet Union. Or even come over to Estonia! That's a safe place to be. By the way, Wuolijoki wouldn't do so well either, if the Germans decided to invade Finland. Brecht told me she too has chosen America.

Klaus Mann: "Everyone wants to go to the United States. Some of my friends are already in Lisbon, out of danger. Others are dead. It started with suicides (for example Hasenclever and Benjamin)." As has been pointed out earlier, Klaus Mann killed himself in 1949. Walter Benjamin wrote (1934): "Being a visionary, Kafka saw into the future, as Brecht says, without being able to specify what would happen, (. . .) Kafka is said to have had but one problem: organization. (. . .) He predicted certain forms of it, for instance the KGB. (. . .) What became of the Cheka, we can see in the form of the Gestapo. (. . .) He thought that Tretyakov was no longer alive. (. . .) In Russia the dictatorship of the proletariat holds sway."

I was on top of a ridge, sweating profusely. There wasn't a cloud in the sky. Maybe one, but so small, it's not worth mentioning. The long grass swayed in the breeze. Somewhere, Hella's cattle were mooing. Far away, across the stretches of grass, I saw someone's white backside rising and falling. This was Brecht, having sex, no doubt. And with who else but Ruth. I went back, sat down under a fir tree and shut my eyes for a moment. The bees buzzed, I would have liked a beer. It's a big manor.

I am compelled to proclaim, or at least share in the proclamation, that enemies of the people will not be allowed to become candidates in the elections for the new Socialist Estonian parliament. Only decent people will be allowed to be candidates. Opposition candidates will be removed from the electoral roll, or if they're not removed, they will do so themselves.

One poet, whose name is Sütiste, says that theater ought to be activated! I ordered the owner of every building to make sure he flew at least two flags. And the length of the red flag has to be exactly the same as the blue-black-white one!

By the way, they've started arresting people.

General Laidoner has already been sent off somewhere far away.

As for Hitler, he said in the Reichstag that the spheres of interest of Germany and the Soviet Union have now been finally delineated.

I drew up, or helped draw up, a list of Estonian artists: we managed to find 142 people altogether.

There was a meeting in the "Du Nord" restaurant. The great performer of monologues, Yakhonov, declaimed Mayakovsky's "The Soviet Passport."

Brecht says that Feuchtwanger has run away to Marseilles.

Ulmanis (the Latvian President) has also gone off to somewhere far away.

Well, I've now shut down the Estonian-British Cultural Society, haven't I? That was one that still had to be shut down—from the time I had to shut all the societies down.

Other men have stopped working for the city and provincial authorities.

Under force of circumstance, we have managed to shut down as much as is humanly possible.

Molotov announced, for his part, to Paasikivi that Väinö Tanner is anti-Soviet and that you can't reason with him, not even when you try to be accommodating. You visit him and visit him again, but it feels as if nothing actually gets done. Why bother associating with him if the cunt is always acting so strangely?! Can anything be agreed upon, given the fact he's so strange? I don't want to bother. No, I just don't want to. At all.

The date of M. Unt's death is unknown. Both the Communists and the nationalists renounced him.

But let him carry on talking for now, while he's still alive.

On 26th July I was compelled to ban the use of the titles Proua (Mrs), Preili (Miss), and Härra (Mr): these three were replaced by one word—Kodanik (Citizen). This declaration has a whiff of the Great French Revolution about it. If only I could understand which.

M. Unt was dismissed from his post as Ministry of the Interior, according to Communist Party Protocol Number 8, dated 21st May 1941, and was then shot. Wicked tongues say that during 1940 or 1941 Unt held a speech on Moscow radio. His picture was in the newspaper. A Ukrainian woman, whom Unt was supposed to have married while he was serving in Denikin's army, and had a baby by him, recognized the photo of the man who jilted her. The woman rang Moscow and the cat was out of the bag.

But Unt doesn't yet know this right now, and so continues his story.

Brecht is busy analyzing politics, as usual. He disputes the claims of those (he didn't say who) that say that fascism will give Europe a measure of stability. He doesn't think it likely. He heard somewhere that a certain Simone de Beauvoir had at that very moment started reading Hegel's *The Phenomenology of the Spirit*. When I (or my double) asked him what the leading author of works on systems theory, Bertalanffy, was doing right now (I happened to have heard his name mentioned during my travels around the world), Brecht was at a loss for an answer. I too am not likely to ever read Bertalanffy's major works, which will reach their final form after my death, which need not be very far away.

Well, I held a speech at a meeting of fishermen in Pärnu, didn't I? I told them that I hoped things would get better.

Brecht thinks it relatively normal that Finns love their country. The landscapes themselves never provide any problems. There are fish in the rivers, berries and birch trees (*Beeren und Birken*) in the woods. They smell nice—roughly as they were intended to do. It is cold in winter, but hot in summer. In summer there are, of course, too many smells, and these occur on account of the heat and the luxuriance of organic material. Even the wind is no longer like a wind, as it wafts through so much grass and so many branches and bushes. It is a harmonious wind, as Brecht tries to explain to me. (*Kaum mehr wahrgenommen wird und dennoch da ist.*) That's what he said to me, but whether he thought it is another matter.

On 27th July I was compelled to shut down all private schools and the newspaper called *Päevaleht* (*Daily News*). Appropriate thing to do. Who ordered the paper to have such a transparent name?!

Oh, how they were rebelling meanwhile in Helsinki, how the left-wingers revolted! There was something they wanted and this demand was good for something.

Not me, but the head of internal security, the bug expert Harald Haberman banned *the whole of* the yellow press.

What a man! Has an interesting appearance, more that of a scientist and a thinker. Biological pragmatism has forced him to be realistic.

He will soon go bald, but that will be greatly to his advantage, especially with the women.

On 22nd July 1940, the Riigivolikogu—the lower house of the Estonian parliament—adopted a bill whereby Estonia would become part of the Soviet Union.

This bill was adopted on the first reading. When the thunderous applause had abated, I made the suggestion that there should not be a long period of time between the first and second readings of the bill but—why not?—announce the second session immediately.

So the first reading of the bill ended at 13:55, there was a smoking break, then the second reading was held at 14:11.

This Brecht is quite happy right now!

As for me, this time I was compelled to annul all former passports which allowed you to travel abroad. They are no longer valid. Do what you like with them.

Well, there you are. Meanwhile the gynecologist Barbarus or Vares, whichever one he really was, I don't care, what do I, a simple wolf, know about barbarians and Barbaruses, and perhaps I should rather not know—the less you know, the better it is for you—anyway, he went off with his delegation to Moscow. He wanted to declare something there, i.e., the wishes of the Estonian people. Barbarus was a writer by nature. He claimed that the Estonian Riigikogu declaration—

I have already mentioned that I was compelled to forbid opposition candidates, and so leave on the electoral roll only those who were politically acceptable and necessary—oh yes, I am also guilty of that too, but state has introduced a new system of government, where there really is no choice. One candidate is always elected from a choice of one, and he usually gets 98.5% of the votes.

This is hard to grasp at first.

But I've lived in Russia, I've been a revolutionary, then I betrayed the revolution, then I became a revolutionary again, so I'm never surprised when there is no choice.

With good luck, you have the choice between life and death, and it is not sure which is better.

—the poet Barbarus claimed the Estonian Riigikogu declaration to join the Soviet Union was "the greatest collective novel ever written in Estonia. And the end of this novel?—against my literary tastes, is a happy one, happier than any novel in which working people have been characters."

Oh, and Päts has also been taken to somewhere far away.

Just for fun, I've been reading Brecht's poems—someone brought them to me or I stumbled upon them myself. Oh I don't know, but one of them seemed to be saying that the food smelled too good and that the milk was in a large and beautiful jug.

Brecht also wrote poems about Finland. Like this one, which is about the Finnish countryside:

Waters full of fish! (Brecht actually said that to me.)
Beautiful forests!
Birken- und Beerenduft!
Vieltöniger Wind (presumably this means that the wind had a variety of tones. A load of rubbish, that they've invented when trying to put winds into words). (. . .) Or this second poem:

Oh schattige Speise! Ein dunkler Tanne / Geruch geht nöchtlich brausend in dir ein. / Und mischt sich mit dem süsser Milch / aus grosser Kanne. (. . .)
   Bier, Ziegenkäse, frisches Brot und Beere.
   Now, that's a poem. I like poetry.

It was decreed that all Estonian vessels were to sail to Murmansk or Vladivostok. It is understandable that they are to sail under the Soviet flag. What other flag would they sail under? Let's try and accept a few things as they are. Hoist the flag, and go where we have to—whether to Murmansk or Vladivostok.

The visas for Brecht and his family were delayed time and time again. Weigel often went to the American consulate. Once, when they had got off the tram and were walking to the harbor, they saw an Estonian ship, now, of course, a Socialist Estonian ship. There was a red flag fluttering from its mast. Mrs Kilpis had mixed feelings about this. But Weigel was glad, and said that in the midst of all this mess it was nice to see something reassuring and hopeful. Weigel gazed for a while at the ship flying the red flag, which had come from eighty kilometers away. After that, Weigel bought a smoked plaice.

Meanwhile, I have been obliged to implement orders given by the President. On 31st July I was compelled to dissolve the navy and also the Home Guard Foundation.

Then I had to dismiss all the elders of the various Estonian provinces. There were no doubt decent people among them, but in times like the present you can't pay too much attention to individuals.

I drafted some law or other which dealt with the details of nationalization.

Also ordered that in the armed forces the word "comrade" would replace "Mr."

I also dissolved the local council for the island of Naissaar. I had no problems with doing so, but some people thought this was over the top.

I've had a reception for artists. Half of them were Latvians and Russians. An international event.

But just imagine—today (2nd August) I am, at the same time, in Helsinki. Some 2,000 people who wanted to be friends with the Soviet Union were dispersed. They were pelted with stones and beaten with rubber truncheons.

I went to Germany and saw there how Goebbels encouraged Gustav Gründgens to make a film about Julius Caesar.

Lithuania has been accepted as part of the Soviet Union (3rd August).

There's still a little time to go before my death.

Yesterday, I was in Finland again for a short while. I don't really want to be there too often, but you have to be there now and again and send the better or worse part of you. On this occasion Brecht was waxing enthusiastic about realism. I've nothing against realism. I'm just a poor boy from out Pärnu way, and those people who come from the countryside arouse a kind of passion for realism as art.

Realism is a game played by us men from forest villages.

Unfortunately, and I no longer know whether for better or worse, I shut down a couple of the last societies which had not yet been closed. Also student societies and alumni associations were shut down. I don't miss these institutions very much—they would have had to be shut down anyway. But there will no doubt be nice young men and women, who won't know what to do with themselves in the future.

Šumakov was bellowing: when are we in Estonia going to get our own Gorky. I wasn't really able to give him an answer to that one. Go and get your own Gorky from wherever you want.

Pravda has been adopting a somewhat millennial tone of late. Today they were writing about how wonderful and nice it is that the foundations of the world are shaking, and the great are falling.

Anyhow, I was talking to old labor veterans in a holiday home in Pärnu. The conversation had been anticipated. I told them that come what may, their lives would improve from now on.

Well, now a really bad thing has happened. I was ordered to proclaim a law covering all those traitors living abroad. I was compelled to say that the law would have retroactive effect. If you don't come home in good time, (i.e., within twenty-four hours) you will be shot, immediately, wherever you happen to be.

On the 5th of August, at midnight, Moscow time was to be adopted. I don't know, but I suppose there must be some blessing to changing the time like this.

(By the way, I'm still alive.)

The theater director Kaarel Ird has written in a women's magazine that a U-turn has occurred in every sphere of life. Instead of prettifying we have the struggle, instead of the West we now have the East, and instead of the Prima Donna we have the Factory Girl.

Well, I was recently compelled to close down the Faculty of Religious Studies at the University of Tartu. They don't have religious studies in Russia and they're not allowing us to have any either. They should actually be allowed. But my opinion no longer counts.

In Russia, two years later, on 8th August 1942, Maria Osten is shot. She was a German Communist who had gone to fight in the Spanish Civil War with Koltsov (shot in 1940). She was arrested in August 1941. So Brecht still managed to see her when they traveled across Russia. The last contact he had with Maria Osten was the handwritten note he received when he was speeding on the Trans-Siberian Express from Moscow to Vladivostok in June 1941: "I'll write to you later about everything that I may have forgotten to write now. I put the black dress on Grete that she had been wearing the last few days she was here. The cremation is at three o'clock. All the best. Auf Wiedersehen. Maria." They did, of course, never meet again, as Osten was declared a spy for Germany and France.

Brecht told me that he has discovered a Finnish sauna and that he goes there often, and has sex with Berlau there. Brecht is, incidentally, extremely frightened of the cold, but when Ruth lashes him with birch twigs, he thaws out. He has written a poem called "Sauna und Beischlaf," in which he writes a detailed account of how he approaches Berlau from behind as she is bent over a bucket and gropes her playfully between her legs.

Jumping into cold water afterwards is of course something that Brecht doesn't like and he doesn't do so.

They are planning to do something about some Jean of Arc type, a contemporary girl who resists the German occupiers, and is then put in a lunatic asylum (or some such place). Steffin has, on the other hand, begun to examine stories by Hella Wuolijoki about some alcoholic uncle or other old man who is a good man when drunk, but a bad one when sober. In the first instance, he's a human being, in the second, a capitalist.

But now for something a bit more exciting.

When I was flying one day over Hella's manor, I heard a horrible shriek and swooped lower into the underbrush to get closer, and saw women engaged in a quarrel.

"I will live where I want to, and I'll sleep where I want to," Ruth was yelling. "What can Grete have against it? Their relationship is a purely platonic one now."

"This is my manor and my house," Hella bawled back. "And I will decide what goes on here! And Grete really has nothing whatsoever against you, but do try to consider Helene as well! She doesn't like the fact that you sleep next to their bed on the rug, in your clothes! Without a pillow! You snore and Brecht snores and Helene can't get any sleep, and in the next room, poor Grete can't get any sleep either and you know what poor health she's in!"

"But I'm not leaving," says Ruth obstinately, "we've lots of work to do. You don't know what I'm going to do?" Ruth says finally.

"No, I don't," shouts Hella.

"I'm going to take my suitcase and pitch a tent under the fir tree over there," Ruth brags, "and you can't stop me, especially being a socialist."

In Estonia, we've introduced house registers. You can no longer be here and there at the same time. The owner of the house will have to register anyone who wants to stay in his house for over a period of twenty-four hours.

Ruth doesn't have to register with anyone out there in her tent and Brecht has gone over there too, and the sound of the typewriter can be heard.

When Brecht came out, he sniffed the resin on the forest breeze, leaned against a birch growing near the tent and said that in the world and his life, there is, at present, *Inzwischenzeit* (an interim period of time).

I was compelled to ban the sending of notices about Estonia to the foreign press.

What Unt doesn't know is that on that very day—this is 20th August—Mercader pays a visit to Trotsky, as if to show him an article. A dagger's been sewn into the lining of his coat. He also has a revolver in his pocket, plus an ice pick. He uses the last of these. Trotsky doesn't die immediately, as Mercader had imagined. He had thought it would be a routine business. Trotsky began to wail. But he did die the next day, so Mercader had completed his task after a fashion. In the "Vanemuine" theater a meeting of the staff is held, where it is decided that neither friendship nor hatred must be displayed during working hours. Friends are for your spare time, as are comrades. It is suggested that feigning and fawning must disappear. The words "Long Live Stalin!" are added. Air raids on Great Britain commence. The concept of being a Stakhanovite is propagated. (This means: you do more work than your strength allows.)

Brecht is prattling on endlessly about his plays. He is in the tent one morning with Berlau; they are having sex. Brecht really is one for the women. In between he has managed to write a few poems too. One goes like this: "My little daughter / comes home one evening hurt, / no other child wants to play with her. She is a German and a member of the nation of robbers." And another one: "This is the year much will be said about. It is the year that will be kept silent about." Or one about his wife: "Actress and refugee, servant girl and woman."

Well, I'm moving between two countries. Sometimes I swim, sometimes I fly. Here in Estonia, I'm submitting for publication the brochure by Yefimov called "Sovetskaya Estoniya."

Hella is standing on the balcony of the manor house and cursing the workers as they have let the bull out among the young shoots. This must not happen again! Besides: this bull is *ilmeinen paholainen*! (Manifestly the Devil.)

Brecht gets up early and goes for a walk in the woods. I follow him. Yesterday, I heard him muttering to himself: "The concept of greatness determines influence. Great is he who exerts influence." Then he lay down and rolled about for a long time in the grass. I fear the worst. On the other hand, I now realize why Berlau says that Brecht smells of the earth.

We have placed an announcement in the newspapers that advertises the fact that busts of Stalin are now available. Seventy-two-centimeter ones cost 25 *krooni*, those only thirty-two centimeters in size cost a mere 6.50 *krooni*.

The play that Brecht is planning with Hella is about the lord of the manor and his chauffeur. (The former is the man who is good when drunk, which all goes to show that human beings are good by nature, which is something that Brecht is muttering under his breath.) The chauffeur is, of course, a member of the working class and nothing can be held against him. A manly type who cracks jokes when necessary.

Brecht is explaining Hegel to me, a philosopher who spoke of the dialectics of master and slave. The only hope is for the slave, as it is he that does the work, and he still has a chance to develop, while the master is the master, and that's all there's to it, and so he will remain.

The foreign ambassadors have to leave Estonia by the 25th August! I've nothing against them personally—they're quite decent guys—but for some reason, my boss doesn't like them.

Funny country, Finland! I'm chatting with the Swedish journalist Sven Landin. He also thinks that the general picture of Finland is a sad one. There are ruins and invalids all over the place . . . Not one happy face.

In Estonia, they say you can see happy faces every step you take.

That's what he said.

Sad ones as well, but as the old adage goes, if you chop down the forest, you have to expect the chips to fly.

Brecht seems to agree.

One Finnish evening, when we were sitting under an old fir tree, he said, thoughtfully:

"You can't get everything at once. If you toss too many loaves to the people, something will go wrong."

Regarding any potential iniquities, Brecht had the following dialectical thing to say: fruitful tendencies can only be triggered off by bastards, and it only happens rarely that virtuous people are on the side of progress.

He fell silent for quite a while, lay on his back and looked up into the leaves of the birch tree. Then he said that he had possibly never been as happy as he was now, here in Finland.

As Minister of the Interior, I have been compelled to end religious studies in Estonian schools. But I haven't done this 100% against my own conscience. I have often myself wondered whether heaven isn't empty. No doubt it is. Who can tell?

Brecht said to me that a work of art is something that enriches the lives of individuals. He suggested that writing poetry is a social practice, despite all its paradoxes, mutability, historical determinism and the creation of history. There's supposed to be some kind of difference between reflection (*widerspiegeln*) and holding a mirror up to someone (*den Spiegel vorhalten*). I was compelled to acquaint myself with the titles of books targeted for destruction. There were two of them. Some people said that I smuggled diamonds into Russia, before I fled to Bulgaria. This may be true, but need not be. They are said to have sentenced me to death. If they do so they can carry out the sentence. It would be easy for them to carry it out.

PART VI

DOCUMENTS

INTERLUDE I

CONVERSATION BETWEEN A.A. ZHDANOV AND THE ESTONIAN AUTHOR VARES (BARBARUS) AS RED ARMY FORCES ARRIVE IN ESTONIA, ON THE SUBJECT OF THE PROPOSAL THAT THE ESTONIAN CABINET MEET

1940

Barbarus thinks that Estonia is now living in a period of breakthrough, and is glad that the time has come when the ideas he has been fighting for with all his strength for twenty-two years are now triumphant. He says that the arrival of the Red Army has been accepted by the population at large with tranquility and understanding.

The population is fearful of German influence, as Germany has been inimical to the Estonians for centuries, so anyone else but the Germans is welcome. The population, the workers, the farmers, the middle-ranking intelligentsia all understand that the Soviet Union is the only country that respects the Estonian people's rights and can guarantee their sovereignty.

Among members of the old government, there were honorable and decent people, but as a whole it was reactionary and not what it should have been. There was no democracy. Relations with the Soviet Union were loyal in formal terms. Initially, it was in fact incomprehensible how the Soviet Union managed to sign an agreement with such a government that always stood on an inimical foot with Soviet Russia.

Barbarus is prepared to work for the good of his people and strengthen friendly relations with us, but feels unprepared for the post of prime minister.

147

He fears that the change will be too abrupt. For twenty-two years, the plutocracy of Estonia has done a great deal to promote Estonian chauvinism. For this reason it is, in Estonian eyes, incomprehensible that a writer and poet, a bohemian by temperament, has been appointed to such an important post. It's imperative that the equilibrium of the Estonian people is not disturbed. Apart from that, he's a sensitive individual, lacks in willpower, and he may not always give orders when necessary.

Barbarus is ready. The direction in which he is going is clear. But it's regarded as necessary, regardless of all the considerations outlined above, that he doesn't refuse to lead the government.

He's thankful for the honor and trust placed in him. He's made the following proposals: Prime Minister or Deputy Prime Minister—Professor Kruus; Foreign Minister or Minister of Social Affairs—Andresen; Minister for the People's Education—Semper; Interior Minister—Unt; Minister of Justice—Jõeäär; Foreign Minister or Ambassador to the Soviet Union—Varman; Minister of Agriculture—Pool; Minister of Transport and Communications—Maddison.

Rossiyski tsentr Hraneniya I Izucheniya Dokumentov Noveishei Istorii. F. 77 (A, Zhdanov), n. 3, s. 124.

BRECHT'S POEM Nº 1

In order not to lose one's daily bread
In times of increasing oppression
Some people choose
To say nothing more about
The crimes of the régime when it keeps exploitation in place
Instead, not to spread the lies of the régime, i.e.,
Not to expose anything, but
Gloss over them either. What went on before
Merely seems to confirm that he is determined
Even in times of increasing oppression
Not to lose face, but in reality
He is nonetheless determined
Not to lose his daily bread. Yes, this decision of his
Not to tell a lie, forces him from now on

To keep quiet about the truth. This can of course
Only be kept up for a short while. But at this time too
While they still work as editors or civil servants
In laboratories and in factories, as people
Out of whose mouth no untruths emerge
Their vulnerability begins. He who does not bat an eyelid
At the sight of bloody crimes, lends them
A veneer of respectability. He designates
The horrible deed as something as unobtrusive as rain
Also as inevitable as rain.
And so he is already lending support, by his silence
The criminal, but soon
He will notice that he, in order not to lose his daily bread
Not only has to keep quiet about the truth, but
Also tell a lie. Not ungraciously
Do the oppressors welcome him, he who is prepared
Not to lose his daily bread.
He doesn't go around like someone taking bribes
As no one has given him anything, nor
Taken anything from him, either.
When the panegyrist,
Standing up at the table of those in power, tears open his gob
And you can see between his teeth
The remains of the meal, you can
Listen to his eulogy with skepticism.
But the eulogy of someone
Who only yesterday was still critical and was not invited to the feast
Is worth more. He
Is, after all, a friend of the oppressed. They know him.
What he says is
And what he doesn't say, is not.
And now he is saying that there is
No oppression.
Best when the murderer
Sends the brother of his victim
Whom he has bought over, in order to confirm
That his brother was killed by a roofing tile. Clearly a simple lie

Will help not get someone who doesn't want to lose his daily bread
Very far. There are too many
Like him. Soon
He gets into line in the ruthless fight fought by all
That do not want to lose their daily bread:
It's not enough to have the will to tell a lie.
The skill is needed and passion too.
A wish not to lose one's daily bread mixes himself
Into the wish by the art of making sense of the biggest load of nonsense
Saying the unsayable.
This means that he has to praise
The oppressor more than other people, as he
Is under suspicion of having once
Having insulted oppression. So
Those who know the truth become the most blatant liars.
And all this only lasts
Until someone comes along that restores
The former honesty, dignity, and then
They lose their daily bread.

PAGE FROM THE LIST OF BOOKS IN ESTONIA TO BE DESTROYED

Birsen, J. *The Coming War*. Tallinn, S.P.A.K. Estonian Union, 1932, 79 pp.

Birsen. J. *Towards a Better Future*. Second revised edition. Tallinn, S.P.A.K. Estonian Union, 1932, 150 pp.

Blackstone, W.E. *Jesus is Coming*. Riga, Awake Publishers, 1928, 272 pp.

Blan, H. *The Red Snake*, Tallinn, Ole Publishers, /1924–1928/, 45 pp.

Blumfeldt, E. *History of the West*, Tartu, Estonian Literary Society, 1938, 57 pp. Eighth volume of *Estonia: Laanemaa Province*.

Bogajevski, G.W. *Preparing the Silos*. With 17 illustrations. Leningrad, 1931, 68 pp.

Bollmann, P. *The Third Way. A drama in 4 acts*,(Part 5), Tallinn, Estonian Educational Society, 1932, 136 pp.

Borgelin, R.G. *Under the Dannebrog Flag. Peace and War*. Volume 1. *Peace*, Tallinn, Loosalu Publishers, 1934, 136 pp.

Borgelin, R.G. *Under the Dannebrog Flag. Peace and War*. Volume 2. *War*, Tallinn, Loosalu Publishers, 1934, 320 pp.

Braks, T. *The Heroes of Eagle Hill. A war play in two acts,* Tallinn, Estonian Educational Society, 1935, 39 pp.

Breschko-Breschowaskaya, E.K. *What Should Be Done in the Constituent Assembly?,* Tallinn, 1917, 12 pp.

Brigader, A. *The Big Catch. A comedy in five acts.* Tallinn, Estonian Educational Society, 1934, 155 pp.

Bubnov, A. *Key Moments of the Development of the Communist Party in Russia.* Saint Petersburg, Russian Communist Party Estonian Branch, 1921, 46 pp.

Buchan, J. *The Thirty-Nine Steps,* Tartu-Tallinn, Loodus Publishers, 1939, 159 pp.

Busch, M. *The History of Awakening in Ridala Parish,* Ridala Baptist Congregation, 1928, 123 pp.

Buxhoewden, D. *How I Protected Myself against Gas Attacks,* Tallinn, Defence League Headquarters, 1928, 48 pp.

Carnegie, A. *Capital and Labor. Problems of Our Time,* Pärnu, Kiri Publishers, 1922, 138 pp.

Christie, A. *The Secret Adversary, Crime novel,* Tallinn, Jutuleht Publishers, 1933, 140 pp.

Coudenhove-Kalergi, R.N. *The Pan-European League, Volume 1* Pan-Europa Publishers, 1929, 12 pp. Author's text at the end.

Coudenhove-Kalergi, R. *Total State - Total Individual,* Tallinn, Tallinn Estonian Publishers' Union, 1938, 158 pp. 1929, 158 pp.

(. . .)

BRECHT'S POEM № 2

When the régime ordered that books with dangerous knowledge
To be burnt in public, and from everywhere
Oxen were forced to take
Cartloads of books
To the bonfires, a refugee poet,
One of the best, discovered a list
And looking at it became angry when he saw that his own
Books weren't on it. He rushed to his desk
With wings of rage, and wrote a letter to the powers that be.
Burn me! he wrote, his pen flying over the paper, burn
me!

I don't care! Don't leave me out! Have I not
Always told the truth in my books? And now
You're treating me like a liar! I command you,
Burn me!

THE OPINIONS OF LECTURER FILATOV OF THE SLAVYANSKI PEDA-GOGICAL INSTITUTE REGARDING THE SECRET PROTOCOL OF THE MOLOTOV-RIBBENTROP PACT

· *To the Deputy Chairman of the Supreme Soviet of the USSR, A. Lukyanov . . .
Since your reply concerning the treaty signed in 1939 worries all Soviet citizens that
have still maintained Leninist Socialist standpoints, please allow me to draw your
attention to the following historical facts . . . ;*

· *Rumors of an addendum attached to the protocol of the meeting between Germany and the USSR are a myth and a falsification, which malicious forces in the
West have repeatedly been trying to spread over the past forty years to fit in with
their strategic plans;*

· *When planning to attack the Soviet Union, Hitler envisaged occupying the Baltic states as well, and there is proof of this from before the war . . . ;*

· *If Hitler has relinquished his plans for the Baltic states (something which is,
however, very unlikely) and if the states had maintained their so-called sovereignty
as bourgeois republics, then they would become his allies in the event of an attack
on the Soviet Union;*

· *There are historical documents that show that all the governments (i.e. of Estonia, Latvia and Lithuania) are pro-fascist. They have secret agreements not only
with Great Britain but with fascist Germany. They have simply not observed the
terms regarding cordon sanitaire vis-à-vis the USSR, but have openly called upon
the West to declare war on the Soviet Union;*

· *The documents show that the governments of the bourgeois Baltic countries are
in complete solidarity with Hitler's policies and have been willing to take part in
the dismembering of the Soviet Union, even naming stretches of territory that they
have laid claim to.*

(From the daily newspaper *Noorte Hääl*)

BRECHT'S POEM № 3

THE EMIGRANTS

I have always found false the name they gave us: emigrants.
That means people who emigrated. But we
Did not leave our countries voluntarily
Choosing a new one where to live, maybe for good.
But we fled. We are refugees, banished individuals.
And the land that has accepted us will be no home, but an exile.
We sit there uneasily, as near the border as possible
Waiting for the day of return, watching the smallest change
Across the border, eagerly asking
Every newcomer, forgetting nothing, giving nothing up
Nor forgiving anything that happened, not forgiving.
No, the present quiet does not fool us! Even here
We can hear the screams from the camps over there. We cling to rumors
That have crossed the border. Each one of us
Walking through the crowds with worn-down shoes
Bears witness to the scandal that sullies our country right now.
But none of us
Will stay here. The last word
Has not yet been spoken.

THE SECRET PROTOCOL ITSELF

23rd August 1939

On the occasion of the signing the non-aggression treaty between the Union of Soviet Socialist Republics and Germany, there was talk of an additional and confidential protocol signed by fully authorized members on both sides, which would define spheres of influence in Eastern Europe.

The results of the negotiations in this area were as follows:

1. In the event of the territorial and political re-organization of the Baltic states (Finland, Estonia, Latvia, Lithuania) the boundary between the spheres of influ-

ence of Germany and the USSR will be the northern border of Lithuania. Both parties acknowledge interests in the Vilnius region.

2. In the event of a territorial and political re-organization, the areas of Poland that adjoin the spheres of influence of Germany and the USSR will be bounded by the rivers Narew, Vistula and San.

With regard to the question as to whether it is the interests of both parties to maintain an independent Poland and, if so, where its borders should run, this will be determined by the course of future political developments.

At any event, both governments will decide on this question by way of amicable agreement.

3. Regarding south-eastern Europe, the Soviet Union asserts its rights in Bessarabia. Germany declares itself to have no claims whatsoever to this region.

4. Both parties will maintain strict secrecy with regard to this protocol.

Moscow, 23rd August 1939

For the German government
J. Ribbentrop

For the Soviet government
V. Molotov

DGFP. Ser. D. Vol VII. P. 246–247. Translated from the English language.

(From the Estonian cultural monthly *Looming*)

BRECHT'S POEM Nº 4

THE MASK OF EVIL

On my wall hangs a Japanese carving
The mask of an evil demon, painted with gold lacquer
I am moved when I see
The swollen veins of the brow that indicate
How much effort you need to be angry.

EXCERPT FROM THE PHRASE-BOOK SUBMITTED FOR PRINTING ON 9TH JUNE 1940

Govorite pravdu!

Speak the truth!

Yesli ne znaete,
skazhite "Ne znayu!"

If you don't know,
say "I don't know!"

Vy ne mozhete ne znat'!

You must know!

Vy dolzhny byli slyshat'!

You must obey!

Vy dolzhny byli videt'!

You must look!

Vy govorite nepravdu!

You are not telling the truth!

Uspokoites'!

Calm down!

Stoi!

Stop!

Sdavaysya!

Surrender!

Slezai s konya!

Get off your horse!

Ruki vverkh!

Hands up!

Ne shumi!

Shut up!

Yesli budesh shumet', ubyu!

If you don't shut up, I'll kill you!

S kakikh napravlyonnyi ozhidayutsya
naleti nashei aviatsii?

From what direction do you
expect our planes to attack?

Yest' li pochtovye golubi?

Are there any mail pigeons?

Kakie imeyutsya bomby?

What kinds of bombs do they have?

Otkuda pozvozyat prodovolstviye?	Where does the food come from?
Sobat' i dostavit' syuda korov (ovets)!	Collect together and bring here the cattle (sheep)!

■

Ne boites' krasnoarmeitsev!	Do not fear the Red Army soldiers!
Za vse vzatoye u zhitelyei voiska Krasnoi Armii zaplatyat!	Everything taken from the inhabitants will be paid for by the Red Army!
Sobrat' zhitelyei dlya ispravleniya dorogi!	Gather the inhabitants to mend the road!
Provedite nas tak, chtoby nikto ne zametil.	Take us by a route where no one will spot us.
Prinesite toplivo!	Bring the fuel!
Yesli sprachite, my sami budem iskat'!	If you hide it, we will search for it ourselves!
Gde imeetsya restoran?	Where is the restaurant?
Gde mozhna kupit' sakharu (myaso, konservov)?	Where can you buy sugar (meat, canned goods)?
Yest' li luchshe?	Isn't there any better?
Yest' li yeshcho?	Isn't there any more?

BRECHT'S POEM N° 5[1]

SPRING III

In the willows on the sound
The screech-owl often cries in the spring night.
Peasant superstition says
That the screech-owl is thus telling people
That they have not long to live. I
Know full well that I have told the truth
About those in power, don't actually need
This bird of death to tell me so.

WHERE DID THEY ALL VANISH TO?

On 30th July 1940, Päts, along with his son Viktor (the latter was a member of the Riigikogu and thus belonged to the group of government officials), and his daughter-in-law Helgi to the city of Ufa, Russia, by way of administrative disciplinary order. The domestic servant Olga Tünder traveled along with them of her own free will. On 26th June 1941, all the Pätses were arrested and were taken to the internal penitentiary of the Bashkir Autonomous Soviet Socialist Republic which was run by the People's Commissar for Security and located in the city of Ufa. Konstantin Päts was incriminated for crimes as set out in Paragraph 58-3, Clause 4 of the Criminal Codex. The President tried on a number of occasions to obtain permission to have himself and his family sent abroad. He was also very concerned about the state of health of his grandson, and made the proposal that he could be exchanged for Thälmann or Rákosi, but his proposal was refused. The small boy died.

On 14th September 1942, the President was taken, along with his son Viktor, to Moscow, so that investigations could be continued and they could be interrogated by the Special Chamber Commission. After the interrogations had taken place, he was sent for a while to the internal penitentiary in the city of Kirov, and on 24th March 1943, without any decision by the courts, he was put on forced medication, in the closed psychiatric hospital in Kazan (Tatarstan). At a special session of the Special Chamber Commission on 29th April 1952, his case was reviewed and he was again subjected to forced medication. By this time, Päts had spent nine years in a closed psychiatric hospital under a special régime, and his son Viktor was no

---

1   *Translator's note: English has been substituted for the Estonian here.*

longer in the land of the living. He had been arrested at the Ivanovo Prison and death had followed on 4th March 1952 in the Butyrka Prison in Moscow.

The organs of the People's Commissioner of the Interior had wanted to recruit Viktor Päts as his assistant and use him in some scheme or other. But his proud and unwavering nature did not allow him to make compromises, and so he paid for this with his life. (. . .)

In June 1941, shortly following his arrest and his being sent to the Pensa Prison, Viktor Päts had been affected so badly by the illegal judgement that he tried to take his life, by hitting his head repeatedly against the wall of his cell.

On 15th November 1954 the Central Commission altered the decision of the Special Chamber Commission regarding Konstantin Päts. On 8th December of that year, his forced medication was stopped and he was sent to the general psychiatric hospital at Jämejala, in his native Estonia. But he was not to remain there for long. On the night of 31st December 1954, he was sent to the city of Kalinin (Tver, on the River Volga, Russia). Here he was to see in the New Year, his last. In my diary I have written the story told to me by the driver of the blue Pobeda automobile, about how Päts was taken away from Jämejala on New Year's Eve.

The Chief-of-Staff of the Estonian armed forces, J. Laidoner, was deported, along with his wife Maria, from Estonia on 19th July 1940. This was done by the head of an observation brigade of the People's Commisariat for Internal Affairs of the USSR, intelligence captain Vladimirov. Laidoner was told that this exile would last some while in connection with his personal security. Until the end of the war, Laidoner would be living outside of Estonia. He was housed at 38 Gogol Street in the town of Pensa in a small detached house with five rooms and was ordered to report once a week to the People's Commisariat for Internal Affairs. In Pensa, Laidoner was awarded a pension. He read a good deal there, and followed the course of the war in Europe (. . .)

On the fourth day after the breakout of the war against Germany, that is to say on 26th June 1941, Laidoner was arrested at the behest of the People's Commissariat for National Security of the USSR. He was taken to Pensa Oblast internal penitentiary run by the Commissariat for National Security, where he was kept until July 1942. His file was then sent the Special Chamber Commission in Moscow for examination, while he himself was taken to the Butyrka prison there. The Special Chamber Commission failed to try his case and he was sent for many years to the penitentiary belonging to the People's Commissariat for Internal Affairs in the town of Ivanovo.

The war came to an end. By this time Laidoner had contracted scurvy, flecktyphus and had suffered a heart attack. In the summer of 1951, prison life became unbearable for him. He was kept on the third floor of the prison and did not take *exercise as it was difficult for the old man to climb the stairs. Laidoner decided to write a letter to Stalin. When Laidoner had been part of a delegation to Moscow in 1939, he had met Stalin, who told him: "If you are ever in difficult circumstances in the USSR, contact me directly and I will help you." Now Laidoner remembered this. The proud general asked the generalissimo to make life easier for him and his wife, who, at that time was in the same prison. Stalin did not keep his word. He wrote, on Laidoner's letter, a resolution concerning Laidoner's plea: "Comrade Golovanov. Arrange an amendment for the group." Nine months later, on 4th April 1952, a certain Levin noted alongside Stalin's resolution: "For filing. According to the command of the authority Laidoner should be put on trial."*

This note was added after Laidoner had been taken from the prison in Ivanovo to the Butyrka, and now intensive interrogation began. When he arrived in Butyrka on 6th March 1952, all his personal belongings were taken from him, the book The Northern War, *plus scraps of writing hidden in the toe of his left shoe and in the shoulder pads of his jacket, which depressed his mood significantly. He tried on several occasions to regain some of these small liberties for himself.*

Between 7th and 22nd March 1952, Laidoner was interrogated fourteen times. On 8th March the doctor stated that he should rest in bed, but the nightly interrogations continued. They did come to an end, however, when Laidoner became seriously ill. On 16th April 1952 the Special Chamber Commission charged Johannes Laidoner with "an active struggle against the revolutionary movement and activity inimical to the interests of the USSR for which the penalty is twenty-five years incarceration." Being a dangerous criminal, he was sent to serve his sentence in the city of Vladimir, to the special prison of the People's Commissariat for Internal Affairs there. This is where the former head of the Estonian armed forces spent the last year of his life. A report drawn up by the governor of the second prison Karpov, and by the warder of Nº 1 post, Arkhireyev, and dated 13th March 1953 states: "this month in Cell Number 215, Prisoner Nº 11, charged according to the Russian Federation Criminal Codex paragraph 58-4 and sentenced to twenty-five years prison régime has died."

On Laidoner's death, the head of intelligence at the Vladimir prison, the junior colonel Zhuravlyov, wrote to the head of the head of prison intelligence at the Ministry of Security of the USSR, Yevsenin, saying: "I would like to inform you that Prisoner Nº 11, born in 1884, has died on 13th March 1953." The cause of death is given as heart failure occasioned by a second cerebral hemorrhage.

On 14th March 1953, at twenty past three o'clock, members of the prison staff Sub-Lieutenant Vorobyov and Staff Sergeant Baranov, plus Sergeant Zemskov buried Prisoner Nº 11 in the cemetery at Vladimir in a joint grave with the Prime Minister of the Polish Government-in-Exile in London, Jan Stanisław Jankowski, who had died that same day and who had been sentenced to 8 years incarceration according to Paragraph 58-8-II.

During the whole of the time that he had been imprisoned in Pensa, Ivanovo, Vladimir and the Butyrka, Laidoner had been referred to in all documents as Prisoner No 11. He was buried under that same number. His name remained a secret.

Junior Colonel Zhuravlyov received a reply from Colonel Kuznetsov of the Prisons Department of the Ministry of the Interior of the USSR, which was contained in an envelope marked "private and confidential" and said: "The personal file of Prisoner No 11 is to be kept in the safe in your office."

It has afterwards been hard, almost impossible, to establish Laidoner's exact place of burial. In those days, people who were held prisoner were not registered with undertakers nor were the numbers of the graves registered under any number. In such graves, the inhabitants of the city of Vladimir were also buried.

Riigivanem (i.e., Prime Minister) F. Akel (he had also been Foreign Minister) was arrested by the organs of the People's Commissariat for Internal Affairs on 17th October 1940 and shot in Tallinn on 3rd July 1941. His final resting place is unfortunately unknown. Friedrich Akel was the last of the former state officials of the Estonian Republic that was shot before the deportation of those arrested began. Before him, four leading state officials had been shot: on the second day of the war, 23rd June 1941, member of the Riigikogu (parliament) Rudolf Riives and Minister of Transport Otto Sternbek were shot, a week later, on 30th June 1941, they were followed by Minister of War Ado Anderkopp and Aleksander Tõnisson.

The Estonian consul in Turkey, Ernst Veberman (he had also been Minister of Trade and Industry) was arrested by the Cheka on 20th December 1940. On the next day, Stalin's birthday, he ended his life by suicide in the prison in Tallinn.

If you leaf through the criminal cases where the Special Chamber Commission sentenced people to be shot, you can find people who were no longer alive when sentenced. In January 1942 material was sent from the Vyatka camp to Moscow for perusal by the Special Chamber Commission concerning the member of the Riigikogu and regional elder for the provinces of Viljandi and Tartu, Hendrik Lauri. The camp commandant recommended that Lauri "be shot." That same February, H. Lauri had died of enterocolitis (he was buried in the cemetery of the 7th camp location in Lesnoi village in the Kraisk region of the Kirov oblast), and yet four months later (in June 1942) the Special Chamber Commission issued an order for him to be shot.

The opposite also occurred: someone could be sentenced to a prison term when, in fact, they had already been shot. This happened to the Minister of Transport Otto Sternbek, who has been mentioned above. He sent a plea for clemency to the Presidium of the Supreme Soviet of the Russian Soviet Socialist Republic, which

160

commuted his death sentence to a ten-year term in prison. (Until 1947, ten years was the maximum prison term, in that same year the term was raised to twenty-five years and in 1950, the death sentence was re-introduced, while the prison term was not reduced—Author's note).

The execution by firing squad of Estonian government officials in the labor camps in 1941 was far from being a rarity. Apart from the five mentioned above, in the first days of the war two more government officials were shot: the 1st September 1941 was the last day in the life of the archbishop of the Estonian Lutheran Church, Hugo-Bernhard Rahamägi (in Kirov). When you think that Rahamägi had also been Minister of Education, his execution on 1st September strikes one as particularly iniquitous. In the same city, on Stalin's birthday, 21st December, Member of the Riigikogu Aleksander Ossipov was shot.

The shooting of the inmates of prisons and labor camps started in April 1942.

(. . .) Most of the government officials of the Estonian Republic lie buried in the city of Sverdlovsk. During the 1930s, 1940s and 1950s, the Urals were turned into one huge labor camp, for the many nations of the USSR. Within the territory of the Sverdlovsk oblast, there were a total of two hundred GULAG prisons and camps. The number of prisoners in these special camps was between 300,000 and 350,000, forming some 10–12% of the total population of the oblast. People from the various regions of the country were ground down in what was like a huge mincing-machine.

In the prison at Sverdlovsk, the following ministers of the Estonian Republic were shot: Jaan Hünerson (5th May 1942), Theodor Pool (25th August 1942), Johannes-Friedrich Zimmermann (24th August 1942), Hugo-Villi Kukke (3rd August 1942). Plus Members of the Riigikogu: Jaan Kokk (10th April 1942), Anton Uesson (13th April 1942), Artur Kasterpalu (2nd June 1942), Oskar Lõvi (2nd September 1942), Karl Jalakas (3rd August 1942). On 13th March 1942 the Defense Minister of the Estonian Republic, Major-General Paul Lill, died of heart failure in Sverdlovsk Prison.

From what we know, the worst camp of all was the one at Sevural whose HQ was situated in the Sosva settlement in the Sverdlovsk oblast. Not one single former official of the Estonian Republic came out of that camp alive, though it held the largest concentration. The following ministers were shot in Sosva: Oskar Kask (13th April 1942), August Kerem (28th May 1942); plus members of the Riigikogu: Jüri Jaakson, Jakob Kalle, Aleksis Tšank, Evald Konno (all on 20th April 1942), Nikolai Viitak (24th April 1942), Ernst Haabpiht (4th May 1942), August Laur (8th May 1942), Elmer Lehtmets (17th June 1942) and Johan Haagivang (30th October 1942).

Nine government officials died in the Sosva camp. Among them were the Prime Minister Ado Birk (2nd February 1942), seven ministers—Jaan Piisak (19th December 1941), Mihkel Juhkam (28th January 1942), Anton Palvadre (16th February 1942), Jaan Kriisa (8th August 1942), Anton Veeperv (19th August 1942), Alfred-Julius Mõttus (4th October 1942), Leopold Johanson (30th November 1942), and member of the Riigikogu, Georgi Orlov (15th October 1941). Several of those who died at the end of 1941, before the start of the mass executions the following spring and summer, were spared execution by dying a natural death.

Next in line after the Sverdlovsk oblast regarding these grim statistics comes the Vyatka (Kirov) Oblast. In the city of Kirov itself the following were shot: Hugo-Bernhard Rahamägi and Aleksander Ossipov (as mentioned above), plus members of the Riigikogu Johan Uuemaa (10th April 1942) and Aleksander Saar (1st August 1942). In the Vyatka camps the following government officials died of dystrophy, tuberculosis and other serious diseases, which the prisoners whose morale had been smashed and were weak on account of hunger, so they could no longer cope with work in the forest : Prime Minister Kaarel-August Eenpalu (27th January 1942); the Archbishop of the Estonian Roman Catholic Church Eduard Profittlich (22nd February 1942); the General-Chief-of-Staff of the Estonian armed forces, Major-General Juhan Tõrvand (12th May 1942); ministers Mikhel Pung (11th October 1941), Karl Terras (25th December 1942), Karl-August Baars (27th February 1942), August Jürimaa (15th June 1942), Aleksander Jaanson (2nd October 1942), Karl Johannes Viirma (11th November 1942), Karl Ibsberg (27th June 1943); members of the Riigikogu Jaan Põdra (4th February 1942), Joakim Puhk (14th September 1942) and Johannes Orasmaa (24th May 1943), plus Hendrik Lauri as mentioned above, who had been sentenced to be shot when already dead.

Fourteen government officials of the Estonian Republic lie in the earth of the Perm province (mostly in the Usol labor camp which is situated in the town of Solikamsk). The following were shot: Minister of War Lieutenant-General Nikolai Reek (8th May 1942); members of the Riigikogu Hendrik Otstavel (11th February 1942) and Nigul Laliste (25th June 1942). Eleven higher functionaries died there (whose cause of death is not known): Riigivanem (in certain years also Foreign Minister and Minister of Education) Ants (Antonius) Piip (1st October 1942); Minister of War Jaan Soots (6th February 1942); Minister of the Interior Richard Veerma (19th February 1942); and other ministers (I shall not give all their posts here as they had different ones over the years) Artur Tupits (28th October 1941), Leo Sepp (13th December 1941), Aleksander Oinas (3rd March 1942), head of the Supreme Court of Estonia Peeter Kann (18th January 1942); members of the Riigikogu Johannes Perens (25th December 1941), August Kohver (19th August 1942), Jarvo Tandre (30th August 1943); the provincial governor of Võru Karl Pajos (25th May 1953).

Top government officials in prisons and labor camps in other oblasts were relatively few in number.

· Karaganda oblast. Here, in the village of Dolinskaya on 15th August 1942, the member of the Riigikogu Ado Roosberg died; on 26th January 1948 in the town of Karaganda, member of the Riigikogu Bernhard Postfeld. The cause of death of both remains unknown.

· Komi Autonomous Soviet Socialist Republic. In the town of Syktyvkar on 16th August 1942 member of the Riigikogu Eduard Arnover died, on 6th November 1942 Vladimir Roopere. Their cause of death also remains unknown.

· Krasnoyarsk Krai. In the town of Norilsk in the on 6th October 1942, Major-General Herbert Brede was shot. On 16th September 1943 in the town of Kansk minister Albert Assor died (cause of death unknown).

· Kemerovo oblast. Here on 28th November 1943 Aleksander Hellat died (Interior Minister, Foreign Minister, member of the Supreme Court, cause of death unknown).

· Novosibirsk oblast. On 1st October 1943 minster Eduard Säkk died (cause of death unknown).

· Nizhny Novgorod (Gorki) oblast. At the Sukhobesvodnaya railroad station in the Semyonovski krai the member of the Riigikogu Alo Karineel was shot (2nd April 1942).

By the autumn of 1942 the members of the Estonian parliament and the members of the government of "plutocrats" (I did not invent this term myself) no longer gave any trouble, as half of them had been shot, the other had died of their own accord.

Only two of the government officials that were deported from Estonia before the war ever came back. There were no other ministers or members of the Riigikogu. The Minister of Education Paul Kogerman who had spent his time in the town of Tavda in the Sverdlovsk oblast was freed early on 2nd March 1945. Member of the Riigikogu Karl Jürisson was arrested on 5th October 1940 and exactly 8 years later, in October 1948 he was freed and served the rest of his sentence in the Vorkuta labor camp.

Member of the Riigikogu Linda-Maria Eenpalu was deported on 14th June 1941 and sent in perpetuity to the Tomsk oblast in the Tainski rayon. She was freed on 21st May 1956 and died in 1967 in Pärnu. As she was not technically arrested, I cannot really count her as being one of those freed. In November and December of 1944, members of the People's Commission for Internal Affairs announced that the following people, had survived the war and had been released from detention and had been members of the Riigikogu were now living in Estonia: Eduard Pedosk, Mihkel Reiman and Minister of Education Aleksander-August Veidermaa. They were immediately arrested. The first of these was sent to Karaganda, the other two to the Dubrav labor camp in the Mordva Autonomous Soviet Socialist Republic. The three were released from the camps exactly ten years later.

There is no clear picture of what happened to eight higher officials of the Estonian Republic.

The Riigivanem (Prime Minister) Jaan Teemant was arrested on 24th July 1940, that is to say before Estonia had actually become a member republic of the USSR. The Special Chamber Commission sentenced him on 21st February 1941 to 10 years deprivation of liberty. There is no information available as to which camps he was sent to or where he died. The second Riigivanem, Jaan Tõnisson, was arrested on 12th December 1940 and deported from Estonia in June of 1941 along with other arrestees. There is no information available as to his subsequent fate. All that can be surmised is that he died en route and his body was left behind at some railroad station. It is rumored that after the war, his birthday was celebrated at the prison in Voronezh. In 1948 he would have been 80 years old. It is hard to believe that such an old man (he was the oldest of all the government officials mentioned) had managed to survive the prison régime under war conditions. I tried to find any traces of Tõnisson in Voronezh, but was unable to find any.

The Minister of Propaganda Ants Oidermaa was arrested on 9th December 1940 and there are no further details as to what happened to him.

Minister of the Interior August Reet was arrested on 19th July 1940. On 8th March 1941, the Special Chamber Commission sentenced him to 8 years in a labor camp. Which camp he was taken to or what subsequently happened to him is not known. It can be surmised that he was kept prisoner in the Arkhangelsk oblast.

Minister of Finance Oskar Suursööt was arrested on 5th September 1940 and on 28th May of the following year, the Special Chamber Commission sentenced him to 8 years deprivation of liberty. It can be assumed that he was sent to Magadan, but no exact detail exist.

Minister Christian Kaarna was arrested on 18th September 1940 and the Special Chamber Commission decided that on account of his membership of the "plutocratic" government of the Estonian Republic, he should be sentenced to 8 years. It can be assumed that Ch. Kaarna was sent to one of the Arkhangelsk labor camps, but no further details exist.

(. . .)

(Published by Vladimir Pool, former Deputy Head of KGB of the ESSR, in the Estonian daily Postimees in October 1991.)

BRECHT'S POEM Nº 6

When in a dream he entered the cottage of the banished
Poet, which stood next to the cottage
Where the banished teacher lived (he heard
Dispute and laughter coming from there), Ovid came to meet
Him at the entrance and said, in a half-whisper:
"Better not sit down just yet. You're not dead. Who knows
Whether you're not going back without anything changing but you."
But, solace in his eyes
Po Chü-yi approached and said with a smile: "He who once spoke
Of injustice deserves the corresponding morality."
And his friend Tu-fu said quietly: "You understand, the banishment
Is not the place where arrogance is unlearnt," but the churlish
Villon was more earthy, asking him: "How many
Doors has the house where you live?" And he went up to Dante
And taking hold of his sleeve, muttered: "Your verse
Are crawling with mistakes, my friend, just consider
All the people who are against you!" And Voltaire cried:
"Watch you, *sous*, otherwise you'll go hungry!"
"And mix in some amusing bits!" cried Heine. "That won't help,"
Mocked Shakespeare, "when Jacob arrived
He could no longer write." "If it comes to a trial
Get a rogue of a lawyer!" shouted Euripides,
"Because he knows the loopholes in the net of the law." They were still
Laughing, when out of the darkest corner
Came the cry: "You, do you happen to know
Your poems by heart? And those you do know,
Can you escape their consequences?"—"Those are
The forgotten ones," said Dante lightly.
"They will have not only their bodies but their works destroyed."
They all burst into laughter. None of them dared look up. The
Newcomer
Grew pale.

ZHDANOV AS THEATER DIRECTOR

Neither the Roman Empire nor Napoleon ever affected Estonia. Not until the mid-20th century did Europe's common roof stretch over our heads too, and since then our common history began, both on Estonian soil, in the parliament on Toompea Hill, and at the parliaments of Europe. On 16th June 1940 the French government resigned and one day later the new head of government asked for a truce from the Germans. That same evening, 17th June, the People's Commissar for Foreign Affairs, Molotov, invited Ambassador Schulenburg to visit him, an unpretentious German aristocrat, almost two meters tall and a genuine admirer of Russian culture, who had already joined, or intended joining, the anti-Hitler coalition and was subsequently hanged for this, and gave this man the "warmest congratulations" on the part of the Soviet government for the brilliant victory of the German forces. It is conceivable, though it has never been proven, that on that cosy evening neither of the conversation partners knew that for the successful Blitzkrieg in France, the German Chief-of-Staff had cleared Poland of armed forces, barring five divisions. The Red Army could have reached Berlin within two weeks, without meeting any significant resistance. But on that day, the Red Army was busy occupying Estonia and by evening there were said to be 130,000 troops present there. These thoughts were going through the head of the People's Commissar when he said to the Ambassador: "It is now time to put an end, in the Baltic states, to the intrigues by which Britain and France have tried to sow discord and mistrust between Germany and the Soviet Union." Schulenburg remembered, from the secret protocol: "Regarding the changes of a territorial and political nature in the Baltic countries (Finland, Estonia, Latvia, Lithuania . . .)." Goodness me, thought Schulenburg, have the Russians already brought 30,000 men into Estonia? And what is Molotov thinking of when he speaks of British and French intrigues? Have not the political changes already taken place in connection with the establishment of military bases in the Baltic countries, bringing these countries into her sphere of influence? Schulenburg's facial expression didn't betray his surprise. Molotov's handshake was warm and firm. "To the end of discord," added the People's Commissar; he had sent his special envoys Dekanozov, Vyshinski, and Zhdanov to the three Baltic countries. Schulenburg knew this trio. The Ambassador had no further questions.

Zhdanov could choose between two types of stage direction.

The embarrassment related to the creation of the People's Republic of Finland was fresh in his mind. The Finnish working people did indeed fight against the "Finnish White Guard," with at their head the people's government set up in Teri-

joki, and the Red Army helped the People's Government by means of an assistance pact, but the Soviet Union was expelled from the League of Nations. Meanwhile, Zhdanov had managed to learn something. When the Germans went to Norway in April, the German Ambassador had published the following text: "In the spirit of the friendly relations between Germany and Norway, the German Government announces to the King of Norway that she has no claims on the territorial integrity of the Kingdom of Norway, nor on its sovereignty, now or in the future." They imposed their fellow party member Vidkun Quisling onto the government, and initially all was quiet in Norway. But on 28th September 1939, when the military bases were imposed on the Estonian Republic, people also promised not to lay claims on that country's sovereignty, or on her form of government or economic system. That part of the agreement is open, known internationally, and from it a new direction sprang. The liquidation of the Estonian Republic had to be stage-directed so that it enjoyed a measure of legitimacy abroad, emerging as it did out of a parliamentary process. To this end, free information was cut off, and Estonia became isolated from the outside world.

In mid-June 1940, the Baltic countries still had a few doors open to the world beyond. For instance, via the joint border that Lithuania had with Germany, it was still possible to leave for neutral Switzerland, Portugal, or the United States. In the other direction, across the sea, loomed the presence of Sweden. There were also airplane flights, linking the capital with the outside world. First these windows were shut. The passenger plane, the Kaleva, *arriving from Stockholm made a stop at Lasnamäe in northern Tallinn, then set course for Helsinki. Seven minutes later it was shot down near the Keri lighthouse by two Soviet fighters. Even before cock's crow a worried constable from Paldiski phoned saying that Soviet vessels had boarded all merchant and passenger vessels flying the Estonian flag, even fishing boats, and towed them off to Paldiski. And on 14th June, that same day, as General Küchler was occupying Paris with the 18th Army, Molotov gave the Lithuanian Foreign Ministry a nine-hour ultimatum, whereafter the Red Army occupied Lithuania and closed the border with Germany. The Baltic countries were in the bag.*

Special Envoy Zhdanov arrived in Tallinn early in the morning of 19th June, two days after the arrival of the Red Army. By police decree, all windows on Pikk Street were kept shut, so that there was safe access to the Russian Embassy, which was located opposite the Georg Stude café (now known as "Maiasmokk"). The Special Envoy lost no time. By one o'clock he was on a visit to the President, Konstantin Päts, and surprised him with the news that the new prime minister would be the physician and minor poet from Pärnu, Johannes Vares Barbarus. The President tried to dodge out of this, but in effect he was a prisoner in his Kadriorg residence and on 21st June Zhdanov softened him up a little with a demonstration combined with a display of armored vehicles. Among those watching stood a thin young sports reporter: "I doubt somehow that this was a revolution," says Ralf Parve, some half-century later. Zhdanov assured Vares that Estonia's sovereignty would be respected and that once the danger had passed, the Red Army would withdraw from Estonia. On Friday 21st June the new government was announced late in the evening. There was not one Communist in it, and this too gave confidence to the public at large. There were at the time 130 Communists in Estonia, and more such people couldn't have been brought in from Russia, because during the years of state terror such people would have been shot, starved to death or had simply disappeared into concentration camps.

Joh. Vares stressed the fact, in both his declaration and his speeches, that Estonian sovereignty was guaranteed and that in the pact that had been signed on 28th September 1939 between the Estonian Republic and the Soviet Union, it was stated that the Estonian Republic would run its own affairs according to the constitution, and that all rumors of Sovietization did not correspond to the truth. That assured people. Only a few days previously, in the ultimatum presented on 16th June, Estonia, Latvia and Lithuania had been accused of plotting to launch an attack on the Soviet Union. Moscow announced in no uncertain terms that the organ of the war-mongering clique in Tallinn was the Revue Baltique! Now the review had been consolidated around members of the cabinet who had been former "war-mongers": the historian Hans Kruus, who had been appointed assistant to the Prime Minister; the archaeologist Harri Moora, assistant to the Minister of Education; and the economist Juhan Vaabel as assistant to the Minister of Finance. Only the Latvian composer Jāzeps Vītols remained in his former job as the director of the Riga Conservatory. It looked as if, after the two cynical ultimata, a little hope had returned. The Estonian opposition politician Jaan Tõnisson saw the hope in a provisional light: "The declaration by the new government is reassuring under the present circumstances if it is implemented under the blue-black-white flag, in other words—on the basis of an independent sovereign Estonia . . . As the radio address on Midsummer's Day by the Prime Minister Dr Joh. Vares-Barbarus, and the explanations by his deputy Hans Kruus in the press show, we can be sure that government activity will occur on the foundation of an independent Estonia, with its duties being performed punctually and honestly, as foreseen in the mutual assistance pact between the Soviet Union and Estonia." ("Päevaleht" 28.06.1940). Those *that preferred suicide to cooperation with an alien power were the Riigivanem O. Strandman and the public officials A. Tuulse and his wife, and S. Kallas, plus, after the war when the name Quisling had also become a synonym for collaboration in Estonia—Dr Joh. Vares and his wife.*

De jure, *the system of agreements between the Soviet Union and Estonia, as mapped out at the Treaty of Tartu in 1920, was regularized in June 1940, so that the Tartu Treaty came to an end on 28th September 1939, when the mutual assistance pact was signed in Moscow. Leaving aside the decisive factor under international law that the 1939 ultimatum came into being under the threat of occupation by armed forces, as well as the fact that one direct result of the ultimatum of 16th June 1940 was the military occupation of the Estonian Republic, the guarantee given by the Soviet government as to the continued constitutional sovereignty of Estonia, plus non-interference in her internal affairs was still valid. The fifth chapter of the pact states: "The validity of this treaty shall in no way breach the right to sovereignty of the Parties, especially with regard to economic structure and system of government." So, the leadership of the Soviet Union stressed on three occasions over the space of nine months, this inviolability: the signing of the pact in 1939 and the ultimatum on 16th June 1940 when the Red Army occupied Estonia were only "in order to ensure the mutual security of the Soviet Union and Estonia" and is said to have ended on 19th June, when Special Envoy Zhdanov held talks with the President and Joh. Vares. At that point, Zhdanov invoked the illusion of a certain amount of legality, something which was to prove fatal to a number of Estonian Quislings.*

The fact that Estonia had been occupied and that the Vares government had appeared out of the blue went unnoticed in the rest of Europe. Western Europe had been shaken to the core. Paris had just fallen, Hitler was expecting to conquer Britain. But the United States was just beginning to understand the full extent of the tragedy in Europe. And Zhdanov did not have as free a hand as he would have liked. In order for the implementation of state terror, of the arrests and genocide, the Special Envoy required the deportation of inconvenient witnesses. But in Estonia, the embassies of, and journalists from, the democratic nations were still present. These had to be sent off as soon as possible, and the Special Envoy decided to simplify the stage directions.

On 5th July 1940, a decree was issued carrying the signatures of K. Päts and Joh. Vares for the formation of the Riigivolikogu (National Representative Assembly) and Riiginõukogu (Senate) to come into effect on 14th and 15th July of the same year, i.e., nine days later.

The law governing the Representative Assembly envisaged a period of thirty-five days between announcement and elections, and §99, Clause 2 of the Constitution stated: "The President of the Republic cannot by decree . . . make alterations to the election for the Representative Assembly, nor the composition of the Senate." So, the elections held under Zhdanov's stage directions were against the Constitution, thus null and void. As the sole author of the Constitution, the President knew this full well. As he, in his incarceration in his presidential residence had no chance to influence the course of political events, he chose to fight against the dictate of the occupying forces, using the only weapon he possessed: constitutional logic.

From a legal point of view, there was not, during the latter half of 1940, either a constitutionally elected Representative Assembly or Senate. The parliament of the Estonian Republic, i.e., the Riigikogu, we should remember, was in those days bicameral.

At this point, quotation marks could be put around this tale, but even falsifications contain a grain of truth in them. Let us read them. By way of manipulation of the electoral law, candidates had four days for the re-election of candidates. Constituency commissions were given the right to either accept or reject candidates. The Electoral Commission itself whose composition was a matter for the Representative Assembly, was made up principally of Communist Party members from Joh. Vares's government. The right of candidates to appeal at the Supreme Court was revoked. The secret ballot involved was manipulated in such a way that only a member of the Electoral Commission was allowed to put the ballot paper in the box. The unusual haste with which the election campaign was conducted was intended to weed out independent candidates, so that in each constituency only one candidate would stand, and that would be one from the electoral bloc of the "Estonian Working People's Union." This electoral bloc used a intimidation and terror as weapons against their opponents: anyone not voting for the bloc was an enemy of the people! Many electoral committees were under the watchful eye of the Red Army, and the members of the bloc were allowed to use the Red Army propaganda machine and resources. Despite the terror and cynical sidelining, independent candidates (seventy-eight of them) managed to register, i.e., in nearly all of the eighty constituencies. This was an unpleasant surprise for Zhdanov. The Prime Minister Joh. Vares was compelled, during the election campaign, to telegraph a further restriction on 9th July: all candidates outside of the "Estonian Working People's Union" were obliged to submit in writing their electoral manifesto by 14:00 hours on 10th July. Those not complying would be struck from the register. In order to insure fraud, the local electoral committee were banned from announcing results, which had instead to be handed over to the constituency commissions. The results were exactly as the Special Envoy had staged them: 92.9% of votes were for the EWPU bloc. This sorcery has been familiar to us now for more than fifty years ...

Let us add here that no Estonian political candidate ever requested an amendment of the Constitution, nor that Estonia should join the Soviet Union. The second chamber of the parliament, the Riiginõukogu or Senate, was never asked to sit. These were not legal elections and no legally constituted parliament emerged from them, one whose decisions would have enjoyed juridical validity. But in truth this was of no significance. Everything that followed was the cynical theater of Quislings. It is the goal that is important, a goal that Zhdanov set for himself, and this affects both the justification of Soviet foreign policy and international law. When the Red Army crossed the border into Estonia on 28th September 1939, in order to "secure" the pact, this was an excuse for occupation. The staging of the reading in the Estonian Constituent Assembly of the illegal declaration was an attempt to clothe the occupation of 17th June 1940 in the garb of a legal annexation. But international law does not recognize decisions taken under the duress of an ultimatum, under the threat of force being used by a foreign army. A few days after the events described here, the Under-Secretary of State of the United States of America, Sumner Welles, noted the following in his diary: "Devious processes whereunder the political independence and territorial integrity of the three small Baltic republics—Estonia, Latvia and Lithuania—were to be deliberately annihilated by one of their more powerful neighbors, have been rapidly drawn to their conclusion." (23.07.1940)

(Lennart Meri, in the daily newspaper *Noorte Hääl*, 1989)

BRECHT'S POEM № 7

I fled the tigers.
Lice fed off me—
I was being eaten up
By mediocrities.

"Den Tigern entrann ich—/ Die Wanzen nährte ich—/ Aufgefressen wurde ich / Von den Mittelmäßigen."

EXCERPTS FROM THE REPORT DRAWN UP BY THE HEAD OF THE BALTIC FLEET OF THE RED NAVY, VICE-ADMIRAL V.F. TRIBUTS

Page 171. being Directive 02622ss, dated 9th June 1940, where instructions are given to the Baltic Fleet of the Red Navy:

1. Capture the naval bases of Estonia and Latvia and all vessels out at sea, capture the Lithuanian navy.

2. Capture the Estonian and Latvian merchant navy and other vessels, cut off sea links between these nations.

3. Prepare and organize the dropping of parachutists in Paldiski and Tallinn; capture the port of Tallinn and the batteries located on the islands of Naissaar and Aegna; make preparations for the capture of the Suurupi battery from the mainland.

4. Close off the Gulf of Riga and maintain a blockade of the Estonian and Latvian coasts from the Gulf of Finland and the Baltic Sea, not allowing these countries to evacuate their national governments or remove military personnel or materiel.

5. Organize a permanent and reliable field security operation. In the Gulf of Finland from the direction of Finland; in Baltic Sea from the direction of Sweden and the south.

6. With the assistance of the Leningrad district forces stage an attack in the direction of Rakvere.

7. Fighters should prevent Estonian and Latvian airforce planes from flying to Finland and Sweden.

Page 172. Taking part in the operations: 120 boats, 1 battleship, 1 cruiser, 2 tugs, 1 gunboat, 7 destroyers, 5 guard boats, 5 base trawlers, 18 heavy trawlers, 17 submarines, 10 torpedo boats.

The air power belong to the Baltic Fleet of the Red Navy consists of:

8th Airforce Base – 7 squadrons of SB and DB-3s.
10th Airforce Base – 64 MBR-2 airplanes, SB.
10th Airforce Squadron – 64 MBR-2s.
73rd Airforce Squadron – 9 MBR-2s.
61st Fighter Base all planes and equipment from the naval base.

Page 173. The coastal defences and ground forces involved: units 11, 12 and 18 from the railroad gun batteries; (. . .) Coastal defences at the Paldiski, Liepāja, Hangö naval bases.

Page 174. The theater of operations has been divided up as follows:

1. The northern coast of the Gulf of Finland, from Bengtskär to Keri Island. The Hangö Naval Base commander Vice-Admiral S. F. Beloussov.

2. The southern coast of the Gulf of Finland from the Bay of Narva to Keri Island. Captain A. I. Matveyev from 4th Submarine Brigade, Second Division.

3. The area between and including Keri Island and the Soela Sound. Baltic Naval Commander, Vice-Admiral S. G. Kucherov.

4. The central Baltic Sea zone. Commander of Light Forces, Vice-Admiral F. I. Telpanov.

5. Liepāja Naval Base. Base Commander Vice-Admiral P. A. Trainin.

6. Swedish Eastern Coastal Area. Commander of 2nd Submarine Brigade, Captain Yakukin.

7. Gulf of Finland, western zone. Squadron Commander Vice-Admiral Nesvitski.

Page 176. During the period of the negotiations and after the treaty has been signed between the USSR and the governments of Estonia, Latvia and Lithuania, the following assignments have been carried out by the Baltic Fleet of the Red Navy:

A. The sea links between these nations have been cut off.

B.   Submarine brigades 1, 2, 3, and 4 coordinated with the lightly armed forces and took up their positions in the Baltic Sea, i.e., in the Gulf of Riga and Gulf of Finland in order to cut sea links and prevent ships from evacuating people and goods.

C.   The squadron consisting of the battleship *Oktyabrskaya Revolutsiya*, 3rd destroyer division and the guard division was stationed to the west of Naissaar Island in order to support the parachutists by providing cannon fire.

D.   The 21st bridge-building battalion started out from the Suurupi battery to the north of Klooga and was supported by the 12th railroad cannon division.

E.   The 1st naval infantry brigade consisting of battalions 1, 3, 5 and 6 was positioned on the vesels the Sibir, the Vtoraya Pyatiletka, the Elton, and moved from Koivisto to Paldiski.

F.   The Gulf of Riga had been shut off and the Gulf of Finland was under blockade. The Estonian and Latvian airforces were prevented from flying to Finland and Sweden.

G.   The descent of parachutists was organized and the operation carried out. Tallinn and the islands of Naissaar and Aegna have been captured.

On 14th June the ships and forces have achieved the following:

A.   Taken up their starting positions for operations.

B.   Made ready for the parachutists to be dropped (backed up by transport vessels, barges, patrol and torpedo boats) onto the islands of Naissaar and Aegna.

C.   Motorized battalion of riflemen and others brought to operation positions by the *Dniestr*, the *Storozhevoi* and the *Silnyi* to Paldiski from Kronstadt. Parachutists ready to descend on Tallinn. Aim: to capture the ports, the naval and merchant vessels and defend buildings.

Page 179b. During our blockade we have captured a total of fifty-two foreign vessels (from Latvia, Estonia, Finland and Sweden).

The agents and intelligence units were already in place on 4th June during the tense period then, and have provided valuable information.

Page 252. Because of the resistance of the merchant fleet, the cruiser *Kirov*, the gunboat, the *Minsk* and the destroyer, the *Lenin*, plus the submarine, the *S-1*, fired warning shots, whereupon the transport vessels came to a standstill.

Source: Estonian Soviet Socialist Republic Central Archive.
Excerpted from: Batch R-92, Number 2s, File 672. Pages 171–252.
Top Secret.

BRECHT'S POEM Nº 8

You, who shall rise from the flood
In which we have been submerged,
Think—
When you speak of our weaknesses,
And of the dark time
Out of which they emerged.

We went, changing our country more often than our shoes.
In the class war, in despair
When there was only injustice and no rebellion.
And we knew only too well:
Even the hatred of lowliness
Distorts your features.
Even anger against injustice
Makes the voice grow hoarse. Alas, we
Who wanted to lay the foundation for friendship
Could not ourselves befriend.

But you, when it has got to the point
When man can help his fellow man,
Think of us
With forbearance.

PART VII

LETTER TO AN ACTRESS

INTERLUDE 2

Dear Mrs Maria Avdyushko!

I would like to give you some idea of the whole matter at hand, and what will now be happening in future. I picked up a quote from someone whose name is John Murray, and is said to date back to 1839: People with a nervous disposition should not go to Finland. And a little later, in 1907, Sylvia Bergström has this to say: *Finland is veiled from the eyes of the globe-trotter*. Well, now there is a "globe-trotter" present, and he is on his way to Hella Wuolijoki's manor at Marlebäck. Brecht cannot in any way take Hella as his wife or mistress or whatever, but the three remaining women are there with Brecht on that white summer's night. They are in Finland. People sometimes say that Finns are alcoholics and interested in the occult. It is, after all, a northern country. Not so much its southern part, but it is a long and vertical country. That which happens up there does, however, manage to reach, say, Helsinki—at least in the sphere of the mind. You would do well to think of "Faust" here. Brecht was, after all, a German! Margareta says something of the sort in this work, about how "once in Thule the crown was worn / by a righteous king" . . .

"If you say that you, and presumably a lot of other people, have been saddened by my decline, then I can say so myself too." (Quote from the novel *Night of Souls* [1953] by Karl Ristikivi, where the novelist has written, in the middle of the book, a letter to one Mrs Agnes Rohumaa. In my case, I have chosen you as my Rohumaa.) So, now I have explained the formal nature of this letter.

They are at Marlebäck and it is still summer, the war is still raging—though the total war, the war to end all wars, has not yet begun.

As for Marlebäck, Hella's manor, I have to tell you in all truth that I have never been there. Not that it is particularly far from Helsinki. There is a railroad station at Kausala. Marlebäck is about 16 kilometers to the north.

I once had the opportunity to go, but I wasn't very interested at the time. Little has been preserved of what it was like in those days.

To you, who are a particularly likeable actress in my eyes, and with whom I have shared both good and bad times professionally over the years, I have this to confess: I had hoped to end this novel quite differently. I have now written what for me is quite a long work. Half of Brecht's sojourn in Finland still lies ahead. And what an eventful time it is! History plays its games, Brecht writes his plays, the women bicker and snarl at one another. Estonia becomes part of, or is made to become part of, the Soviet Union. Great importance has been put on Brecht's play *Puntila and His Hireling, Matti*. He wrote the script, based on a play by Hella. But since this play has recently been re-staged in Estonia by Katri Kaasik-Aaslav, I'm not going to go into great detail here. It's not the job of a novel to start analyzing plays! The place for a play is on stage, isn't it? Let the analysts analyze it when it's staged.

Actually, there is another theme, that I want to bring up—and, in fact, write about—and that is how Brecht and Hella cooperated, but nothing to do with a play. This is an epic, written by Hella and entitled *The Song of War*, which Brecht translated (along with his women) into German. But something irritates me about the work as a whole and exposes something that has been hidden. (Maybe I've exposed goodness knows what is already here. The majority of it with the author's permission, and citing my sources relatively precisely, though the majority of the authors are dead, and even history itself is dead at times.) You can say this much about *The Song of War*: in Brecht's opinion it was one of the most pacifist poems in the world. "It is a great work," is what Brecht said. And they set about translating it. Now it has been published in both Helsinki and Tallinn (in parallel text in both instances).

Hella wrote an afterword for *The Song of War*, translated by Brecht and Grete:

"[The Estonian nation] has its own songs from its twenty-year period of independence, which it has brought along as an offering when becoming part of the Soviet Union."

Neureuter mentions that "offering" (i.e., *Mitgift*) implies a dowry.

Wuolijoki has in this work brought out one important theme from Estonian folk poetry:

"Brother bright brother / if you go to war / or if you go to press the foe / this I will teach you: / Do not go to war at the front / nor go to war at the back—/ at the front the fire is red, at the back the smoke is blue! / Stay in the middle when going to war, / near to the ensign bearing the colors. / Those at the front will perish, / those at the back will fall, those in the middle will get home safely."

What is expressed here in its idiosyncratic way is something that Estonians still possess. Brecht also, of course, translated these lines. When he was completing his *Caucasian Chalk Circle* in 1944, a play about Georgia, another Soviet republic—although after the mention of kolkhozes in the prologue, the play then moves back a long way in history—Brecht adds this fragment as a Georgian folk song putting it into the mouth of Grushe (. . . *halt dich in des Krieges Mitten / halt dich an den Fahnenträger. / Die ersten sterben immer / die letzten werden auch getroffen / die in der Mitten kommen nach Hause*).

The same theme occurs in our national epic, the *Kalevipoeg*. Oskar Loorits has said that you can't vanquish anyone if you have that attitude of mind, and we haven't vanquished anyone either. But Professor Felix Oinas has pointed out that although he has found this motif in Ukrainian texts, it just doesn't fit in when put in the mouth of a Caucasian highlander. Hella was said at first to have been very peeved at this theft, but managed to forgive Brecht. But the greatest battle was yet to commence: in 1948, Brecht forgot Hella as being one of the authors of the *Puntila*. (But when Hella arrived in Berlin in 1949, she really liked the staging of the play; they made up, and Hella received her due share of the fee.)

I'll touch here briefly on parallelisms, something which are basic features of Estonian folk poetry.

At first glance, there appears to be no clear explanation why they occur. You get the impression that the bards just churn out the first thing that comes into their head.

In one of his articles, Jaan Kaplinski gives an example:

"Võttis puusta naista teha,
tammepuusta tahuda,
haavapuusta Annekesta,
maarjapuusta Marikesta,
kasepuusta Kaiekesta."

i.e.,

Wanted to make a woman out of wood,
hewn from oak she would be,
from aspen wood an Anneke,
from beech wood a Marike,
from birch wood Kaieke.

I chose this example because your name appears, as does that of your foster-father's second wife, i.e., the actress Kaie Mihkelson. But there is a serious question to be asked here: did the man that carved you out of wood (Kaie Mihkelson and for example your colleague, the City Theater actress Anne Reemann), did this man really make all three women at one time, and what did he then do with them? As you'll understand, I'm alluding here to Brecht's three women, as depicted in this novel which to my mind isn't at all about Brecht or Hella or even the three women, the three norns or weird sisters, is not about the three weavers of fate, nor about you or any other actress, who has ever played in our performance of *The Murderers* and *Norbert* (derived from Ibsen's Nora in *The Doll's House*).

But these allusions say little to anyone except ourselves, because who attends Estonian plays much anyway? Let us return to the parallelisms of folk poetry. Following Kaplinski's model, I'd like here to talk about Boolean algebra. Everything encloses something else. If you mention the word "berry" you can mean blackcurrants, blueberries or strawberries. Or other types of berry. We don't think of berries as being simply "berries" (the Estonian for berry—"mari"—this is another reference to you). But folk poetry doesn't just mention the word "berry" once, but lists lots of different types. It won't just mention that an "animal" is approaching but starts listing all kinds of creatures. It's always safer to say what's coming towards you, and there's certainly a difference, if it's a lion or an earthworm. But when we start writing poetry (and I'll try here to write a poem in the style of a Finno-Ugrian folk bard):

A lion came towards me,
The hare in the woods grew afraid.
The earthworm—it attacked,
the swallow—it swallowed.

Kaplinski has pointed out that the parallelism enhances the everyday reality of the poem. In fact, such a view of the world—this is now my own opinion—everything is one and the same. Everything is different and comparable to different things. Even human beings. This is a somewhat Buddhist idea, thought I'm no great expert in the field of Buddhism. Kaplinski has termed the parallelisms in the Finno-Ugrian *regivärss* type of poetry as disjunctive, and that it cannot, therefore, readily be translated into "more Western oriented" languages, as disjunction is natural to a mythological kind of thought.

Brecht is fascinated by poems containing paradoxical parallels (Golden smoke rises from the kitchen / from the yard silver smoke, / from the chimney gray smoke.—*Aus dem Kuche auf stieg der goldene Rauch, / aus dem Hofe aus der silberne Rauch, / aus dem Schornstein der Graurauch, aus dem Badestube der Rauch von den Wunden der Knechte*). Here we see a dialectical moment in Brecht's thinking. A certain diffuseness adds to the imagery, the singer is not pinning down everything exactly, is simply hinting at fantasy and memory, adding an epic breadth, seemingly addressing every listener individually, making the imagery all the clearer, looking at the object from various angles at the same time. This contains the alienation effect.

Maria, you understand what I'm driving at.

We have touched upon these subjects before—even if only in passing. For Brecht, that sort of duality or bipolarity existed, which could be expressed in such antitheses as reason versus instinct, providential self-preservation vs. romantic self-destruction, states of being vs. morality, facts vs. passion, agency vs. result, stupidity vs. spontaneity.

We Estonians, perhaps we do not want to have either of the poles of the dilemma.

But I don't know, am I an Estonian and what right do I have to talk in their name?

There are other explanations. Uku Masing refers to the fact that there is no future tense of a verb in the Estonian language: "Since we have no future, we have no time, philosophically speaking, to either the time to move or the need to attack. Because the future and the movement of objects are in very close proximity. We presuppose that the future is the present, and since we do so, we live in the eternal present (. . .)."

It's quite possible that ancient Estonian folk poetry was acted out in a mythological, not a historical space. Everything occurs at one and the same time and recurs, does not develop in any direction in the way an arrow would. In the *regilaul* songs, not a word is used to describe historical events. Everything tends to happen simultaneously:

"Läksin metsa kõndimaie / pühapäeva hommikulla, / äripäeva õhtaalla, / laupäeva lõuneella."

(I went for a walk in the woods / in the morning on Sundays / in the evening on workdays / in the afternoon on Saturdays.)

People don't walk together all the time, they just walk. Period.

Brecht, who lies buried along with Hegel in the same graveyard, perceived the world differently, as something that develops.

For example, he enjoyed dialectical thoughts.

A couple of random quotes:

"Without dictatorship (without suppressing the peasantry who do not support industrialization) you cannot create a situation where dictatorship is superfluous." Or: "There is no freedom at present in Russia, only liberation." Or: "The *Ding an sich* (thing in itself) is immeasurably inconvenient." Or, more about dictatorship: "You have to support dictatorships that tear up their own roots." Or, the idea that popped up from somewhere that "causality (the interplay of cause and effect) should only be acknowledged where it can be detected."

And so (according to Uku Masing): "To those whose feelings have been corrupted by European modes of thought and feeling, our people appear boring and sleepy, people whose soul consists of a hum of monotony defined by the boundaries of the body. What can this have in common with a person whose soul always strives to escape the body, not to disperse like mist or smoke, but try find the direct road to infinity?"

In reality, this is all melancholy or nostalgia. Melancholy has to be a manly trait. (According to Seppo Knuuttila, clergymen, professors and schoolteachers are melancholic, as they know everything and feel the grief of losing everything; their melancholy is more directed in time than in space.)

Greetings,

Mati

PART VIII

LATE SUMMER

1940

RHEUMATISM

Brecht has rheumatism. He's trying to cure himself at Hella's manor. How does he do it?

He goes into the woods.

It's a hot summer and the woods are full of the fragrance of pine trees.

Brecht finds an anthill. In it, and around it, there's a special kind of life that is even dialectical.

On a sudden impulse, he grabs a large sack, which he just happens to have with him. He wants to take the anthill with him, as he has been taught to do at the Marlebäck manor. Not by Hella. But by some war refugee. But where can he find a shovel?

At he very last moment, when Brecht has already been seized by despair, he has a brainwave, and the thought strikes him that he has brought a spade with him. A small one, but it's better than nothing. You can't really imagine someone stuffing a whole anthill into a sack with his bare hands.

And that is why Brecht has the spade with him! He shovels the anthill into the sack.

Then he puts the sack over his shoulder. It's moving slightly. The mass of ants is moving around in the sack. Brecht doesn't make a big thing of it, as movement is a sign of development, and development isn't a bad thing—with the exception of such occasions where development enhances the power of the ruling classes and powers that be.

On Hella's instructions, he pours out the anthill into his bathtub, which is full of hot water. The pine needles, the ants and their eggs. Brecht is sitting in the bathtub. They all come and stand around the bathtub: Hella, Helene, Grete, even Ruth who nobody has managed to throw out yet. Brecht stares out from the depths of the bathtub and the steam. The women, as if they are the guardians of hell. This thought is caused by the steam which wafts up: when the water cools, someone adds a little warm water.

Afterwards, Brecht feels some relief.

"Women, do this again for me," he says in a very serious voice and promises to go off into the woods once more to find an anthill so that he can boil himself again, if necessary.

Later, he forgets his promise.

He's begun to recover.

MUSHROOMS

Helene often goes mushroom-picking. She doesn't salt the Field Mushrooms, but lets them simmer in butter and lemon juice. She marinates the Yellow Milk Caps too (*Lactarius scrobiculatus*). Brecht feels they ought to pick other types of mushroom as well. Surely not only Agarics and the Penny-Bun Boletus (*Boletus edulis*) are edible!

Other types are no doubt are just as suitable.

Brecht writes the following tirade in his *Puntila* play: "Have you salted any mushrooms yet this year?—I don't salt them, I dry them.—How do you do that, then?—I cut them into large chunks, thread them onto a piece of string, and hang them out in the sunshine. (. . .) And I don't salt the Field Mushrooms either, just let them simmer in lemon juice and butter. They have to be as small as buttons. I marinate the Milk Caps.—Milk Caps are not exactly delicate little mushrooms, but they do taste nice. In general, Field Mushrooms and the Boletus are popular.—First, I peel them.—You don't really have to, all you have to do is get rid of the dirt.—How long do you let them simmer for? —I just bring them to a boil.—And you add salt right away?—Right at the start."

Early morning. The dew is still on the grass. Delicate bunches of undergrowth are plaited together. When you go though them, you can trip up. Brecht is walking close on Helene's heels, gathering mushrooms. He is picking both Field Mushrooms and Boletus type mushrooms. But dialectically speaking, it's not possible to divide the world of mushrooms into only two types: white ones (Field Mushrooms) and red ones (Boletus)! Brecht is also picking Russula mushrooms and even Paxillus ones. These last ones need a good deal of boiling. West European people are usually quite surprised when they hear that in Eastern Europe people eat *Paxillus involutus*. This is a poisonous toadstool, West Europeans will cry. But they simply aren't familiar with parboiling—this idea is quite alien to West Europeans. With regard to meat, this is different. While a number of snobs may eat raw meat (*bœuf à la tatar—steak tartar*), the majority of West Europeans think that meat has either to be boiled or fried. Strange that such a mental muddle is present in the case of mushrooms and meat.

Brecht starts to pick Inky Cap (*Coprinus atramentarius*) on a dung heap.

Night has fallen. Brecht is boiling mushrooms. The air is full of the compounds to be found in mushrooms, especially milky sap, bitter almonds and carbide, whose smells constitute the bouquet of various types of mushroom. The mushroom water in the pan is frothing. Brecht is watching this and thinking: do I actually exist? Various other gnoseological or ontological questions enter his head, but they are not important. Brecht refuses to think anymore about them. We *do*, all the more!

Is he struck by a sudden thought? An impulse? Why doesn't the thought arise? It always arises. With Brecht as well. The thought of picking mushrooms and going into the tent with Berlau. He takes only the Inky Caps out of the boiler. They have collapsed during boiling, but are still inky and proud nonetheless. He takes out ten Inky Caps, then opens the cupboard and takes out a bottle of wine. He wraps up the mushrooms in a piece of newspaper, slips the bottle of wine into his inside pocket.

Then he plunges into the night, wades through the grass, almost falls into a ditch, but doesn't, and lo—there is the tent, and in it Red Ruth!

When Brecht has had sex with Berlau, he unwraps the Inky Caps and brings out the wine. They eat the mushrooms. They are happy.

Unexpectedly, Brecht's face goes bright red. The same happens to Berlau. A minute or two passes and they turn violet. Completely violet. Two violet-colored people! It's as if they're at a masked ball! Brecht has always greatly appreciated the theater of masks. Brecht doesn't like a full mask. He likes a half-mask. But a mask, nevertheless. He who wears a mask cannot say *Me*. He is no longer egotistical and egocentric, he is something else, he is objective, he is functional, not emotional. Brecht's face, his violet colored face, is now a mask. A violet mask.

This can naturally be blamed on the Inky Cap.

Mushrooms are closely associated with the theater, because the great Russian actor Shchepkin went gathering mushrooms at night with a lantern. One Russian eccentric even thought that Lenin was a mushroom—this was proven by his appearance standing on an armored car (1917). It's possible that the photo of Lenin and the armored car beneath him reminded people of mushrooms and the spiny construction of mushrooms.

Be that as it may, but—ignoring the fact that the gills of mushrooms can be compared with the metro, the telephone network and even with Lenin, it is clear in our work here that Brecht ate the Inky Caps and drank wine with them.

And that is why his face has now become an oriental mask.

Brecht, who greatly appreciates masks, especially oriental ones, and who is constantly looking for links with oriental theater, because they lack that damned empathy technique of method theater, has now himself become like a mask. This is caused by the coprine in the Inky Cap. It is a poison that only affects people in conjunction with alcohol.

The poisoning is not life-threatening, it is, in the first instance, theatrical.

"You look like a Chinaman with your blue face," says Ruth.

"I know, that's the effect I'm aiming at," says Brecht, putting on airs.

"But the color's already fading."

"It is only but a temporary effect."

Brecht gets to his feet.

"Sit here a while, I'm going for a stroll."

He goes under the trees where it's dark.

They are fir trees, and under them no grass grows.

Brecht feels something brush against his back. He looks round. There's no one there. Did someone throw a fir cone at me? thinks Brecht, or maybe it was a squirrel. Or a lynx. He listens. The forest is silent.

In front of him, a dense alder grove.

Couldn't have come from there.

Brecht turns to his right. He goes downhill and feels the coolness of the mist. Brecht ends up in the long grass. The mist thickens. Best to turn back, thinks Brecht, otherwise I'll lose my way. Or should I go there "where boundlessly (*ilman reunalta*) the blue Terimäki hill arises"?

But then someone hails him.

A man is standing there, half his body shrouded in mist.

"My name is Aapo," is what he says, "do you want to listen to what I have to tell?"

Brecht can't speak Finnish, but he manages somehow to understand. First of all, the fact that the man wants to say something, maybe he understands literally—Brecht can't really understand, but somehow he does.

"Speak," says Brecht, half of his own body also shrouded in mist.

"It's an old story," warns Aapo.

"Never mind, tell it anyway."

"And you'll listen?"

"Of course I'll listen."

Aapo says that it was a mild summer's evening and that the Youth was sitting on the grass. What youth? asks Brecht. A youth that was cuddling a dear young maiden who was leaning on his chest like a glowing rose. I understand, says Brecht. Aapo continues: the young man had to travel away. Like me, I have to constantly travel from one country to the next, to escape the revenge of What's-His-Name. The young man promised to be away for a hundred days. The maiden is said to have replied: "The sun, as it sets, does not cast so loving a farewell glance on its lover on leaving, nor does the rising sun shine so beautifully, as do my eyes, when I rush towards you. And what fills my mind over the length of the day, but it's the thought of you as I walk with you in the hazy world of dreams." Thus spoke the young maiden according to Aapo. Brecht asks: but does the young man reply? Aapo says that indeed he does. The young man is supposed to have said that you speak beautifully, but why does the soul have presentiments? The young man is said to have sworn to be eternally faithful to the maiden. That's what they did: swore to be faithful for all eternity before God and heaven. And holding their breath, the woods and hills listened to their words, Aapo added. Then the young man left, but thought all the while about his beloved. But the maiden went in the opposite direction. Then she met a prince. OK, thinks Brecht, class relations are tough and amoral even in northern climes. Aapo says that the prince has a purplish red belt. Yes, a purple belt was what this prince or sovereign had, but who are you, the teller of the tale? I am Aapo, replies Aapo. Is the name not enough? If it's not, I can add the fact that I'm the twin brother of Tuomas. May I go on? asks Aapo. Brecht nods. It's getting dark in one way or another. The gaze of the prince radiates love and he has sworn to bring boundless happiness to the young maiden. He has a great deal of money and many jewels.

He promises to take the maiden to his castle. The maiden is surprised and a curious confusion fills her mind. That's exactly how a woman is bought in capitalist society, however romantic she thinks the whole matter is. "When you raise your tail, lower your eyes, / you teach us every time—/ give us to eat first of all, / then say, for that is how what follows occurs." Yes—"however you justify, however you twist—/ food comes first, then morality." Aapo says that the maiden is supposed to have turned to the man, shading her face as from the blazing sun. And all of a sudden, she leaned against the chest of the prince. The prince snatched up his sword and broke into a run. The maiden is supposed, as if in a fever, to have rested her hand on his supporting arm. They crossed steep hills and deep dales as the woods grew ever darker around them. And now, as Aapo's tale progresses, it grows ever darker. For that reason, Aapo doesn't see that Brecht's face is growing ever redder and ever more like an oriental mask. Anyway, then high mountains and dark caves came into view. And something ghastly happened! The man in the royal coat changed suddenly into a hideous devil: he sprouted horns, his real self was revealed, the mask fell away, he had been exposed, rough bristles grew on his neck and the poor maiden felt his sharp claws against her cheek. And the maiden is said to have cried out, struggled and writhed, but all in vain. The Devil roared like a lion (*jalopeura*) and dragged the maiden into his cave and drank her blood. But then a miracle occurred! The maiden didn't die! What did it matter that she was now bloodless and as white as snow. Even the Devil grew amazed, then thought that he would stay with her. In the daytime, the maiden sat on the summit of a mountain like a snow-white statue, her arms across her chest, her head bowed. She didn't complain, nor get up, nor did sighs oppress her praying breast. She's said to have sat there for a hundred years. Then suddenly a mysterious light descends from heaven, and when this light was quite close to her, the maiden understood that it was neither a fallen star nor a comet, but the youth, his face transfigured, sword in hand. The heart of the maiden began to beat vigorously as she had seen that it was her betrothed. But why was he carrying a sword, if he was coming from heaven? Do you want to kill me? asked the young maiden. Brecht has always been interesting in the killing of women. He had, admittedly, never actually killed any himself, but you never know when such impulses and motifs might come in handy. Aapo then went on to tell that the betrothed kissed the bride and this brought the blood back to her body. And, well, then morning broke. The birds twittered in the spruce trees on the hillside and a fiery ray of sunshine came from the northeast. The evil Devil had appeared. But the youth killed the Devil: his sword pierced the Devil's chest, whereupon the Devil's black blood spurted forth, ridding the world of this hideous monster. Thereafter, the young maiden and her betrothed vanished, as if in a puff of blue smoke.

While this tale was being related, they had managed to walk quite some distance. Suddenly, Aapo's tale came to an abrupt end. Nothing could be seen to warrant this. Just the soughing above them, around them, even beneath them. Everything was in pitch darkness.

"Stretch out your hand," said Aapo.

Brecht does as requested. He stretches out his left hand and touches a plank wall.

He pushes against it. It moves. He can hear a creaking sound, it's a door. Fumbling before him, Brecht enters. He doesn't know whether Aapo is following behind, or is leading the way.

Brecht shuts his eyes, what does it matter that it's as dark in here as outside?

They sleep a while.

Now a pleasant warmth is coming from the stove, a little light too. But the soughing outside has now become a howling sound.

"The northern wind is gusting from the star-glittering heavens," whispers Aapo, who is lying there, "and the pale moon looks down smugly, as if to say, what are you doing so far up in the north?"

Then an exhausted Brecht falls asleep once more.

Suddenly a rustling sound can be heard as if someone is moving. Brecht asks:

"Are you all awake?"

"We are," replies a voice, which does not sound like Aapo's.

Brecht thinks for a while.

"How many of you are there?" he then asks.

"Seven," replies yet another voice.

Brecht can make them out against the stars. They're standing in a clump against the window.

He wonders why they're not asleep, but are looking out of the window.

"Come and look for yourself!"

"Who are you?"

"It is I, Simeon."

"Why are you standing there by the window, Simeon?"

Simeon says that "it" only has one eye that glitters like that of a wolf in the darkness. Brecht goes over to the window. There's something there. Three sisters? A unicorn? Ghastly! Aapo too says: ghastly! From a corner of the room emerges Juhani, yawning. Brecht is startled, and asks abruptly: who are you? Juhani doesn't reply. From the darkness appear Lauri and Eero, finally Timo too.

There's some kind of creature outside. Brecht dare not go right up to the window. Maybe Hitler (or even Stalin) has turned up again.

Lauri suggests someone get some matches and "tenderize the adversary."

Finally, the adversaries (or adversary) move off.

None of them can see it anymore. But they go and have a look now and again, just in case. Now Brecht too goes right up to the window.

There's nothing out there in the night that could possibly be frightening.

The wind too has dropped, as if it has anticipated the creatures (or whatever they were) and their arrival, and disappears along with them.

But a faint soughing can still be heard.

"Tell me a story, Simeon," says someone, a short while later.

Simeon begins to tell his tale. He tells of some kind of devil or demon. It's about his height, but can change into anything it wants. Sometimes it's a whirlwind. It moves with a rush through the thickets. At that point Simeon always cries out. Later on, the creature wanders over ground covered with stones and thistles. It keeps changing, now one way, now the other. It sometimes romps in front of Simeon like a small mewing kitten, sometimes it towers like a tall man, reaching up to the clouds. Soon Simeon's own tale gets tangled and he cries: Oh, my sinful tongue can no longer tell this story!

It's clear that Simeon has no intention of continuing to tell his story.

This displeases Brecht.

"You ought to carry on telling your tale," shouts Brecht, "so what if the critical attitude will seem useless to some! That's because those reactionaries can't manage anything in their own countries! Just get on with your story!"

Juhani also supports Brecht, though he is unable to express himself clearly. But the idea is this: principally, you have to deal with the behavior of large groups of people, and laws can only be valid for the movements of large groups of people.

Brecht agrees, but adds that this should also be done in the case of individuals.

But Juhani changes topic and asks Simeon:

"Is walking on the Moon with the Devil and up in some tower too the right way of going about things?"

"And in a tower made of boot leather as well," Timo adds.

Simeon doesn't reply. His eyes are ablaze when they meet those of his companions. On all fours like an animal, he goes off to his corner and rolls up into a ball.

The sun rises. When they open the door, cool air enters the room. It's completely silent, no soughing of the trees. Maybe one single bird or something similar.

No one is in the mood for talking.

Each one puts on his own bast shoes and ties the laces. Without anyone taking the lead, they all walk half a verst through the thickets of fir trees and begin to go uphill. Because of the undergrowth, it's impossible to see how high they have climbed, but it soon turns out that the hill is a pretty low one. It's in fact a very large boulder, the height of two men, and as long as four.

Atop the Great Giant's Stone, Aapo tells the history of this boulder. A proud elk (this time not a *jalopeura* but a *peura jalo*) began to cry when a hunter was about to shoot it, but the hunter had no mercy and shot it nonetheless. But the grim giant of Pärapõhja somehow knew, obviously by telepathy, that something was amiss with his proud, golden elk. When Brecht asks, as if in passing, what the giant then did, Aapo explains that the giant got very angry, pulled a huge rectangular stone from out of the castle wall and threw it at the bowman. "The remains of the bowman lie under the boulder, on which we now are sitting," says Aapo finally.

The rustle of branches makes the men look round. The thicket is full of eyes.

On every side.

How did these men suddenly end up on the stone!

"What creatures are these?" asks Brecht, already standing on the boulder.

"They are *jalopeuras*," replies Simeon, grimly.

The lion or jalopeura (i.e., large elk) in Finnish is a word that Mikael Agricola invented. The lion is an impressive elk. In the Estonian language, there is the word "lõukoer" (i.e. jaw-dog), a dog with a large jaw, something a good deal smaller than a noble elk. But what the hell!

The jalopeura is a lion and a deer at one and the same time, and it also means Leo, the sign of the horoscope. "Behold he shall come up like a lion from the swelling of the Jordan, against the habitation of the strong: but I will suddenly make him run away from her: and who is the chosen man that I may appoint over her?" (Jeremiah 49:19).

This lion or jaw-dog or jalopeura *could very well be the Devil. In the olden days, the Finns would sometimes say:* mine macan Sieuni cansa Jalopeurain seas *(i.e., I am sleeping with my soul amongst bad people).*

Juhani makes a sign to indicate how good it was that the giant cast the stone here.

With eyes ablaze the jaw-dogs watch Brecht and his seven brothers. They discuss whether anyone ought to get a little sleep meanwhile. But Brecht thinks that a man befuddled by sleep could become the prey of the jaw-dogs. Two have to stay awake at any one time.

To keep up their spirits, Simeon tells yet another tale, about what happened with the Devil in the leather tower.

It was like this. The Devil whistled, and a pair of leather trumpets pressed their way through the wall. They began to roar hideously, like those same savage jaw-dogs that had just laid siege to the men in the woodland thicket. Someone had started driving smoke, pitch fumes and sulfurous gases out of their jaws. Both Simeon and his companion the Devil had begun to cough. Simeon was still talking about the leather tower, which was swaying and slowly beginning to collapse. Simeon himself began to sway.

Let us not forget for a moment that the whole of the dialogue taking place on the boulder was being observed by a ring of voracious jaw-dogs. The conversation did therefore sound as a way of keeping up good spirits.

Brecht thinks that Simeon's story is strange, idiosyncratic, and scary at one and the same time. People have said that when the Moon is created the New Moon holds the Old Moon in its embrace for one whole night. The wavering of fearful people announces the new age, adds Brecht, in which not only brothers but hundreds of jaw-dogs are listening. All that is to be done is assign the Still and Already. The class struggle, the old and new discussion—all of these rage in the innards of every individual.

Juhani begins to actually weep at this story. But he soon pulls himself together. In fact, Brecht begins to yell at Juhani to stop crying. He says that Juhani must not try to captivate anyone! He should not try to entice people from everyday life into higher spheres, and says that feudal relations must be presented simply. This final sentence determines everything.

The men take their guns, which they had wisely taken along that morning.

The Giant's Stone is hidden in swathes of smoke, but death is flashing and crashing on all sides in the form of the pride of jaw-dogs. And now here, now there, a large-maned beast roars. They fall, shot through, and pant out their last breath of their powerful lives.

One lion, whose brain is pierced by a bullet, falls suddenly silent, struggles but briefly, stretches out its strong paws; and there and then it expires and blackish-red blood spurts into the air in an arc out of the wound, then falls to the ground. But a lion that is wounded in the chest, but whose heart Brecht and the seven brothers didn't manage to hit, rages on, staggering here and there, bloody among those of its companions that bullets have not yet struck, until, finally, it does a somersault down into the heather and falls there, gurgling, its paws waving in the air.

Aare Kinnunen considers that the boulder on which the brothers defended them-
selves against the lions is like an island under siege—both social relations and na-
ture itself protect it from the outside world, although these may be two altogether
different things, but at one particular moment they fuse.

And anxious haste, hurly-burly and a horrible scrimmage arises among the re-maining lions, when they smell the steaming blood of their companions and they attack wildly as one fell pack. Their tongues hanging out, their eyes rolling and filling the forest with their roaring, something that cannot yet frighten Bre-cht—he knows only too well from whom he is fleeing—and so, with a hideous roar the lions kick dead wood and turf up over their backs. But on the boulder, in the cloud of smoke, stand Brecht and his brothers like pale phantoms, load-ing, firing by turns, and at the same time the lions are bounding forward. The guns flash, crack.

But Brecht feels that the lightning flashes, and the thunder on high rumbles all the louder, as the thunderstorm rushes ever onward in the mountains of cloud.

Brecht thinks up a poem: "A man is dying deep in the forest, where the dark-ness roars and sways. Nails in the roots of the trees, there the man is dying."

Then the smoke and grim darkness envelops the boulder. Through this dark-ness the roar of the lions can be heard. Brecht suddenly cries out the words of a poem that came to mind right there: "I cannot die in darkness, / when there is lightning above, / when there is the blue sky above!"

As if in answer to this, a dull rumble can be heard, the roar of the lions, the howl-ing of the dogs, the reports of the guns and the storm in the tops of the fir trees.

Through all this Lauri has been sleeping. He now wakes up when there is a great crash above his head. Grim thoughts enter his head and he says: "This is how you enter the fiery stove of hell, this is how it is, when we go thither—what more can save you?" He has spoken, and now he rolls over, and falls once again into a deep sleep.

It seems as if this Giant's Stone where Brecht has just been is swathed like a proud castle or palace, he does not know what was done, what was said, yes— this Giant's Stone is wrapped in a mantle of smoke, and reiterates the language of lightning.

Around it flows blood and they are writhing by the hundreds, their paws in the air. The thunder roars, from where a fierce battle had broken out, water is poured down onto the seething forest. The forest groans through its beard of moss.

Brecht and the Seven Brothers stand there, surveying the rich slice of death there before them; and like so many steaming rivulets, the blood flows forth beneath Brecht's gaze, down from the Giant's Stone in all directions.

When the rain ceases to fall, Brecht says: let's go and have a look. And they step out of the shadows into the light. Brecht silently bares his teeth, likewise the Seven Brothers: they walk around the lions, look at them with disgust, shaking their heads from time to time.

Brecht says that there's meat to be had here. And Timo replies that there is blood here too.

Juhani gives a meaningful cough and all of a sudden pictures an incident that is said to be about to occur around 1993. Brecht has never noticed that Juhani has the gift of divination. He is pretty skeptical about soothsaying. But on this occasion, he does want to know what older brother Juhani is foretelling.

Juhani says that he feels that before the century is out, a great lone lion will cross the eastern border.

And so it came to pass that in Ruokolahti, Finland, in 1992, a man saw a lion in the forest. A short while later, what could have been lion's paw prints were discovered, ones coming from the east. The Somali refugees Abdi Mohamed and Osman Ismail Mohamed told the Finnish tabloid Iltasanomat *that lions do not eat human flesh, since it smells bad. But a lion will, of course, eat a human being if it is really hungry.*

Osmo Pekonen also refers to a strange incident: in 1992 a creature was resembling an abominable snowman or Martian was spotted. It was said that ABCs, i.e., Alien Big Cats, had arrived in England. Businessmen known for their level-headedness and others had seen what looked like huge cats in broad daylight. This had happened in Surrey, on Exmoor and in the Peak District.

A Finn, a 41-year-old forest ranger, saw the eyes of a lioness in the short grass. He snuck away and didn't dare to look over his shoulder. He got lost. This gave rise to yet another question put by Pekonen: why did the ranger think that this had to be a lioness? He referred to the Estonian-Finnish writer Aino Kallas, who was in the habit of talking about the dying Eros.

The Estonian writer Jaan Kaplinski once said to me in a private conversation that Brecht's poetry reminds him of the tread of a lion's paw.

The police never did find the lion.

HOME AGAIN

Hella says afterwards that various things have happened to her. "I was in the forest once," she says, "and all of a sudden right in front of me is a great big—what looks like a hen or turkey, some sort of *ilmestys*, i.e., a manifestation of something, its wings stretched out, waddling, kihkadi-kahkadi, kihkadi-kahkadi, with a huge load of hay behind it and then—whoosh! It was quite foggy, and I didn't manage to get a good look at it, but there it was burbling along . . . You can imagine how I broke into a run and came home quite out of breath!"

"Sometimes, dead children cry in the forest," adds a farmhand sitting nearby. "They have no souls and they yell as if from the bottom of a well."

"Those are hoopoes," a servant girl manages to say, someone whom Brecht has somehow suspected of following him, right through the summer—a secret agent, no doubt.

"They're bitterns, birds that boom in the reeds, *Botaurus stellaris*," says Hella, trying to pour oil on troubled waters. "Lost bones have got nothing to do with it."

The farmhand nods.

"What's called a 'lost bone' is the thighbone of a human being, which has lain for seven years in water and now appears to jump up emitting a kind of bloody froth. There's one in the stream over there, a couple of versts from here."

"It's not a lost bone, but a bittern," says Hella didactically. "For us Estonians, the bittern is a kind of Pontius Pilate. When he had given the order to have Christ crucified, they drove Pilate out to the banks of the Danube and put him into a deep mash tun. There Pilate was turned into a bittern."

Grete is writing this all down.

"Who cares whether it's a lost bone or a bittern," says the farmhand, and spits, "all kinds of things happen round here. One evening, kitchen maids saw the heads of children on fence posts. Then on the floor of the byre a human head was seen rolling along like a gray ball. I myself saw some kind of white mass two nights in a row."

CLASSICAL STYLE

Brecht is thinking about brevity.

If you leave out enough, then that one word, for instance "night" in the phrase "when night falls," will begin to reverberate. It will correspond exactly to what the reader is imagining, become its equivalent. Because inflation is the death of every economy. Words can drop their retinue and meet one another with the greatest dignity imaginable. And it is quite wrong to think that classics in this instance have forgotten about the reader, quite the opposite—they respect the reader.

Hella gives me little omelettes made from calves' blood, to which a little thyme and sour cream is added. She calls them blood cakes (*Blutkloss*).

The scene on the boulder, which the animals have sieged, is out of control, Brecht is thinking. I feel that I became too emotional there, lost my critical faculty and self-control.

Brecht doesn't really want to eat blood cakes. He wants to go to the sauna. Hella says that Finnish soldiers would build saunas even on the front line.

Puntila *is beginning to take shape. At first, Hella is very surprised. She thinks the work lacks drama and humor. All the characters talk in the same way. Brecht nevertheless tries to allay her fears. (Later, they send the play to a competition, but it is awarded no prizes.)*

THE WORKER

Brecht is watching through the window how a worker is hewing a block of wood.

He feels that the worker's rhythm is perfect and very light at one and the same time. When his left hand is holding the log upright, his right arm is already rising, axe in hand; it chops through the log like butter. When two blows are needed, e.g., when there is a knot in the wood, the man strikes, without needing to aim, into the first cut. When the log falls over, the man no longer rights it: he picks it up later, or ignores it. At any rate, his hand has already seized a new log.

What Brecht likes especially is that the man can't see himself at work: he works in a dark shed, and Brecht can clearly see his hands at work, but not his face.

Hella says:

"I'll always remember that summer. Just think: peace reigned, the oats were rustling in the fields at Marlebäck . . . the scent of clover in the meadow, and the lavender and other herbs on the banks of the stream, with the evening the sky arched over the silken blue of the River Kymi, like a huge snail's shell, and the evening wind kissed us with its pastel-colored sighs, when we met in my room, into which the breath of the Kymi wafted over the verandah, and in through the windows . . ."

*Later, in prison, Hella writes her famous description of evening meetings, which also appear in several works by other authors (for instance, Peter Weiss's The Æs-*thetics of Resistance*). Someone, who is speaking of Brecht, cannot resist describing how Brecht is smoking his eternal evening cigar in his rocking chair on the veran-dah, while Helene is pouring the coffee from a silver coffee jug, Berlau is sitting, pretty as a picture, under a copy of a Titian, smiling her Mona Lisa smile at Brecht, and behind a clump of roses, Grete is stenographing away as Brecht speaks and the mistress of the house is lounging comfortably on the corner of the divan. And when Brecht has finished relating his theater passages, they take a short break, and Helene sings some Eisler songs. And sometimes things remain like this till the first rays of dawn.*

But fall is approaching. The trees are beginning to turn yellow. It rains a lot, on several occasions the cattle are left inside in the byre.

Then it emerges that Hella is forced to sell Marlebäck, as there is a gasoline shortage, so that taking the milk to market takes four hours by horse instead of one hour by truck; and there is also a shortage of workers.

In 1965, journalist Manfred Gebhardt of the German periodical Das Magazin *gave a romantic description of his return to town. "None of the blessings of the Häme province, its sky, its rivers, the beauty of its inhabitants and forests could keep him back from returning to Helsinki to be among the workers there, stand elbow to elbow with men on the street as they talked with him—so what if misfortune and shortages were part of that life."*

RAIN AND SUNSET

It is drizzling today—the air is soaked through. Especially when someone turns their face up to the sky and closes their eyes, their brow grows wet. There are no large drops. Only under the old fir tree can you feel how the air has condensed, and a few large drops fall from the branches. In the west, a single, clear bloody streak of sky can be seen, a kind of knife wound over the forests of Finland; but the east is sinking into blue darkness.

Brecht comes back from the forest before it has grown pitch dark; he dislikes extremes or excess. Irrational phenomena sap his last strength, adventures are concentrated, but luxurious! Now Brecht is standing in the long grass, behind him the primeval forest, before him the low alder bushes and the lights of Marlebäck have already been lit. Hella is making food, Grete has hidden her face in her rough pillow and Ruth is nervously rubbing together her slender, slightly bony fingers. They are all people and night will soon hide them, but around them, in their immediate vicinity, they have lit small lamps. A twinkling light is reflected in their faces, a little by the walls as well, but it does not reach far—the damp air reflects nothing, although it could in theory.

A silent breeze is stirring something or someone in the darkness, everything looks the same. Yes, this is no longer *ilma* it is *sää*, as you can no longer ignore it (*sää* is the Finnish for weather in the regular sense, but also a rule or law, and the latter of these two cannot be blithely ignored forever).

Brecht is walking across the water meadow. The breeze blows through the long grass, comes and brushes Brecht, then goes off into the forest. Brecht glances over his shoulder, and is convinced that the wind is brushing against no other living being.

Now the last bloodline must also end.

WHERE HELP IS NEAREST AT HAND . . .

Under the eaves of the shed, a man is smoking a cigar. Brecht wants to skirt round him with a nod, but the man, in the darkness, addresses Brecht in the English language. Brecht understands that this must be one of Hella's guests, one who has been here before.

Brecht takes a cigar from his breast pocket and Terentyev offers him a light. The cigar hasn't become damp. They stand there under the eaves and watch how the landscape finally fades into night.

When Brecht meets this man in August 1945, by this time in Santa Monica (California), where he (now called Yakovlev) is being employed by Julius Rosenberg in order to pass on information about the atomic bomb program, he asks whether Brecht wouldn't perhaps be interested in seeing Berlin again. Brecht is interested. The war has just ended and the situation in Germany is very confused. Yakovlev says that he will have to be patient for a while, but that a trip home would be possible. Brecht understands the realities of the matter. Yakovlev says that he is prepared to help Brecht. Brecht writes to Ruth in New York about it: "You know, I will make no plans without you," swears Brecht, adding: "e.p.e.p.d."

As the automobile turns out onto the highway from Marlebäck in the darkness of late autumn, and drives through the forest, Brecht spots a bonfire at the edge of the road. Around the blazing bonfire dog-snouts are sitting. These creatures occur when a woman has intercourse with a dog, and now they are sitting around the fire playing cards. Brecht says nothing to the others. But he keeps looking out of the back window of the car, until the falling dusk swallows them up.

PART IX

EPILOGUE

At the end of that summer, in Helsinki again, Hella and Brecht wrote their *Puntila* together, after which they started to quarrel, but made up again.

When Brecht had already left quite some while before, the female parachutist Kerttu Nuorteva happened to be sent from Russia in order to visit Hella. The young woman was caught and admitted everything. Nuorteva went back to the Soviet Union—that could be arranged—and she spent some time in prison there, then in a mental hospital. Then she worked in Karaganda as a construction engineer and died in 1963 of meningitis.

Hella was also caught. In 1943, she was sentenced to death for espionage, then the sentence was commuted to life in prison. She was freed in 1945 (partly because of pressure from the Allies). Until 1949, she worked as the Director-General of Finnish Radio, then as a member of the Finnish parliament, the Eduskunta. She died on 2nd February 1954. She left behind a mass of plays, which are staged to this day—even beyond the Finnish cultural orbit—and many books of memoirs.

We have already mentioned above that Berlau died an alcoholic, poisoned by the fumes of the stove, in 1974, as she has foreseen in a dream.

There was also prediction involved in the case of Grete Steffin. A gypsy had predicted (when she was seventeen) that she would die at the age of thirty-three. And that is what happened. Brecht got his visa and left on 13th May 1941. They traveled through Russia. Grete's tuberculosis took a turn for the worse when they were in Moscow, and Brecht left her behind at a Moscow hospital. Along with the elephants. Brecht got to hear of her death when traveling through Siberia by train (4th July 1941). Steffin died in a ward at the Central Tuberculosis Clinic, 53 Chalovskaya Street. For the last part of her life she had stenographed everything that Brecht said about his odyssey through life. Some of these notes disappeared in Moscow, some were taken to Berlin. I haven't seen them, and if I had, I would not have been able to decipher them. (Brecht: In the ninth year of fleeing from Hitler, worn out from wandering around / from cold and hunger / our comrade Steffin died / in the Red city of Moscow. / My pupil (*mein Schüler—masculine?!*) is gone. / My life is over. / My career is gone. / My charge is gone.)

Helene ran Brecht's theater the "Berliner Ensemble" until her death (1971).

Brecht died on 14th August 1956. At about 23:45 as is estimated, before midnight. He had demanded that after his death his heart was to be cut out of his chest with a stiletto. (This reminds you of vampire tales.) One doctor did as requested. When the sculptor Fritz Cremer came to take the death mask, it seemed as if Brecht's bloody lips moved, as if he were trying to say something. Cremer could not complete his task and fled from the room. Brecht was buried at his own request in a metal coffin—he was afraid of snakes—buried in the same cemetery as the one where Hegel lies buried, the greatest *ilmaisija* (expounder) of the dialectic.

Afterword

The original Estonian version of this novel contains a few appendices that the advent of the internet, still in its infancy when the book was first published, has rendered redundant. Nowadays, you can find a great deal of the information included there by using a search engine. The translator has therefore taken the decision to omit these as they are not intrinsic to this postmodernist novel with its irony and synchronicity.

First, there was a bibliography of books about Brecht consulted by Mati Unt; this focuses on German, Estonian, Finnish and Russian sources. Next came an article by Ernst Bloch, already in English, entitled *Entfremdung, Verfremdung: Alienation, Estrangement*; this version was originally published in *The Drama Review*. It was followed by three poems by Brecht, still in German, called "Finnischer Tanz," "Finnische Landschaft" and "Finnische Gutspeisekammer 1940." A fragment of Brecht's 1955 will and testament came next. And then a brief article by the Estonian poet and theologian, again already in English, about the words "ilma" and similar, derived from Estonian and Livonian, and meaning "un-" or "lacking."

Finally, there are a number of photos. First, Brecht as a baby, then a portrait gallery of Helene Weigel, Ruth Berlau and Margarete Steffin, and, inevitably, Brecht himself. Plus, the rotund and round-headed Hella Wuolijoki, the Finland-Swedish poet Elmer Diktonius, and Finnish workers' theatre director Eino Salmelainen. Wikipedia and other online literary sources can enlighten here. Last but not least, a curious set of snapshots of Hitler "dancing," as his odd stamping footsteps are termed, dated June 17, 1940.

Eric Dickens, Blaricum, Netherlands, April 2009

MATI UNT's novels *The Autumn Ball, Things in the Night,* and *Diary of a Blood Donor*, among others, established him as one of the most prolific and well-regarded novelists in Estonia. He was also instrumental in bringing avant-garde theater to post-Soviet Union Estonia and was well-known as a director.

ERIC DICKENS is a translator and reviewer of Estonian and Finnish-Swedish literature. He is currently translating work by the novelists Toomas Vint and Hannele Mikaela Taivassalo.

SELECTED DALKEY ARCHIVE PAPERBACKS

HARRY MATHEWS,
The Case of the Persevering Maltese: Collected Essays.
Cigarettes.
The Conversions.
The Human Country: New and Collected Stories.
The Journalist.
My Life in CIA.
Singular Pleasures.
The Sinking of the Odradek Stadium.
Tlooth.
20 Lines a Day.
ROBERT L. MCLAUGHLIN, ED.,
Innovations: An Anthology of Modern &
Contemporary Fiction.
HERMAN MELVILLE, *The Confidence-Man.*
AMANDA MICHALOPOULOU, *I'd Like.*
STEVEN MILLHAUSER, *The Barnum Museum.*
In the Penny Arcade.
RALPH J. MILLS, JR., *Essays on Poetry.*
OLIVE MOORE, *Spleen.*
NICHOLAS MOSLEY, *Accident.*
Assassins.
Catastrophe Practice.
Children of Darkness and Light.
Experience and Religion.
God's Hazard.
The Hesperides Tree.
Hopeful Monsters.
Imago Bird.
Impossible Object.
Inventing God.
Judith.
Look at the Dark.
Natalie Natalia.
Paradoxes of Peace.
Serpent.
Time at War.
The Uses of Slime Mould: Essays of Four Decades.
WARREN MOTTE,
Fables of the Novel: French Fiction since 1990.
Fiction Now: The French Novel in the 21st Century.
Oulipo: A Primer of Potential Literature.
YVES NAVARRE, *Our Share of Time.*
Sweet Tooth.
DOROTHY NELSON, *In Night's City.*
Tar and Feathers.
WILFRIDO D. NOLLEDO, *But for the Lovers.*
FLANN O'BRIEN, *At Swim-Two-Birds.*
At War.
The Best of Myles.
The Dalkey Archive.
Further Cuttings.
The Hard Life.
The Poor Mouth.
The Third Policeman.
CLAUDE OLLIER, *The Mise-en-Scène.*
PATRIK OUŘEDNÍK, *Europeana.*
FERNANDO DEL PASO, *News from the Empire.*
Palinuro of Mexico.
ROBERT PINGET, *The Inquisitory.*
Mahu or The Material.
Trio.
MANUEL PUIG, *Betrayed by Rita Hayworth.*
RAYMOND QUENEAU, *The Last Days.*
Odile.
Pierrot Mon Ami.
Saint Glinglin.
ANN QUIN, *Berg.*
Passages.
Three.
Tripticks.
ISHMAEL REED, *The Free-Lance Pallbearers.*
The Last Days of Louisiana Red.
Reckless Eyeballing.
The Terrible Threes.
The Terrible Twos.
Yellow Back Radio Broke-Down.
JEAN RICARDOU, *Place Names.*
RAINER MARIA RILKE,
The Notebooks of Malte Laurids Brigge.
JULIÁN RÍOS, *Larva: A Midsummer Night's Babel.*
Poundemonium.
AUGUSTO ROA BASTOS, *I the Supreme.*
OLIVIER ROLIN, *Hotel Crystal.*
JACQUES ROUBAUD, *The Form of a City Changes Faster,*
Alas, Than the Human Heart.
The Great Fire of London.
Hortense in Exile.
Hortense Is Abducted.
The Loop.
The Plurality of Worlds of Lewis.
The Princess Hoppy.
Some Thing Black.
LEON S. ROUDIEZ, *French Fiction Revisited.*

VEDRANA RUDAN, *Night.*
LYDIE SALVAYRE, *The Company of Ghosts.*
Everyday Life.
The Lecture.
The Power of Flies.
LUIS RAFAEL SÁNCHEZ, *Macho Camacho's Beat.*
SEVERO SARDUY, *Cobra & Maitreya.*
NATHALIE SARRAUTE, *Do You Hear Them?*
Martereau.
The Planetarium.
ARNO SCHMIDT, *Collected Stories.*
Nobodaddy's Children.
CHRISTINE SCHUTT, *Nightwork.*
GAIL SCOTT, *My Paris.*
DAMION SEARLS, *What We Were Doing and Where We*
Were Going.
JUNE AKERS SEESE,
Is This What Other Women Feel Too?
What Waiting Really Means.
BERNARD SHARE, *Inish.*
Transit.
AURELIE SHEEHAN, *Jack Kerouac Is Pregnant.*
VIKTOR SHKLOVSKY, *Knight's Move.*
A Sentimental Journey: Memoirs 1917–1922.
Energy of Delusion: A Book on Plot.
Literature and Cinematography.
Theory of Prose.
Third Factory.
Zoo, or Letters Not about Love.
JOSEF ŠKVORECKÝ,
The Engineer of Human Souls.
CLAUDE SIMON, *The Invitation.*
GILBERT SORRENTINO, *Aberration of Starlight.*
Blue Pastoral.
Crystal Vision.
Imaginative Qualities of Actual Things.
Mulligan Stew.
Pack of Lies.
Red the Fiend.
The Sky Changes.
Something Said.
Splendide-Hôtel.
Steelwork.
Under the Shadow.
W. M. SPACKMAN, *The Complete Fiction.*
GERTRUDE STEIN, *Lucy Church Amiably.*
The Making of Americans.
A Novel of Thank You.
PIOTR SZEWC, *Annihilation.*
STEFAN THEMERSON, *Hobson's Island.*
The Mystery of the Sardine.
Tom Harris.
JEAN-PHILIPPE TOUSSAINT, *The Bathroom.*
Camera.
Monsieur.
Television.
DUMITRU TSEPENEAG, *Pigeon Post.*
The Necessary Marriage.
Vain Art of the Fugue.
ESTHER TUSQUETS, *Stranded.*
DUBRAVKA UGRESIC, *Lend Me Your Character.*
Thank You for Not Reading.
MATI UNT, *Brecht at Night*
Diary of a Blood Donor.
Things in the Night.
ÁLVARO URIBE AND OLIVIA SEARS, EDS.,
The Best of Contemporary Mexican Fiction.
ELOY URROZ, *The Obstacles.*
LUISA VALENZUELA, *He Who Searches.*
PAUL VERHAEGHEN, *Omega Minor.*
MARJA-LIISA VARTIO, *The Parson's Widow.*
BORIS VIAN, *Heartsnatcher.*
AUSTRYN WAINHOUSE, *Hedyphagetica.*
PAUL WEST, *Words for a Deaf Daughter & Gala.*
CURTIS WHITE, *America's Magic Mountain.*
The Idea of Home.
Memories of My Father Watching TV.
Monstrous Possibility: An Invitation to
Literary Politics.
Requiem.
DIANE WILLIAMS, *Excitability: Selected Stories.*
Romancer Erector.
DOUGLAS WOOLF, *Wall to Wall.*
Ya! & John-Juan.
JAY WRIGHT, *Polynomials and Pollen.*
The Presentable Art of Reading Absence.
PHILIP WYLIE, *Generation of Vipers.*
MARGUERITE YOUNG, *Angel in the Forest.*
Miss MacIntosh, My Darling.
REYOUNG, *Unbabbling.*
ZORAN ŽIVKOVIĆ, *Hidden Camera.*
LOUIS ZUKOFSKY, *Collected Fiction.*
SCOTT ZWIREN, *God Head.*

FOR A FULL LIST OF PUBLICATIONS, VISIT:
www.dalkeyarchive.com

SELECTED DALKEY ARCHIVE PAPERBACKS

PETROS ABATZOGLOU, *What Does Mrs. Freeman Want?*
MICHAL AJVAZ, *The Other City.*
PIERRE ALBERT-BIROT, *Grabinoulor.*
YUZ ALESHKOVSKY, *Kangaroo.*
FELIPE ALFAU, *Chromos.*
  Locos.
IVAN ÂNGELO, *The Celebration.*
  The Tower of Glass.
DAVID ANTIN, *Talking.*
ANTÓNIO LOBO ANTUNES, *Knowledge of Hell.*
ALAIN ARIAS-MISSON, *Theatre of Incest.*
JOHN ASHBERY AND JAMES SCHUYLER, *A Nest of Ninnies.*
DJUNA BARNES, *Ladies Almanack.*
  Ryder.
JOHN BARTH, *LETTERS.*
  Sabbatical.
DONALD BARTHELME, *The King.*
  Paradise.
SVETISLAV BASARA, *Chinese Letter.*
MARK BINELLI, *Sacco and Vanzetti Must Die!*
ANDREI BITOV, *Pushkin House.*
LOUIS PAUL BOON, *Chapel Road.*
  Summer in Termuren.
ROGER BOYLAN, *Killoyle.*
IGNÁCIO DE LOYOLA BRANDÃO, *Anonymous Celebrity.*
  Teeth under the Sun.
  Zero.
BONNIE BREMSER, *Troia: Mexican Memoirs.*
CHRISTINE BROOKE-ROSE, *Amalgamemnon.*
BRIGID BROPHY, *In Transit.*
MEREDITH BROSNAN, *Mr. Dynamite.*
GERALD L. BRUNS,
  Modern Poetry and the Idea of Language.
EVGENY BUNIMOVICH AND J. KATES, EDS.,
  Contemporary Russian Poetry: An Anthology.
GABRIELLE BURTON, *Heartbreak Hotel.*
MICHEL BUTOR, *Degrees.*
  Mobile.
  Portrait of the Artist as a Young Ape.
G. CABRERA INFANTE, *Infante's Inferno.*
  Three Trapped Tigers.
JULIETA CAMPOS, *The Fear of Losing Eurydice.*
ANNE CARSON, *Eros the Bittersweet.*
CAMILO JOSÉ CELA, *Christ versus Arizona.*
  The Family of Pascual Duarte.
  The Hive.
LOUIS-FERDINAND CÉLINE, *Castle to Castle.*
  Conversations with Professor Y.
  London Bridge.
  Normance.
  North.
  Rigadoon.
HUGO CHARTERIS, *The Tide Is Right.*
JEROME CHARYN, *The Tar Baby.*
MARC CHOLODENKO, *Mordechai Schamz.*
EMILY HOLMES COLEMAN, *The Shutter of Snow.*
ROBERT COOVER, *A Night at the Movies.*
STANLEY CRAWFORD, *Log of the S.S. The Mrs Unguentine.*
  Some Instructions to My Wife.
ROBERT CREELEY, *Collected Prose.*
RENÉ CREVEL, *Putting My Foot in It.*
RALPH CUSACK, *Cadenza.*
SUSAN DAITCH, *L.C.*
  Storytown.
NICHOLAS DELBANCO, *The Count of Concord.*
NIGEL DENNIS, *Cards of Identity.*
PETER DIMOCK,
  A Short Rhetoric for Leaving the Family.
ARIEL DORFMAN, *Konfidenz.*
COLEMAN DOWELL, *The Houses of Children.*
  Island People.
  Too Much Flesh and Jabez.
ARKADII DRAGOMOSHCHENKO, *Dust.*
RIKKI DUCORNET, *The Complete Butcher's Tales.*
  The Fountains of Neptune.
  The Jade Cabinet.
  The One Marvelous Thing.
  Phosphor in Dreamland.
  The Stain.
  The Word "Desire."
WILLIAM EASTLAKE, *The Bamboo Bed.*
  Castle Keep.
  Lyric of the Circle Heart.
JEAN ECHENOZ, *Chopin's Move.*
STANLEY ELKIN, *A Bad Man.*
  Boswell: A Modern Comedy.
  Criers and Kibitzers, Kibitzers and Criers.
  The Dick Gibson Show.
  The Franchiser.
  George Mills.
  The Living End.
  The MacGuffin.
  The Magic Kingdom.
  Mrs. Ted Bliss.
  The Rabbi of Lud.
  Van Gogh's Room at Arles.
ANNIE ERNAUX, *Cleaned Out.*
LAUREN FAIRBANKS, *Muzzle Thyself.*
  Sister Carrie.

JUAN FILLOY, *Op Oloop.*
LESLIE A. FIEDLER, *Love and Death in the American*
  Novel.
GUSTAVE FLAUBERT, *Bouvard and Pécuchet.*
KASS FLEISHER, *Talking out of School.*
FORD MADOX FORD, *The March of Literature.*
JON FOSSE, *Melancholy.*
MAX FRISCH, *I'm Not Stiller.*
  Man in the Holocene.
CARLOS FUENTES, *Christopher Unborn.*
  Distant Relations.
  Terra Nostra.
  Where the Air Is Clear.
JANICE GALLOWAY, *Foreign Parts.*
  The Trick Is to Keep Breathing.
WILLIAM H. GASS, *Cartesian Sonata and Other Novellas.*
  Finding a Form.
  A Temple of Texts.
  The Tunnel.
  Willie Masters' Lonesome Wife.
GÉRARD GAVARRY, *Hoplla! 1 2 3.*
ETIENNE GILSON, *The Arts of the Beautiful.*
  Forms and Substances in the Arts.
C. S. GISCOMBE, *Giscome Road.*
  Here.
  Prairie Style.
DOUGLAS GLOVER, *Bad News of the Heart.*
  The Enamoured Knight.
WITOLD GOMBROWICZ, *A Kind of Testament.*
KAREN ELIZABETH GORDON, *The Red Shoes.*
GEORGI GOSPODINOV, *Natural Novel.*
JUAN GOYTISOLO, *Count Julian.*
  Juan the Landless.
  Makbara.
  Marks of Identity.
PATRICK GRAINVILLE, *The Cave of Heaven.*
HENRY GREEN, *Back.*
  Blindness.
  Concluding.
  Doting.
  Nothing.
JIŘÍ GRUŠA, *The Questionnaire.*
GABRIEL GUDDING, *Rhode Island Notebook.*
JOHN HAWKES, *Whistlejacket.*
AIDAN HIGGINS, *A Bestiary.*
  Bornholm Night-Ferry.
  Flotsam and Jetsam.
  Langrishe, Go Down.
  Scenes from a Receding Past.
  Windy Arbours.
ALDOUS HUXLEY, *Antic Hay.*
  Crome Yellow.
  Point Counter Point.
  Those Barren Leaves.
  Time Must Have a Stop.
MIKHAIL IOSSEL AND JEFF PARKER, EDS., *Amerika:*
  Contemporary Russians View the United States.
GERT JONKE, *Geometric Regional Novel.*
  Homage to Czerny.
JACQUES JOUET, *Mountain R.*
  Savage.
HUGH KENNER, *The Counterfeiters.*
  Flaubert, Joyce and Beckett: The Stoic Comedians.
  Joyce's Voices.
DANILO KIŠ, *Garden, Ashes.*
  A Tomb for Boris Davidovich.
ANITA KONKKA, *A Fool's Paradise.*
GEORGE KONRÁD, *The City Builder.*
TADEUSZ KONWICKI, *A Minor Apocalypse.*
  The Polish Complex.
MENIS KOUMANDAREAS, *Koula.*
ELAINE KRAF, *The Princess of 72nd Street.*
JIM KRUSOE, *Iceland.*
EWA KURYLUK, *Century 21.*
ERIC LAURRENT, *Do Not Touch.*
VIOLETTE LEDUC, *La Bâtarde.*
DEBORAH LEVY, *Billy and Girl.*
  Pillow Talk in Europe and Other Places.
JOSÉ LEZAMA LIMA, *Paradiso.*
ROSA LIKSOM, *Dark Paradise.*
OSMAN LINS, *Avalovara.*
  The Queen of the Prisons of Greece.
ALF MAC LOCHLAINN, *The Corpus in the Library.*
  Out of Focus.
RON LOEWINSOHN, *Magnetic Field(s).*
BRIAN LYNCH, *The Winner of Sorrow.*
D. KEITH MANO, *Take Five.*
MICHELINE AHARONIAN MARCOM, *The Mirror in the Well.*
BEN MARCUS, *The Age of Wire and String.*
WALLACE MARKFIELD, *Teitlebaum's Window.*
  To an Early Grave.
DAVID MARKSON, *Reader's Block.*
  Springer's Progress.
  Wittgenstein's Mistress.
CAROLE MASO, *AVA.*
LADISLAV MATEJKA AND KRYSTYNA POMORSKA, EDS.,
  Readings in Russian Poetics: Formalist and
  Structuralist Views.

FOR A FULL LIST OF PUBLICATIONS, VISIT:
www.dalkeyarchive.com